P9-BYK-241

Highest Praise for
John Lutz

"John Lutz knows how to make you shiver."
—Harlan Coben

"Lutz offers up a heart-pounding roller coaster
of a tale."
—Jeffery Deaver

"John Lutz is one of the masters of the police novel."
—Ridley Pearson

"John Lutz is a major talent."
—John Lescroart

"I've been a fan for years."
—T. Jefferson Parker

"John Lutz just keeps getting better and better."
—Tony Hillerman

"Lutz ranks with such vintage masters
of big-city murder
as Lawrence Block and Ed McBain."
—*St. Louis Post-Dispatch*

"Lutz is among the best."
—*San Diego Union*

"Lutz knows how to seize and hold the
reader's imagination."
—*Cleveland Plain Dealer*

"It's easy to see why he's won an Edgar
and two Shamuses."
—*Publishers Weekly*

JOHN LUTZ

THE HAVANA GAME

A Thomas Laker Thriller

PINNACLE BOOKS
Kensington Publishing Corp.
www.kensingtonbooks.com

PINNACLE BOOKS are published by

Kensington Publishing Corp.
119 West 40th Street
New York, NY 10018

All Kensington titles, imprints, and distributed lines are available at special quantity discounts for bulk purchases for sales promotions, premiums, fund-raising, educational, or institutional use.

Special book excerpts or customized printings can also be created to fit specific needs. For details, write or phone the office of the Kensington sales manager: Kensington Publishing Corp., 119 West 40th Street, New York, NY 10018, attn: Sales Department; phone 1-800-221-2647.

ISBN-13: 978-0-7860-4095-7
ISBN-10: 0-7860-4095-5

First printing: February 2019

10 9 8 7 6 5 4 3 2 1

Printed in the United States of America

Electronic edition: February 2019

ISBN-13: 978-0-7860-4096-4
ISBN-10: 0-7860-4096-3

For Barbara, always

Yemayá is the mother of the Orishas. She rules the oceans, and like them, can be either peaceful or violent.
—KATIE MCKERNAN, St. Michael's College

CHAPTER ONE

Don't look at anybody.

His trainers had told him that. All of them. He'd been trained by both sides in this war, and considering they were enemies, it was funny how similar the training was. Especially the dictum *When you're operational, don't look at anybody.*

The danger was that they would look back. Make eye contact with some stranger, and he might remember you. And when he was asked, be able to describe you.

So he kept his eyes on the square of worn linoleum floor, smeared with slush and mud, between his boots. He'd memorized the route, counted the stops, and knew that there was one more stop before his. It wasn't necessary for him to look up at signs.

The tram was crowded. It was one of the narrow, old-fashioned cars they used in the city center to please the tourists. He was one of the standees, holding onto a loop of worn leather, allowing his body to sway as the tram turned left or right, slowed down or speeded up.

He didn't have to look at his fellow passengers to know they were all white. Which meant he was conspicuous. In a country of white people, he was olive-skinned and black-haired. Lucky for him the weather was so cold. He could keep his cap pulled down on his forehead, his scarf wrapped around his mouth and cheeks. His face was almost as well covered as that of a woman wearing a burqa. Only the eyes showed, and he was keeping them fixed on the floor.

A small object wobbled and rolled into his field of view. Bumped into his left boot and lay there. Yellow ring and pink bulb: a baby's pacifier. He suppressed the impulse to look up. No need to do anything about this. In a moment, an arm would appear, as the mother bent to retrieve the pacifier. He would not look up at her.

Seconds went by. The pacifier just lay there against his boot. Without raising his head, he peeked out from under his cap brim. Four paces to his left, a baby was sitting on a woman's knee, a pretty woman with bright blue eyes and cheeks flushed from the warmth of the car. She was wearing a knit cap with a yellow ball on top. The baby was fretting, waving his fat little arms around, but the mother hadn't noticed that he'd lost his pacifier. She was talking with the man beside her. Possibly the baby's grandfather. He had a full white beard, round steel spectacles, and a jolly smile. He looked like Santa Claus. A lot of the old men in this country did.

Someone was looking at him. He could feel the gaze, as palpable as an icy draft. Forgetting his training, he raised his head and looked.

It was a middle-aged woman in a head scarf squinting at him, thin lips pursed in disapproval. She'd noticed the pacifier and was wondering why he didn't return it. Maybe thinking he was going to pocket it. She was going to remember him. She'd be telling her friends, "There was one of *those* people in the tram, and you know, they'll steal *any*thing."

Maybe she was about to point him out to the other passengers. Or address him, loudly demanding that he return the pacifier. Then the whole car would notice him and remember.

Letting go the strap, he bent and picked up the warm, sticky pacifier. Holding it up with the tips of his fingers to show he had no designs on it, he made his way up the crowded aisle. The child's mother and Santa Claus were laughing and talking and did not notice him, even when he was standing over them. He extended his arm, offering the pacifier.

The mother's cheeks flushed even pinker, and she covered her mouth in embarrassment. Santa Claus took the pacifier and made a show as if he was about to put the grimy bulb back in the baby's mouth. The mother batted it away in mock horror. Both of them looked up at him, laughing, inviting him to share the joke.

He nodded and turned away, moving carefully on the tilting floor. He felt sick to his stomach. That was another reason you tried not to look at anybody. One they didn't dwell on in training. If you started seeing the targets as people, it was harder to carry out the operation.

The tram shuddered to a stop. His stop. The doors folded open, and he stepped out onto the platform, into the cold wind. This was the broad avenue that ringed the ancient center of the city. Spires and domes looked black against the dark-gray sky. It was almost night-fall.

The platform was a bright and aromatic island. It was a large and busy one, because this was where the city and suburban lines crossed. It had a roof with electric heaters hanging from the beams, their coils glowing orange. On long counters, merchants had laid out treats: roasted chestnuts, pastries filled with meat, sausages, smoked herring, fruit, and candy. Funny how the cold air made the smells especially delicious.

On his earlier visit he'd noticed the anti-terrorism precautions. The trash receptacles were just steel rings from which clear plastic bags hung. He couldn't read the notices, but knew they warned people to watch for abandoned parcels. CCTV cameras were perched under the eaves of the roof.

Nothing to hamper him.

He walked around the counter where two women were selling hot chocolate. They had a line of customers and didn't notice as he paused beside the stack of cardboard boxes containing marshmallows. Counting down to the sixth box, he slid it halfway out, inserted one finger in the cut-out from the cardboard flap, and flicked a toggle-switch. Then he slipped the box back in place and walked away. It had taken only a couple of seconds.

Descending the steps to the snowy street, he took from his coat pocket a rectangular plastic object, which he held to his ear. Anyone giving him a second glance would assume it was a cell phone. It wasn't.

He wished that flicking that toggle switch had set a

timer counting down. That would have meant it was all out of his control now. He might even be caught in the blast himself. He'd be thinking only about getting away from here quickly.

But the switch had only armed the detonator. The cell phone was really the transmitter he would use to set off the bomb. The planners had told him it had to be done that way, for maximum effect.

No need to look at his watch. He could hear the other tram approaching. The city had excellent public transportation; the trams always ran on time. He glanced over his shoulder. The suburban tram was pulling in. It was newer and sleeker than the one that ran around the city center. The old tram was still sitting on the opposite track, doors open. The controllers always held it so that passengers could switch lines.

He was passing an old church. Ducking behind one of its pillars, he took the detonator away from his ear and rested his finger lightly on the button. On the platform, the doors of the suburban tram slid open. Passengers poured out. People were stepping out of the old tram, too. They'd been enjoying its warmth until the last moment before they had to change. The platform was thronged with people.

Now.

But as he was about to press down, a yellow dot caught his eye: the ball of wool atop the cap of the mother. Holding her baby in one arm, she used the other hand to raise the lapel of her coat to shield his face from the wind. The old man limped behind her, a shopping bag in each hand.

He lifted his finger from the detonator. In a few seconds they would be aboard the new tram. The doors would close. Steel and safety glass would protect them. If he just gave them a couple of seconds.

He fought off the wave of weakness. Turning his back, he pressed the button.

A brilliant flash made the snow sparkle. The pillar at his back shielded him from the shock wave, but the roar of the explosion hurt like ice picks thrust into his ears. He was deafened, but only for a moment. Sooner than he wanted to, he could hear the screams.

CHAPTER TWO

"How would you like to go for a Sunday drive on Rock Creek Parkway?" Laker asked.

Ava put her book of crossword puzzles on her lap and looked at him. "You sound almost indecently smug. This is no casual invitation, is it?"

"No."

"You finally finished the Mustang?"

"Yes."

"Congratulations. I mean it. I was afraid you'd never get it done."

He *was* proud. Restoring the 1964 Ford Mustang had consumed all his free time for the last year and a half. But with Ava one had to be precise. "It's not *quite* done."

"You're inviting me out in an unsafe vehicle?"

"She drives like a dream. Brakes, steering, drivetrain, suspension all working beautifully. Only one thing. The top is stuck."

"In the up position?"

"Um—no."

"Laker! I'll freeze to death."

He looked out the row of windows that ran across the front of his loft. The Washington Monument glistened in the sunshine against a cloudless, pale blue sky. "Just look. It's spring."

"Just listen. It's March."

The wind was rushing around the old building, rattling the window sashes, whistling through the cracks. "I'll lend you the fur hat my friend on the Montana Highway Patrol gave me," he offered.

"I don't think so."

She picked up her book and a pen. She was one of those people who did crossword puzzles in ink. Did them quickly. And always in foreign languages, today French. She told him it was a way to build her vocabulary. He wasn't sure how that worked, since he'd never seen her pause to look up a word.

His cell phone pinged as it received a text message. It was sitting on his desk, on the other side of the vast loft, and was barely audible over the wind.

"I didn't hear anything," Ava said, without looking up.

With a sigh, he pushed himself up from the sofa and headed for the desk.

"I wouldn't, Laker. Suppose it's your boss?"

"Maybe he'll want a ride in the Mustang."

"Ha. Only one reason he calls on Sundays. To destroy our weekend."

Laker picked up the phone and looked at the screen. It *was* his boss. Samuel Mason didn't care for most technological innovations, but he loved text messaging. It saved him many a phone call. Mason didn't like to waste time talking to people if he could help it.

"It's Mason, but our weekend is safe," he called to Ava across the loft.

"What does it say?"

"'My office Mon 0730. Bring your toothbrush.'"

"Meaning what?"

"I'll be going directly from the briefing to the airport."

"Couldn't he tell you where you're flying to? How're you supposed to pack?"

"He doesn't give unnecessary information over cell phones."

Ava put the book down and tucked her pen behind her ear. Or he assumed she did, because it disappeared entirely behind a heavy curtain of auburn hair. When she went to work at the NSA, she gathered it in a nononsense bun, but on weekends she allowed it to hang free to just below her shoulders. Laker liked to look at it. Liked to look at her face, too, her long straight nose and wide-set brown eyes. She had heavy, arched, expressive eyebrows, and at the moment they were signaling concern. Laker hadn't been out of Washington on assignment in two months, but now their lucky streak was ending.

She said, "Laker, wherever they send you, whatever the job is, look for a bear under the bed."

He returned to the sofa and stood looking down at her. "I love it when you go all cryptic and portentous."

"I shouldn't be saying anything at all. I've been reminded many times that at the NSA, committees issue cautious, well-supported recommendations. Individuals keep their opinions in the building."

"But your opinion is?"

"The Russians are planning something big."

He sat down beside her, with his left ear toward her. He'd lost most of the hearing in his right ear due to an IED blast in Iraq.

"There've been interesting developments in sigint, concerning the FSB," Ava began.

Sigint was signals intelligence, and the FSB was the Federal Security Bureau, the successor to the KGB, which had inherited all its parent agency's ruthlessness and duplicity. Laker got that much, but when she plunged into the complexities of cryptography, he was quickly lost. He held up a hand, palm up. "Please. No more stochastic progressions and algorithms. Tell me in baby talk."

Ava leaned forward, eyes alight. She loved her work. "Moscow sent out a message to all stations worldwide. Things that general are usually low security. Junk mail, really. But this one was in a new code. Innovative and much denser than any we've seen in a while. I talked the committee into cracking it, even though it took hours and hours of expensive supercomputer time."

"And you were right. It turned out to be a vital message."

"I was wrong. It was a memo to all employees not to shop online using their office computers."

"Oh. Sorry."

But he was clearly missing something, because she was now perched on the edge of the sofa, eyes wide and glistening, full lips parted in a half-smile. Ava looked particularly lovely when she had a hunch. "It wasn't a waste."

"You mean you've cracked the code. You'll be able to read other messages."

"No. They changed it right away."

"You'll have to explain, then."

"It's a phenomenon that sigint experts call down-creep. Codes that would normally be used only for top secret messages are extended to lower levels of importance. That makes it harder for code breakers to spot the important messages, because they're hidden in the stream of low-level stuff. When you see downcreep at an agency, you should assume they're preparing a major operation. Frequent changing of code is another sign."

"I see. But this is not the official recommendation of the NSA."

"Not yet. I sent a memo. Hope somebody will read it."

"Okay. I'll look for the bear under the bed, wherever they send me, even if it's Las Vegas." It would not be Vegas. But he didn't want to think about that until tomorrow morning. "Sure you won't reconsider the ride in the Mustang? As our hours together dwindle to a precious few?"

"If they're dwindling, I want a nice warm shower. With a nice warm you."

She stood up and began to unbutton her blouse. The movement dislodged the pen, which fell to the floor.

Laker didn't notice.

CHAPTER THREE

While the CIA and NSA had sprawling suburban campuses, the Gray Outfit was small enough to fit into a Victorian-era row house on Capitol Hill. Its chief, Samuel Mason, had his office in a converted top-floor bedroom. The front windows looked out over neighboring rooftops to the Capitol dome. It seemed huge from so close at hand. You got a clear view of Freedom, the twenty-foot tall statue standing atop the dome, sword in one hand, laurel wreath in the other. As Laker set down his suitcase and took his usual chair in front of the desk on Monday morning, he found himself staring at it. Even though Mason himself was a riveting sight.

He had a large bald head, short thick neck, broad sloping shoulders. Sitting behind his desk, he resembled a mountain with a necktie. In an enemy attack on the Outfit last year, he'd lost the sight in his left eye. He wore a black patch over it, the straps crossing his bare, gleaming scalp above the ears. He also had a natty gray-and-maroon glen plaid patch, which he wore sometimes, just to discomfit people. It amused him to see whether they would compliment him on it or not. Mason had a strange sense of humor.

As usual, he skipped the small talk. "You heard what happened yesterday in Tallinn, Estonia?"

"A streetcar platform was bombed. Fifty-two killed, at last count, and more than twice that number injured. Last I heard, no claim of responsibility."

"Death toll is up to fifty-four now. Still no claim."

"Unusual. If it was ISIS or some other Mideast terrorist organization, they'd be boasting about it."

"Maybe it wasn't."

Laker considered. "I was thinking, after the Muslim extremist attacks in Belgium and France—"

"Estonia's not like Belgium and France. It's small and rather isolated. Has little contact with the Mideast."

"Then who are the top suspects?"

"It may not be an organized group. Just a couple of crazies. That's the thinking in Tallinn, I hear. Estonia has a sizeable minority of ethnic Russians, who immigrated when Stalin occupied all the Baltic states after World War II. They've never assimilated. They claim the Estonians are prejudiced against them."

"Not surprising. The Estonians didn't ask to be part of the USSR."

"They were sure happy to regain their independence when the Soviet Union broke up. Tensions between the natives and ethnic Russians have gotten worse since then. There have been recent incidents. Vandalism of patriotic sites and churches. Street brawls. Demonstrations turning into riots. But nobody had been killed. If this bombing is the work of the ethnic Russians, it would represent a major escalation."

Laker smiled bleakly and muttered, "Look for a bear under the bed."

"What?"

"Something Ava said."

"About Estonia?"

"About the general world situation these days. She thinks the Russians are getting ready to flex their muscles."

"Your girlfriend has the best brain in the NSA. Which actually isn't much of a compliment. My colleagues in Fort Meade and Langley are discounting the possibility of direct Russian involvement in the bombing. I am not."

Laker said, "Moscow's in an expansionist mood these days. They'd like Estonia back."

"And the rest of the Baltic republics."

"Why wouldn't they be using the same strategy as in Crimea and Ukraine? Encourage the ethnic Russians to make trouble. Then announce, we've got to restore order. Protect our fellow Russians. And send in the troops."

"Because Estonia is not Ukraine. It has a stable democratic government and a growing economy."

"And it's a member of NATO."

"Yes. You know what that means. An attack on one NATO member is an attack on all. Meaning if Russian troops invade, American soldiers will be among those fighting and dying for Estonia."

Mason sat back, closed his eye, and rubbed his brow. His injury had left him prone to painful and debilitating headaches. Friends and rivals had urged him to retire. But Mason said he was as competent as ever, and only a little more ornery. "My fellow agency heads think I'm being alarmist. Sure, Moscow doesn't like to have

NATO allies along its borders. Sure, there's civil un-
rest in Estonia. And Moscow is encouraging the ethnic
Russians. But that's all they're doing. They're not
planning to invade. They're not going to risk starting
World War III."

"Duly noted," Laker said. "But you don't think this
streetcar bombing was the work of a couple of crazies."

"The bomb was a small but powerful explosive surrounded by ball bearings. The type that would do the
most damage. Its placement and the timing of the blast
were meticulous. And whoever planted it has vanished
without trace."

"Seems like a professional op."

"FSB. In my alarmist opinion. And I admit, I don't
have much to base it on."

"So you want me to go to Estonia and establish that
the bombers were FSB agents. Good way to do that, of
course, would be to catch them."

Mason raised both hands and put them on either
side of his head. It was as if his headache was literally
splitting. He was trying to hold the two halves together. "Laker, we've talked about this before. From
an agent of your seniority, I expect finesse. Judgment.
Not single-handed heroics."

"Right."

"Just because I suspect Moscow of direct involvement in Estonia doesn't mean Washington can do the
same. Remember, the bosses of the other spy shops
think I'm out on a limb already. If anybody is going to
start World War III, it's not going to be the Gray Outfit."

"Okay. So I'm just going to liaise?"

"That's the word. You put on your suit and tie. Go to meetings. Listen. Fly home and report. Got it?"

"Got it."

"My secretary has your plane ticket."

Laker rose, took a farewell glance at Freedom atop the dome, and turned toward the door.

"Laker?"

He turned back. Mason was putting on his glasses, reaching for the next report in the stack on his desk. The next problem. He said, "Leave your Beretta in your office safe, will you? You're not going to need it. And it's bad taste, packing heat while sitting in conferences with our allies."

Laker considered pointing out that Freedom had a sword as well as a laurel wreath. Decided it wouldn't do him any good. Went out.

CHAPTER FOUR

As she arrived at work, Ava North received a text message from Laker: "On my way. Won't be gone long. NRS."

NRS stood for No Rough Stuff. He didn't want her to worry. Which was nice of him. If only he hadn't said it before, about an assignment from which he'd returned on a stretcher.

She walked down the corridor, ran her pass card through a reader, and opened a door marked J-22. If you didn't already know where you were going, the National Security Agency preferred that you not get there. Its signs were deliberately unhelpful. J was the cryptography directorate, and 22 was the section that dealt with the Russian Federation. It was a large room, with a tier of glass-walled offices from which the supervisors could look down on the underlings. The mid-level analysts were in a cube farm. Junior analysts like Ava didn't even rate partitions. They sat in rows of desks.

Hers was the last in the row, meaning that she had a view of the flags flying before the main entrance and the vast parking lot. She also had the satisfaction of knowing that while she could see out, no one could see in. NSA headquarters was a big cube of black reflective glass.

She switched on her desktop computer and waited for it to boot up. Stern memos circulated regularly, reminding employees to turn off their computers when they went home. NSA was the most voracious devourer of electricity in the state of Maryland, but her bosses deplored waste. She entered her password and the screensaver, the shield of the NSA, appeared on the monitor: a bald eagle, perched like a parakeet on a gold bar, which on closer inspection turned out to be a key.

Ava gazed at it gloomily. She enjoyed the intellectual challenge of her job, but most of her assignments were low-level tasks. Unlikely she would make any discovery worthy of being symbolized by a gold key on this gray Monday in March.

She touched keys and her schedule for the day appeared. On top, in flashing red letters, was "0930 MTG IN DD HARDIN OFC."

Ava sat back and sighed. She'd never met the Deputy Director but had heard about her. Rear Admiral Victoria Hardin was one of those people from the military who didn't believe in coddling the civilian employees. Summoning Ava at the last moment with an entry in her schedule rather than a call or email was typical. From what colleagues had told Ava, she could expect the actual meeting to be even chillier. But it was 9:25 now, and tardiness wouldn't be appreciated. She rose, smoothed her skirt, and headed for the door.

One long corridor, a flight of stairs, and another, longer corridor, and she arrived panting before a door that said only, DD J and K Directorates. She knocked.

"Enter."

Admiral Hardin was sitting at the head of a small rectangular table. She wore Service Dress Blues. Her hands were folded on the table, and the sleeves of the uniform were ringed with gold most of the way to the elbow. She had short gray hair and one of those faces that don't reveal much. Ava's informants had told her you didn't get anywhere trying to read Hardin's eyes or mouth. The thing to watch for was a Y-shaped vein down the middle of her forehead, which popped out when she was angry.

She said, "Sit down, North."

There was one other person at the table, a middle-aged man in suit and tie. Ava was always glad to have at least one fellow civilian at a meeting. In a movement that became habitual at NSA, she glanced at the ID hanging from a lanyard around his neck: Rahmberg S. K-14, it said. She didn't know what that section did. His dark hair was going thin on top, and he had heavy bags under his eyes and a mouth pulled down by sagging jowls. She took him for a lugubrious fellow, but then he smiled and put out his hand. Maybe he was just unhappy about being in this meeting.

"Stan Rahmberg. Pleased to meet you."

"Ava North. Hi."

Hardin said, "Your superior showed me that memo you wrote last week."

Ava didn't know which memo it was. But the telltale vein was showing in Hardin's brow, so she decided not to say anything.

"Thing that amazes me about NSA," Hardin went on. "We have people here with doctoral degrees, and they don't know things every recruit learns in his first week at Great Lakes Naval Station. Like when you get a reprimand from a superior, you accept it and move on. You don't shoot back a memo full of bullshit excuses."

Rahmberg was embarrassed for Ava. He pushed back his chair. "I'll just step out if you're going to discuss classified material."

"Sit down. It's nothing classified. Far from it. North flagged what looked like a routine message from a foreign agency for decoding. After spending a lot of time and money on it, her section established beyond a doubt that it *was* routine."

"Oh," said Ava. So it was the one from Moscow to all overseas offices, about online shopping during office hours. "I was mistaken, but—"

"No, I don't want to hear the part that comes after *but*. I read your memo, I told you. It was very ingenious. All that crap about downcreep. With footnotes even. You just about convinced your superior that you weren't wrong after all. That you hadn't wasted hours of supercomputer time. That this memo had significance nobody but you had seen. You need to learn when to let a thing drop. It's not hard to figure out. All you need is a bit of humility."

"Yes, ma'am." Ava had noticed that calling military types sir and ma'am had a soothing effect on them.

Not Hardin. "I realize humility doesn't come naturally to you. You're one of *the* Norths, aren't you?"

"I'm not sure what you mean. My father was undersecretary of state for a time."

"And your grandfather was Ephraim North, confidant of presidents, and your grandmother was Tillie North, Washington's most famous hostess. How come you're not a multi-millionaire lobbyist? Or married to one?"

Don't say it, Ava commanded herself. But she did anyway. "Maybe patriotism had something to do with it."

Hardin's close-set eyes widened dangerously, but before she could speak, the phone on the table rang. She picked it up, listened for a moment, and said, "All right, bring him up."

A manila folder was resting on the table next to the phone. Hardin opened it and scanned a page. She asked Ava, "Did you meet with Kenneth A. Brydon, Directorate K, Section 14, late Friday afternoon?"

The change of subject threw Ava. She said, "Well, yes, Ken and I chatted in the third-floor lounge for a few minutes. I guess it was about five. Why do you ask?"

"Apparently you were the last NSA person to see him alive."

"Oh God—what happened?"

"Sorry to have to tell you this," Rahmberg said. "I was Ken's supervisor. It's a terrible thing. He was mugged in Baltimore Saturday night. Stabbed to death."

"When you talked, did he mention his plans for the weekend?" Hardin asked.

"No. We're members of the Math Club. We were talking about a program for tutoring public school kids."

"Yeah, that program meant a lot to Ken," Rahmberg said. "Did you know him well?"

"No. I mean, I liked him, but we were just office acquaintances."

"Did you talk about your jobs?" Hardin asked.

"No, never."

"Oh? So you're a stickler for the rule that employees in different directorates shouldn't talk shop? Or was he?"

"He just said his job was too boring to talk about."

Rahmberg bowed his head to hide a smile.

Hardin glanced at her watch again. "Okay. I don't foresee any problems, then. What's happened is that Detective Sal Amighetti of Baltimore PD showed up at the gate an hour ago and said he wanted to question Brydon's supervisor and the last person here who spoke to him. He should've put in a request through channels. But since he's here, we might as well—"

A knock at the door interrupted her.

"Enter," said Hardin, rising from her chair.

A black Marine sergeant opened the door and stood back to let the Baltimore cop enter. Amighetti had to be near retirement age. His face was all seams and pouches, but his coarse gray-black hair was still abundant enough to be brushed straight back. It made Ava think of the quills of a porcupine. He was short and broad-chested. His visitor's pass hung around his neck. Hardin rose and gripped his hand hard. He winced. Ava guessed that like a lot of men his age he had arthritis in his thumbs. She shook his hand more gently.

"Sit down," commanded Hardin.

Amighetti did not. He said, "I'd like to interview each of you separately."

Hardin's thin lips formed a grim smile. "Detective, this is the NSA. You do not barge in and start grilling people as if you were in the Baltimore slums."

"I noticed it was the NSA," said the Detective mildly. "Somewhere between being searched and handing over every piece of ID in my wallet before they'd issue me this." He flicked the visitor pass with his forefinger.

"This is a secure facility. The procedure we're going to follow is that you familiarize us with the facts of the case, and I decide how best to assist you within the framework of security requirements."

Amighetti looked at her in silence for a while. Then he said, "You know, Admiral? I really like your striped pants."

Ava and Rahmberg exchanged a sideways glance and kept their faces straight as the detective craned his neck to get a better look at the broad gold stripe down Hardin's blue uniform trousers. "I was in the Marines in the Gulf War. Never did get to wear striped pants."

Hardin gave him her beady-eyed glare. Realizing it wasn't having any effect, she said, "Let's sit down."

They took their chairs. Amighetti pulled a notebook out of his pocket and flipped it open. "Mr. Brydon was killed Saturday night in the parking lot of the Calle 57 Casino, near the Baltimore waterfront. A man walking to his car found the body and reported it at 11:49 P.M.

We don't have the M.E.'s final report yet, but he hadn't been dead long. Cause of death was a stab wound, entry in the back, deep enough to pierce his heart. No wallet, watch, or phone found on the body. We assume robbery was the motive."

"So it was an ordinary mugging," said Hardin. "Obviously it had nothing to do with Brydon's work. I wonder what you're doing here, Detective. Wouldn't your time be better spent on the streets of downtown Baltimore, looking for the perp?"

Ignoring the question, Amighetti turned to Rahmberg. "Was Brydon a regular gambler?"

"I didn't know a lot about Ken's life away from work. But he never talked about it."

"I'm surprised that he would go to a casino," said Ava.

Amighetti turned to her. "Why?"

"Well, he was a mathematician. He'd know the odds favored the house."

"The floor supervisor said he was playing blackjack between nine and nine-thirty. He won eighteen dollars."

"So as a mathematician, he knew to quit while he was ahead," said Hardin.

Rahmberg's face had turned sad again. "I hate to think the poor guy was killed for eighteen bucks."

"Did he wear expensive jewelry?" asked Amighetti.

"Can't see Ken wearing anything you could call jewelry. He did wear a wristwatch. I never noticed what brand, but it wasn't a gold Rolex."

Amighetti turned to a fresh page in his notebook. "What was Brydon's job, Mr. Rahmberg?"

"Stan, don't answer," Hardin said. "Detective, you've given us no reason to think that Brydon's murder had anything to do with his work at the NSA. This is a routine crime. The mugger was lurking in the parking lot, hoping to waylay some gambler who'd won big. He just chose the wrong victim. It's sad, but that's all there is to it."

"Muggings in the parking lot of the Calle 57 Casino are not as routine as you seem to think, Admiral," said Amighetti.

"The casino's in downtown Baltimore, you said."

"Yeah, but the parking lot is fenced, lighted, and patrolled. Aside from patrons getting in occasional drunken brawls, there's no crime there."

"So this was an unusually brazen mugger."

"He's unusual, all right. When somebody gets hurt in a mugging, it's generally because he resisted. Mr. Brydon didn't get a chance to. He was stabbed in the back." Amighetti looked at each of them in turn. "That's why I'm looking into the possibility that he was targeted."

Hardin glanced at her watch. "I have another meeting to get to. Let's wrap this up. Stan, what was Brydon's security clearance level?"

"He was a Four."

"All right. That settles it. He wasn't cleared for sensitive material. Detective, many of the lower-level people at NSA might as well be working for an insurance company. Including Brydon. You'll have to take your investigation elsewhere. You won't find any answers here."

"Maybe if you'd allow me a few more questions—"

But Hardin was already on her feet. She walked to the door and opened it. The waiting Marine spun smartly on his heel to face her and snapped to attention. She seemed to enjoy that more than anything that had happened during the meeting, except perhaps reaming out Ava.

"Sergeant, escort Detective Amighetti to his car."

CHAPTER FIVE

Crawling along with Baltimore's rush-hour traffic, Ava had a good view of the Calle 57 Casino Hotel as she approached. It was a slim skyscraper in blue reflective glass, with giant LED screens that flashed ads for loose slots and cheap drinks, intermixed with Caribbean scenes. She'd read somewhere that Calle 57 was a street in Havana, and the images were of '50s American cars cruising the Malecón, sailboats off Morro Castle, fishermen with Hemingway beards standing beside marlin they'd caught.

There had been a lot of controversy about those screens in the columns of the Baltimore *Sun*. People complained that they upstaged every other building in the skyline and distracted drivers on the interstate.

At the end of the working day, Ava had headed straight for Baltimore. She was still trying to work out a sound justification for this decision. She hoped she wasn't going to check out the casino just because Admiral Hardin annoyed her.

There was something else. She felt that she owed it

to Ken Brydon. They'd never gotten to know each other very well. He flirted with her at first, but when he found out that Thomas Laker was her boyfriend that ended right away. Nobody in the lower levels of NSA knew what Laker actually did, but he had a formidable reputation. So Brydon was just a work buddy, but he was witty and irreverent, and the prospect of bumping into him was enough to brighten a dreary day.

She'd worried about him sometimes. Never that he'd be killed, only that he'd be fired. The NSA was a high-pressure bureaucracy with no tolerance for mischief, and employees who sat at computers all day doing jobs they were too smart for could easily get in trouble.

She didn't know what Ken did, exactly, but she knew it bored and frustrated him. He was an imaginative pro-grammer who could have been making a lot more money in the private sector. Occasionally she would see him sitting alone with his laptop in the employee lounge, his tousled blond head propped on one hand as the fingers of the other hand tickled the keyboard. She would hope that he wasn't trying out passwords, pok-ing and prodding at firewalls.

It was dark by the time she turned into the casino's parking lot, which was as Detective Amighetti had de-scribed it. Lamps atop tall stanchions cast a bright, even light. The surrounding fence was eight feet high. As she walked to the casino entrance, she was passed by two golf carts driven by uniformed guards.

In the casino, she didn't know what she was looking for. So she just wandered. Artificial palm trees sprouted from the floor. Exuberant fountains splashed into broad pools. Stuffed giant parrots gripped overhead perches. Other parrots, smaller but real, groomed themselves in cages. Murals depicted beaches and jungle-covered hills.

She passed bars where bands were playing *pachanga* and customers were sipping daiquiris and mojitos. The waitresses were dressed in short frocks in vibrant hues with Carmen Miranda headgear. The waiters wore white guayaberas and black pants.

The gamblers didn't seem to be giving the decor much thought. Pallid, paunchy, dressed in the drab, bulky clothes appropriate to late winter in the North, they had their eyes fixed on the cards or the wheel or the little windows in the slot machines. They might as well have been in a concrete basement. She wondered what it would take to make them look up.

Only a couple of minutes later, her question was answered.

Gazes lifted, heads turned, faces broke into excited grins. She turned to see customers backing out of the way while taking pictures with their phones as a celebrity and his entourage swept past. Living in Washington, you got to be a good judge of entourages, and this was an impressive one. But she didn't recognize the celebrity in the lead.

He was a man of about forty, short and broad-shouldered, with gleaming black hair and liquid brown eyes. He was wearing an elegant cashmere topcoat. On his right was a face she'd seen on television when Laker was watching sports. A pro golfer or maybe a race car driver. On his left was a tall, skinny woman whose hip-pumping walk indicated she was a fashion model. Her eyelashes were so thick she seemed to be squinting, possibly from the glare bouncing off the gems in her necklace and bracelets.

But it was the man directly behind the celebrity who riveted her. Everybody else was smiling and chatting in the usual entourage fashion, but this man was watching the crowd. His eyes were scanning the casino customers, alert for unfriendly faces or sudden moves. His gaze passed over her like a shadow. She felt chilled.

He had a long, deeply lined face and a tall, lean body. His head was bald on top, but he wore his hair long at the sides, covering his ears. It looked odd, but she was willing to bet that no one ever made jokes about it. Not to his face, anyway.

An aide had run ahead of the group, cardkey in hand. He unlocked an elevator. The doors slid open. He stood back and held them as the entourage trooped in.

"Going to the helipad on the roof. 'Copter's waiting to take them to D.C."

Startled, she looked at the man beside her. It was Detective Amighetti.

"Who is that?" she asked.

"*El patrón*. Rodrigo Morales. Owner of the Calle 57 casino chain. And other properties."

"Oh. Who's the man with him?"

"Obviously you don't follow golf."

"I mean the one behind him. Is he a bodyguard?"

Amighetti seemed pleased by the question. "Acting as one at the moment. But he has a long and distinguished past. Arturo Carlucci, formerly of the New Jersey Mob. Once their top enforcer. The reason for that goofy haircut is to cover the top half of his left ear."

"Why?"

"Because it isn't there. But he left wet work behind

long ago, when the *capos* discovered his diplomatic and managerial skills. He rose high enough to be swept up in a RICO prosecution. Did five years. Released early for good behavior. Appeared to go straight. Got a legit job from Morales. Personal security."

"*Appeared* to go straight?"

"I mentioned the diplomatic skills. Unsubstantiated rumor is, he's the Mob's ambassador to the court of Morales."

The entourage was boarding the elevator. Carlucci's cold eyes swept the room one last time before he stepped in. Ava glanced at Amighetti. His coarse swept-back hair again reminded her of the quills of a porcupine as he gazed impassively at Carlucci.

She said, "You didn't mention at the meeting this morning that the casino's owner is mobbed up."

"I can't prove anything of the kind. Nobody can. Even if he was, what would it have to do with Brydon? A guy like Carlucci would never mug somebody for eighteen bucks. What are you doing here, Ms. North?"

"I'm not sure."

"Admiral Fancypants didn't send you to check out the scene of the crime?"

"The Admiral has no further interest in what happened to Ken Brydon."

"Why should she? A low-level employee is the innocent victim of a mugging. But you're not satisfied with that?"

"No. I liked Ken. I feel bad about what happened to him. But I'm not completely sure he was innocent."

Her answer seemed to satisfy the detective. He said, "I'll tell you what I'm doing here. Trying to tie up a loose end. You'll remember, the floor supervisor said Brydon quit playing blackjack and cashed in his chips about nine-forty."

"Yes."

"So how come he didn't go out to his car until two hours later? Presumably he was somewhere else in this building. What was he doing?"

"I don't know. Having a drink or dinner, maybe? It must be easy to find out. Don't they have surveillance cameras all over casinos?"

"Sure. We're probably on a screen somewhere right now." He gave her a look to see if this discomfited her. It did.

Amighetti went on, "I've been going back and forth with the head of security, guy responsible for the cameras. He said there's an awful lot of videotape and it would take a long time to review it and is this really necessary?"

"He's dragging his feet? Is that suspicious?"

"I'm sure there is an awful lot of videotape. Maybe he's just lazy." Amighetti's gaze was roaming around the big room. Was he looking for the camera that was aimed at them? Ava was certainly thinking about it. He glanced at his watch. "You want to take a little walk with me, Ms. North?"

"Where?"

"Out of here."

Shoving his hands in the pockets of his battered parka, he headed for the exit. Ava followed at a slower pace, allowing a gap to open and other people to pass between them. It probably wouldn't matter if the casino got her on video leaving with Detective Amighetti. On the other hand, maybe it would.

They went out through the main entrance, which was bustling with taxis and airport vans, disgorging arriving hotel guests. Amighetti crossed the street, and she followed. Away from the lights of the casino, the block was dark and quiet. All the shops were closed, with steel gates over their windows. A cold wind drove litter past their feet. It was only half a mile to Harborplace, Baltimore's tourist area, but this was a desolate block.

Amighetti zipped up his coat as she caught up with him. "We'll go around the corner, make sure we're out of camera range. Suellyn's kinda hinky about that."

"Suellyn?"

"Friend of mine who works in the casino, as a blackjack dealer."

"I wouldn't have picked you as a blackjack player."

"We met under other circumstances."

Ava took a guess. "You arrested her?"

"Not for anything serious. And it was a long time ago. Still, if the casino found out she has a criminal record, they'd fire her."

"But they're not going to find out from you. And to show her gratitude, Suellyn gives you information from time to time."

"This time it's about Brydon. She said I'd be very interested. You're pretty quick on the uptake, Ms. North. Considering we're far from your usual *muhloo*." It was Amighetti's way of saying milieu. "You're one of *the* Norths, aren't you?"

Before Ava could reply, a woman came around the corner and headed for them. The tails of her thin raincoat, inadequate to the weather, flapped around her legs, bare to the mid-thigh under sheer pantyhose. The pile of blond hair atop her head was so stiff with hairspray that the wind had no effect on it. The corners of her bright pink lips turned down as she looked Ava over.

"Who's she?"

"Friend of Ken's," said Amighetti. "She'll tell you her name, if you want to know."

Suellyn shook her head. Again the pile of blond hair was undisturbed. "I'm supposed to be on a smoke break, so let's get to it. That Brydon guy was in the casino before Saturday."

"He was a regular?"

"No. Just once before. A week earlier."

"So why am I supposed to find this interesting?"

"He won big at blackjack. Like, ten thousand dollars."

"Ten thousand dollars." Amighetti gave Ava a sideways look. "What did you say about Brydon? You didn't think he'd gamble because he was a math whiz and wouldn't like the odds?"

"I don't know what to tell you."

Amighetti turned back to Suellyn. "Was he at your table?"

"No. Not at any of the regular tables. That's the part that's weird."

"Go on."

Suellyn looked over her shoulder, up the street. There was nobody there, but even so she bent forward and lowered her voice. "They opened a table. Brydon was the first to sit down at it. The dealer was a guy I'd never seen before. Not long after Brydon left, one of the regulars took over for him, and I haven't seen him since."

"You're saying, he was brought in to deal winning cards to Brydon? Why would the casino arrange for Brydon to win?"

"You don't believe me."

"I'd just like them to arrange something similar for me."

"Look, I don't know what was going on for sure. But it was not normal. When somebody's on a lucky streak, the casino likes to make a big deal of it. Make all the customers think it can happen to them, too. The floor supervisor or some other big shot comes over to shake the guy's hand. The PR department takes his picture. And of course the winner's all smiles."

"Brydon wasn't."

"He looked nervous. Like he couldn't wait to cash his chips in and get out." She looked over her shoulder again. "Look, I got to get back. Don't come in the casino again tonight, okay?"

"Okay. Thanks."

Suellyn moved away with a clatter of high heels and disappeared around the corner.

"What do you think, Ms. North?"

"I don't know what it means. But obviously it's important. You'll have to get hold of the video of Ken's earlier visit."

"Like I said, the casino is being uncooperative. I'd probably have to get a court order. Which means producing Suellyn, which I don't want to do. And even then I might not win. Ruy Morales has a lot of pull in this city." Amighetti hunched his shoulders. "How about we get out of this wind, Ms. North? I know a place for coffee."

They walked to the next corner. This street was wider,

with more traffic. A McDonald's stood on the corner. They went in and ordered coffee. Amighetti said it was his treat. A few minutes later they were seated in a booth.

"If you had to take a guess," Amighetti said, "what would you say is going on here? Why would the casino arrange for Ken to win?"

"It was a payment."

"Yeah. What did Ken have to sell? It would pretty much have to be information from his office, wouldn't it?"

"You heard what Admiral Hardin said. His security clearance was low. He didn't have access to secrets."

Amighetti patted his coarse pelt of hair. "I'm not talking about state secrets. Kind of thing the fate of nations turns on. The NSA collects all kinds of information, right? Maybe Brydon stumbled on something that could help Ruy Morales's resort chain make money."

"It would still be illegal. Ten thousand wouldn't be enough, for the jail time Ken was risking."

"Maybe that was just a down payment. Ken told somebody in the Morales organization what he had. Or could get. They made the deal, and Ken got his first payment. The next week he was back, with the goods. He did some penny-ante gambling for a while, passing the time before his meeting with the persons unknown. Only instead of getting paid, he was killed. How come?"

"I can't think of an explanation."

"No? But you're pretty smart. Think again." He sat back and took a sip of coffee. He seemed to be in no hurry.

"Maybe Ken's information wasn't as useful as he thought."

"They wouldn't kill him for that."

"No. Well, I guess it's possible they told Ken, now that he'd broken the law, they owned him. He'd have to keep producing information. And he tried to walk out."

"That's a possibility. There's another one."

"You'll have to tell me."

"Ken's information was much, much hotter than he realized. Morales's people couldn't risk leaving him alive."

She took a swallow of coffee and set the cup down, with a loud clunk that told her how nervous she had suddenly become. "We're just spinning theories, Detective."

"Yeah. But it's sort of a troubling chain of events, isn't it? You think the NSA can afford to walk away from this?"

Ava sighed. "I think I'm not going to get much sleep tonight."

CHAPTER SIX

The first thing Laker realized on awakening was that he was alone in bed. Ava must be making coffee in the kitchen. He dozed and waited. No gurgle of water, no scent of Arabica. He was not at home. He was in Tallinn, Estonia.

The previous day came back to him: a seemingly endless, turbulence-ridden flight over the Atlantic, a tedious layover at Heathrow Airport, the last leg over the North Sea and the Baltic. He'd been practically comatose by that time, but his driver was excited to have an American in the cab and insisted on conversation. He spoke fluent English and had an extensive knowledge of American television and pop music. Laker was unable to add much.

At the hotel, the desk staff wouldn't let him go up to his room until they'd offered him a nightcap of the local liqueur, Vanna Tallinn, a bedtime snack of smoked herring and potatoes with sour cream, a visit to the sauna. Laker got to make extensive use of one of the few Estonian phrases he knew: *"Ei, tanan,"* No, thanks.

He threw off the covers and swung his feet to the floor. That seemed to go okay, so he rose and walked to the window.

The desk staff had told him they were giving him a room with a view of Old Town. Opening the curtains, he found that it was true. He could see dormered roofs dusted with snow and a varied assortment of towers: a conical fortress, a pointed medieval church spire, and a cluster of onion domes. Farther away, he could see the blue of the harbor, and the funnel and communication masts of some cruise ship docked there. The idea of cruising the Baltic in March didn't appeal to him, though he'd heard it was the best time of year to see the northern lights.

Glancing at the clock, he decided to skip breakfast. He didn't have much time to get to his first meeting. He showered and stepped up to the mirror to shave. He had a good face for his profession, meaning that it wasn't the kind people remembered. Black hair, brown eyes, regular features. His nose showed no sign of its numerous breakages, and the IED blast that had partially deafened him had left no visible scars. His only distinctive feature was his cleft chin. Ava often teased him, saying it was like Cary Grant's, or Kirk Douglas's, depending on her mood. Spreading foam over it, Laker considered growing back his beard. He liked covering up that Hollywood cleft. Liked not having to shave, too.

He was in good time as he crossed the bedroom to the closet. His last act of the night before had been to hang up his suit bag, so he wouldn't go to the meeting in wrinkles. Laker owned only four suits, and they were all old. But they were good. Years ago, when stationed in London, he'd had them tailored on Savile Row, justifying the expense because he was hard to fit, owing to his height and the width of his shoulders.

He'd chosen the charcoal pinstripe for this trip. After knotting his tie, he slipped into the jacket and buttoned it, then paused feeling that he'd missed a step.

He hadn't strapped on his gun. That was it. He'd followed Mason's order to leave the Beretta M9 and its shoulder holster in his office safe in Washington. Diplomatic finesse, not weaponry, was what this mission would require of him. He hoped Mason was right about that.

Outside, it was a lot colder than Washington. He was grateful for his heavy wool topcoat. The concierge was holding open the door of a black Volvo taxi. He got in and told the driver where to go.

"Ministry of Justice?" The driver repeated doubtfully, with a glance at Laker in the mirror. The face in the mirror was north European, broad cheekboned and long-jawed, with blue eyes behind steel-framed spectacles, but the cap was American, adorned with the Y of the New York Yankees.

"You know where it is?" Laker asked.

"Sure, that is not the problem. Okay if I take detour?"

"Something going on?"

"Big demonstration on Suur Karja Boulevard."

"Use your best judgment."

The driver turned into the street. The Volvo was warm and comfortable. Laker sat back and buckled his safety belt. He asked, "Who's demonstrating?"

"The Russians."

Here was an opportunity to sample local public

opinion. Mason would be interested. "You mean the ethnic Russians? They're Estonian citizens, aren't they?"

The driver shrugged skeptically. He was good at expressing himself with his back turned. "Stalin moved them in, when he occupied the country. Yeltsin should have moved them out, when he let us go."

Laker's briefing book, which he'd read on the plane, had forty pages on the situation with the ethnic Russians. The cabbie's statement summed it up pretty well.

They were driving down a wide boulevard. Traffic thickened and slowed to a stop. Laker looked out the side window as an old-fashioned streetcar rolled past. He said, "You'd think the ethnic Russians would lie low for a while. What with the bombing."

"Their leaders say they had nothing to do with it. For them, issue is settled. It's back to their usual demands."

"Stronger anti-discrimination laws?"

"Today, is language. They want Russian to be made an official language of Estonia. Taught in all schools."

"You mean, they want their children to keep speaking it?"

"No, they want rest of us to learn it. We'll need it when we're part of Russia again."

The topic seemed to be making him irritable. He checked his mirrors and spun the wheel. The Volvo accelerated into a narrow, cobbled side street. For a few hundred yards, traffic was light and moving well. Then they turned a corner and entered a small square that was packed with cars. After a few minutes of immobility, the driver took his hands off the wheel and slumped in his seat. "Sorry," he muttered. "Turn was bad idea."

Laker heard a noise louder than the thrum of engines.

He pressed the button to lower his window a few inches. It was a din of shouts and running footfalls. The sound of a demonstration going bad, familiar to him from many years in the world's trouble spots. It was coming from somewhere off to their right.

Laker's eyes filled with tears, his nostrils with mucus. Pulling out a handkerchief, he said, "We need to get away from here. Turn left."

The driver was coughing and wiping his eyes. "What is it?"

"Tear gas."

He closed his window. Not that it would help much. People who knew tear gas only from movie scenes in which characters ran through dense clouds of it unaffected didn't realize how potent the stuff was. It got to you before you even smelled it. Tears were gushing down his cheeks, rivers of snot running from his nose.

The driver, gasping and coughing, was having a hard time maneuvering the car. He managed to get it pointing toward a street opening to their left, but then he had to stop. Cops in riot gear, carrying Plexiglas shields and wearing gas masks, were running toward them. They streamed past the car on both sides.

Laker swiveled to look out the back window. Beyond the line of motionless cars, the street was filled from one building wall to the other by demonstrators. They were making the transition to rioters as he watched, throwing down their signs, tying handkerchiefs around their faces. They met the police charge with a hail of rocks. One bounced off the roof of the Volvo. A bottle fell on the cobbles next to the car and broke. A pool of blue flame began to spread. Molotov cocktail.

"We have to get out of here!" the driver yelled.

But a car had come to a standstill right in front of them. Laker said, "We can't. We'll be okay. Just concentrate on breathing."

The melee spread through the traffic jam as the outnumbered cops were pushed back by the rioters. Only paces to Laker's right, a cop went down, one rioter seizing his shield while another kicked him. The Volvo shook. Out the back window Laker saw jeans-clad legs as a man mounted from the trunk to the roof of the car. His feet clomped overhead and he started shouting.

Laker turned back to see the driver shift the gear lever into reverse. "No!" he shouted. "Don't move!"

The car lurched backward. The man toppled onto the hood, then rolled to the street. His cry of surprise and pain drew the attention of the rioters. Their eyes glared at Laker. Rushing the car, shouting, they beat on its windows with their fists, kicked its doors.

"We're okay," Laker told the driver, with more confidence than he felt. "They can't get at us."

The car was completely surrounded. It shifted on its springs, one way, then the other. Its left side rose. The wheels lost contact with the ground. Laker's safety belt held him, but the driver slid from his seat as the car settled on its right side.

Another sickening jolt and it was upside down, resting on its roof. Over the din he could hear impacts of metal upon metal. Some pointed tool, clanging against the exposed gas tank? No way to be sure. Just in case, he wasn't going to wait until the car exploded. "Try to get out!" Laker called to the driver. That was all he could do for the man.

He opened the catch of the safety belt, tucking in his head and letting his shoulders take the impact as he dropped to the roof of the car. His fingers scrabbled at the unfamiliar door lever. It was only seconds but felt much longer. Finally he pushed the door open. Turned over and began to crawl out on hands and knees. He'd be completely helpless. He braced himself for blows.

They came. Fists in his back, kicks in his ribs. He watched helplessly as a boot stamped down on his right hand. The din all around him was so tremendous he couldn't hear his yelp of pain.

As soon as he was clear of the car, he flipped onto his back, coiled his legs, and drove both feet into the groin of the nearest attacker.

More blows fell on his shoulders as he surged to his feet. A woman with long dark hair snarled something at him and swung a rock at his head. Laker stepped inside the swing and tapped her on the chin. She went over backward.

A riot was no place for gallantry.

He put his back to the upside-down car and raised his fists. But apparently there were no more bouts on today's card. The rioters were taking to their heels. Either the police had deployed more tear gas or the wind had shifted, because it was getting harder to breathe. Pausing only to see that the driver was crawling out the front door, Laker staggered away, weeping and wheezing. His handkerchief was gone. He mopped his face with his scarf.

A running man bumped into him, knocking him against a motionless car. He felt his way along its fender. Looked up to see, through his tears, the mouth of a narrow street straight ahead. He ran toward it, bent over, head down, as a shower of rocks and paving stones fell all around him. One struck him a painful blow in the shoulder.

Once he reached the street, not even wide enough to qualify as an alley back home, it was better. The tear gas was no longer incapacitating. Apart from a few running figures in the distance, no one else was around. Blinking and wiping his face, he strode steadily away from the clattering and shouting in the square.

He turned a corner into a wider street. Ahead, a line of riot police stood shield to shield. Laker approached slowly, arms at his sides, hands open. The police watched, unalarmed. He called out, *"Räägi inglise keeles?"*

The cop directly in front of him raised the visor of his helmet and said, "Yes, I speak English."

"I'm a representative of the U.S. government," Laker said. "Can you get me to the Ministry of Justice?"

It wasn't necessary to show his creds. Four policemen were detailed as his escort. They set down their shields, surrounded him, and set off at a brisk pace. He assumed they were taking him to a car, but they just kept walking. "Is the Ministry of Justice nearby?" he asked the cop on his left.

The helmeted young man raised his plastic visor to answer. "You'll be able to see it once we get past the Linnahalle," he said. Everybody in Tallinn seemed to speak English. He pointed at the building they were about to walk by, an enormous bunker with blank concrete walls. After a hundred paces or so, they came to the first break in the wall, a wide staircase with crumbling steps and rusting railings. It led to boarded-up doors and windows. The boards were embellished with colorful graffiti.

Laker recalled seeing similar buildings in Moscow. He said to the cop beside him, "One of Stalin's architectural gems?"

"Nazi bombing left a lot of vacant lots in the city," the cop replied. "When the Soviets occupied us, they put up buildings like that. We preferred the vacant lots."

Passing the concrete hulk, they came into a square lined with government buildings. The cop pointed out the Ministry of Justice. It was a couple of centuries old, Laker, guessed, made of white stone and red-orange brick, with tall round windows, a tier of over-life-size statues of national heroes on plinths, and a clock with a deep blue dial. The facade was made even busier by stone scrolls and iron fretwork. At its summit, the blue, black, and white Estonian flag furled and unfurled in the wind.

His escort left him at the door. *"Head aega,"* Laker said, with a grateful nod, and went in. A functionary in tailcoat and breeches, lacking only a powdered wig, approached. Laker told him he was here for the meeting on the terrorist attack, but he already seemed to know that and led the way up broad marble stairs.

At the top stood three men in the olive uniforms of U.S. Army soldiers in NATO. The one in the middle had his cap under his arm. Its bill was encrusted with gold curlicues; he must be the superior officer. He certainly had a superior smile, as he looked down at Laker.

Only now did Laker notice that his coat was hanging open, having lost its buttons, his tie askew and white shirtfront spotted with grime and blood. He wasn't sure where the blood had come from. At least it wasn't his. His trousers were torn at both knees so that his hairy kneecaps showed.

"We heard that an American got caught in the riot. That would be you," said the senior officer. His shoulder boards carried the gold eagles of a colonel. The badge on his chest read ANTROBUS.

"It would. Tom Laker, Colonel. Pleased to meet you."

"Creds, please," said the young lieutenant on Antrobus's right. Laker handed over his ID. The lieutenant glanced at it and handed it to Antrobus.

"Department of Homeland Security," he said. "That doesn't narrow it down much. But never mind. I'll call Washington later and find out what agency you work for. And why you're here. Just to pass the time, though, what's your version?"

Laker had worked extensively with the military during his Middle East postings, and had come to know many types of officers. Antrobus seemed to be the type who was always performing for his aides. The smooth-faced, bright-eyed lieutenants on either side of him were listening intently, and tonight they'd be telling their mess-mates, "You should have seen the old man rip into that spook from D.C." Or at least Antrobus imagined they would be.

"I'm just here to listen and learn, Colonel."

The smug smile hadn't left Antrobus's face yet. Maybe it never did. He was about to say something skeptical when the aide on his left looked down the hall and said, "Excuse me, sir? It looks like they're going in."

"Let's join them by all means." Hands clasped behind his back, he sauntered down the hallway. Laker fell in beside the aide on the right.

"I doubt you're going to learn anything this morning, Mr. Laker," Antrobus went on. "The Minister calls a big meeting every day, whether anything's happened or not. And I have to come in." He glanced sideways at Laker. "Base is *an hour* away."

Laker chose not to express sympathy for the colonel's wasted time. "There's still no claim of responsibility?"

"It will be in the media when it comes. No need to hold a meeting. Anyway, no one doubts that it's the Russian minority. Those charming people who just roughed you up. I realize you can't do anything about the state of your trousers, but at least straighten your tie. Also, take off your overcoat and hang your creds on your breast pocket." He remembered belatedly that he was talking to a civilian and added, "Please."

The meeting was evidently a formal affair. People in suits and uniforms were preceding them through tall double doors at the end of the hallway. Sentries in old-fashioned dress uniforms, armed with new assault rifles, stood on either side of the doors.

Passing through them, Laker found himself in a huge room with a lofty ceiling, a row of tall windows on one side, and a vast painting of a Napoleonic-era battle, with flashing swords and plunging horses, on the other. He assumed Estonia had fought on the winning side.

The attendees were gathering around a long, highly polished table. Antrobus sat down. One lieutenant, who'd been carrying his briefcase, laid it in front of him, while the other poured a glass of water for him.

Then they retreated to join the line of flunkies along the wall.

A slender man in a dark blue uniform with rows of bright buttons approached Laker. He had a neatly trimmed dark goatee, high forehead and large, heavily lidded eyes that gave him a mournful look. "Mr. Laker, sorry for your misadventure. Telliskivi, Commissioner of Police."

For a policeman, he had a soft, gentle voice. They shook hands and Laker winced. It was the hand that had gotten stomped on. "I'm okay. Your men were very helpful."

"Should you need to travel around the city again, please feel free to call on me for a police car."

"You're expecting the disorders to continue?"

Telliskivi flexed his eyebrows noncommittally and went to his seat up the table. A man who had to be the Minister of Justice was taking the chair at the head of the table. He was a portly old fellow in a vested suit, with longish gray hair tucked behind his ears and round spectacles. He had a benevolent air. Laker could imagine him carving nutcrackers for little girls, which would turn out to be enchanted.

"Thank you for coming," he said. "We will speak in English for the benefit of our friends from NATO, if there are no objections?"

He looked down both rows of faces; there were none. "Commissioner, your report, please."

"Two more of the wounded have died, bringing the toll to fifty-six," said Telliskivi. Even when he was speaking loudly enough to be heard by the entire table, his voice kept its gentle tone. "We are withholding the names until we notify the next of kin. There has been no credible claim of responsibility for the attack. I have received the laboratory report on the explosive residue found at the scene. I asked the technicians to look for taggants."

Colonel Antrobus gave an audible snort.

A woman with a cap of short gray hair, seated beside the Minister, leaned forward. "Taggants?"

"Chemical agents inserted into explosive during manufacture, to make it traceable to its source." Telliskivi explained.

"I don't know why you bothered to ask, Commissioner," said Antrobus. "I could've told you you weren't going to find taggants. Amateur terrorists like the Russian ethnics use homemade explosives."

Telliskivi's mournful eyes rested on the Colonel for a long moment after he finished speaking. Laker felt something. A faint vibration of incoming bad news.

"In fact, it was a sophisticated plastic explosive called Semtex." Telliskivi's voice was gentle as ever. "It had taggants showing it was manufactured by Dover Chemicals, Inc., of Fort Wayne, Indiana, which sells 100 percent of its output to the U.S. armed forces."

Antrobus's breath rushed out of him like the air from a punctured tire. He sagged back in his chair. His face was white. Laker glanced around the table. All eyes were on the Americans, awaiting a response. It was pretty obvious what it had to be, and just as obvious that Antrobus wasn't up to making it.

Laker said, "Commissioner, do you have any information on how the terrorists got hold of the explosive?"

"We do not," said Telliskivi.

Antrobus's mouth was open, but no words were

emerging. Laker said, "Obviously, there's a possibility that it came from the NATO base. Colonel Antrobus will immediately launch a full investigation."

"I'll immediately launch a full investigation," Antrobus repeated. "As soon as I get back to base. Commissioner, I must ask you to put your own investigation on hold, pending our report."

"I'm afraid that will not be possible," said Telliskivi.

"Minister, I insist—" Antrobus began.

"The Commissioner is in charge of the investigation," said the Minister, glaring at Antrobus.

"Very well," said Antrobus. "But you are in charge of this meeting, and I insist that you remind everyone at the table of the importance of security. I will hold you responsible, sir, if anything said at this meeting leaks to the media."

Telliskivi dropped his eyes. So did Laker. He was embarrassed for the Colonel.

The Minister gazed at him. He no longer seemed like a benevolent wood-carver. "Colonel," he said. "Leaks are the least of your worries."

CHAPTER SEVEN

Laker returned to his hotel to shower and change and eat a sandwich from room service. He put Band-Aids on his scraped knees and took aspirin for the pain in his hand. Then he hired a car to take him to the NATO base, an hour outside the city.

He was held up at the gate for a long time. The explanation was that civilian vehicles were not allowed on base, but Laker suspected there was more to it. Antrobus might not welcome his visit.

Eventually a Humvee arrived, driven by a soldier in a uniform so sharp, Laker figured he had to be French. Sure enough, when he got out in front of the command post, the soldier said, *"Je vous attendrai, monsieur."* Maybe that was a hint to keep it short.

Antrobus had changed uniforms. He was now in camo fatigues, with high laced combat boots. The boots rested atop a pile of files, on a large, cluttered desk. He did not rise when Laker entered. Nor did his lieutenants, who were sitting at a side table with more paperwork.

"Laker," he said. "Why am I not surprised to see

you here? Having committed us to an internal investigation, which you were not authorized to do, you've come to get a report on its progress, which you're not authorized to have."

"It was obvious that the investigation had to take place."

"Quite. But you allowed the Estonians to pressure you into blurting out the promise they wanted. If you'd only kept your lip zipped for a minute, I could have . . ."

Antrobus dried up, like an actor who'd forgotten his lines. The lieutenants exchanged worried looks. But he recovered. He steepled his fingers, so that his West Point ring caught the light from the window, and said, "I could have required that the Minister make his request through the usual channels. Which would at the very least have bought us some time."

"I don't think time is on our side," Laker said.

"I've been on the phone to contacts in the Pentagon, who told me a great deal about you. You were a star running back for Notre Dame. You could have turned pro. Instead you went into the CIA. Saw active service in the Middle East. When you returned, you were being talked about for a high post in the Operations Directorate. Instead, you vanished into the mists beyond the CIA."

Antrobus's sources weren't very good, Laker noted with relief. This was old information. He said, "I'm with a small agency. We work in the cracks between the big agencies. Do things that would otherwise go undone."

"What a smooth way of saying that your successes always come at someone else's expense." Antrobus glanced sideways at his lieutenants, to make sure they'd caught this penetrating insight. "Why should I cooperate with you, when you're going to try to get the glory and make me the goat?"

"My hope is that a thorough investigation and prompt report will establish that the Semtex did not come from this base. Which will reflect well on everybody."

Antrobus considered. Then he unlaced his fingers and swung his feet off the desk. "All right. What are your questions? Not that I'm promising to answer."

"I'd just like to know the status of the investigation."

"We are conducting an inventory of all plastic explosive stores in the base armory."

"Good. What else?"

"If nothing is missing, we can file a report and we're done."

"I would suggest that you call your MPs for a report on personnel who are AWOL. See if any of them had access to the armory."

Antrobus smiled. He looked at his aides. They smiled, too.

"Here's the situation, Laker," Antrobus said. "We are less than a hundred kilometers from the Russian border. Too close for the Kremlin's comfort. They've been demanding that this base be closed for years. But Estonia has been standing firm, because we are the first line of defense against a Russian invasion.

"Once the news leaks about American Semtex being used in the terrorist attack, the ethnic Russians and other hostile elements will jump to the conclusion that it came from this base. That's bad. Now you're suggesting something even worse. That it was an inside job. A NATO soldier was involved in the theft. There's no sense turning over that stone unless we have to."

"It's something we can quickly check out. A possibility we can eliminate. I think that'll be all to the good."

Antrobus shrugged. The gold eagles on his epaulets glinted. "Very well," he said. "I assume you want to wait for the results. Cowan?"

One of the lieutenants jumped to his feet.

"Put Mr. Laker in one of the unused meeting rooms. Offer him coffee."

A slow half-hour passed before Laker was summoned back to the Colonel's office. An officer was sitting in front of the desk. He had ginger hair and moustache, and a muscular neck that bulged from his tight collar. He was wearing a tan uniform jacket with oversize pockets and a Sam Browne belt. Laker guessed he was British.

Antrobus said, "This is Captain Tyburn, head of the Military Police detachment on this base."

Tyburn stood and shook hands. Laker's fingers were able to take it. The aspirin must be working.

"Tyburn, your report," said Antrobus.

"As of 1300 hours, we have seven personnel classified as Absent Without Leave, sir."

"Are any of them cleared for access to explosives stored in the armory?"

"No, sir."

"Short and sweet," said Antrobus. "You're dismissed."

Tyburn hesitated, then said, "There is one soldier

who is late returning from a 72-hour leave. He won't be officially classified as AWOL, if we hear from him before 1700 hours."

"Then why are you bringing him up?"

"Because he's a clerk in the armory, sir."

Antrobus shot a venomous look at Laker. "A fellow Brit, Tyburn?"

"No, sir. He's U.S. Army."

"What's his name?" asked Laker.

"Mr. Laker's hoping he's a likely collaborator with the ethnic Russian terrorists," said Antrobus bitterly. "Does his name end in -vitch or -ski, by any chance?"

"His name is Mohammed Barsinian."

"Wait till the media get hold of that," Antrobus said. "Now we have a fucking Arab terrorist in the mix."

"Specialist Barsinian is not an Arab," Tyburn said.

He and Laker were in the back of a Humvee, headed for Barsinian's barracks to meet with his sergeant. Laker was glad that he had his good ear toward Tyburn. The base was noisy. A troop of soldiers jogged in file past them, heavy boots clumping. Helicopters passed overhead. The dry crackle of small-arms fire drifted in from some faraway range. Big engines were churning somewhere, either very large trucks or tanks.

"It's an Iranian name," Laker said.

"His father is Iranian, mother American. He was born in Detroit."

Tyburn's manner was stiff. He was sitting erect, looking straight ahead. All he needed was a swagger stick tucked under his arm, Laker thought. He said,

"Captain, I'm not jumping to any of the conclusions Colonel Antrobus is."

"Oh, the colonel's got a point. The media will hear the name Mohammed and start a fracas about Islamic terrorism. Especially media allied with the Russian separatists. They'd welcome a chance to shift the blame for the tram bombing."

"At this point, he's just an American soldier who's a little late returning from leave."

This seemed to reassure Tyburn. He unbent a little. "Barsinian's record is a bit odd. Joined up straight out of high school. Excelled in training. Showed a talent for languages. Knew Farsi and learned Pashto. That made him very valuable in Afghanistan."

"He worked in Intelligence?"

"At a low level, yes. But he looked set to rise. Unfortunately, he came up against prejudiced fellow soldiers, and he wasn't the type to back down. After a number of incidents, he and the Army agreed on an honorable discharge. Four years later, he applied to re-enlist."

"Unusual. I assume they put him through stringent background checks and interviews?"

"Yes. He claimed that he'd changed. And that has certainly turned out to be true."

"He doesn't get involved in fights with bigots?"

"Doesn't get involved in anything. Specialist Barsinian will never make corporal. He sleepwalks through his duties and seems interested only in having a good time on leave. His tardiness today is typical."

The Humvee turned into a long, straight road running between low prefabricated buildings. It stopped in front of one of them, and they got out.

"We'll find out more from Sergeant Johnson," Tyburn said. "He's a good man."

Tyburn pointed down the street. A lone soldier was coming toward them, double-time.

Tyburn turned to Laker. "Are you the Tom Laker who played for Notre Dame?"

"I didn't know the British followed American football."

"For some of us, rugby isn't violent enough."

Johnson reached them. He wasn't breathing hard. He came to attention and saluted Tyburn. Johnson was black, an average-size man but powerfully built. The hair that showed under his forage cap was salt-and-pepper. He had a chin like a brick.

"This is Mr. Laker from Homeland Security. It's about Specialist Barsinian."

Johnson's gaze shifted to Laker and back to Tyburn.

"It's all right, you can speak freely," Tyburn said.

"In that case, sir, I'm planning to ream Mo out. Kick his fat ass from here to Kansas City. He'll never be late returning from leave again. You don't have to worry about that, sir."

Tyburn smiled but made no comment. He said, "We'd like to see his personal effects."

The Sergeant opened the door of the barracks, and they went in. The sun shone through narrow windows set high in the walls onto the linoleum floor, which wasn't just clean but polished and flashed like a mirror. Walking between the rows of bunks, Laker noticed the blankets were so taut he could have bounced a quarter off every one. It was hard to believe forty men lived here, snoring and shitting and showering. There wasn't the slightest tinge of fug, only a tang of disinfectant. You could tell a lot about a sergeant from the condition of his men's quarters. Laker figured Tyburn was right. Johnson knew his trade.

"You called Barsinian 'Moe,'" Laker said to him.

"That's what he always goes by." Johnson allowed himself a slight smile. "Tells people he was named for one of the Three Stooges."

"Not a very dutiful Muslim?" Tyburn asked.

"Never seen him with a Koran. Or praying to Mecca. I make it clear to all my Muslim soldiers, they're as entitled to their religious observances as anybody else. But Mo's not interested."

"Does he drink and smoke?" Tyburn asked.

"Yep. He's a total pussy hound, too. Pardon my language, sir."

This to Laker. Funny how prim military people were around civilians. Especially ones from Washington. "Sergeant," he said, "I have a feeling you know why we're here. You've heard there's an inventory going on at the armory, including the section where Barsinian works, and you've put two and two together."

"Mo would have nothing to do with any missing Semtex," said Johnson. "He's a good soldier. The troubles he gets into are chickenshit. Pardon—"

"You're pardoned."

"Some soldiers just can't do peacetime. But if I ever have to go into a combat zone again, I'd want him with me."

Tyburn looked pleased by this endorsement. He was rooting for Barsinian to come out clean. So was Laker.

"This is his bunk," said Johnson.

"Open his locker please, Sergeant."

Boots squeaking on the linoleum floor, Johnson went down on one knee and pulled a metal trunk out from under one of the beds. It wasn't locked. Laker and Tyburn knelt and rummaged through Barsinian's clothes. His taste in off-duty clothing was colorful, verging on flashy. There were catalogues of expensive watches and car magazines. Like Laker, he had a fondness for muscle cars of the '60s and '70s, though he preferred Corvettes and Camaros. There was also a small box in green gift wrap with silver trim.

"Chocolates for the girls," Johnson said. "They're a special kind, filled with the local liqueur."

"Vanna Tallinn?" asked Laker. "I've heard of it."

"Can't say I care for it," said Tyburn. "But chocolates filled with it are a delicacy. You can only get them from one shop, place in the Old Town called Klein & Grossberg. Expensive."

"Mo says they do the trick," said Johnson. "With the girls, I mean."

They'd reached the bottom of the trunk. As they got to their feet, Tyburn said, "Thank you, Sergeant, that'll be all. You can return to your duties."

But Johnson hesitated. He said, "Sir, when they get finished with that inventory, could you let me know?"

"It's likely to take a long time before they know for sure if any Semtex is missing. Barsinian is a clerk in the office. They have to check out the possibility that he altered records to conceal his theft. Not that we're assuming there even were any thefts."

Johnson looked stricken.

Tyburn put a hand on his shoulder. "It's still possible all he did was miss his bus. He could walk through the gates anytime."

"Yes, sir. Thank you, sir."

They left Johnson kneeling before Barsinian's locker, carefully replacing its contents.

CHAPTER EIGHT

As darkness fell, Laker was back in Tallinn, riding the tram that ran along the modern boulevard toward the Old Town. The narrow car was crowded, the benches along its side filled and a lot of people standing, holding onto the leather straps. Laker had been lucky enough to find a seat, and he was studying pictures of Specialist Barsinian.

He was good looking, in a brooding way. His head was shaved practically to the skin on the sides, but he had a heavy lock of glossy black hair topping his forehead. Both his upper and lower eyelids were heavy. His eyebrows nearly met over his nose. He had full lips and a fleshy chin. The front full-figure shot showed a broad-shouldered, slim-waisted soldier at attention, but the rear view revealed the fat ass that his Sergeant had joked about. The MP who'd given Laker the pictures had pulled Barsinian in a couple of times. He said you could always spot him from behind. He had a pigeon-toed stride that made his ass wag in an unsoldierly fashion.

By the time Laker had returned to his hotel from the

base, five o'clock had passed and Barsinian was officially AWOL. What that meant, Tyburn explained by phone, was that he notified the NATO criminal investigative service to open a case file. But he would not send Humvees full of MPs to search the streets of Tallinn.

"How about the inventory at the armory?" Laker asked.

"Still going on. If we find that Semtex is missing, we have to assume the worst."

"Which is?"

"From what we've learned about Barsinian, it seems unlikely he's motivated by Islamic fanaticism."

"More likely he's motivated by money."

"Yes. He sold the Semtex to the highest bidder. Some ethnic Russian group, or whoever it was who blew up the tram station. Meanwhile Barsinian took the money and ran."

"Deserted."

"Yes. If that's correct, he's far away by now. He certainly wouldn't hang about in Tallinn, waiting to be arrested."

Which meant that the sensible course of action for Laker was to relax in his comfortable hotel room, watching CNN and sipping a single-malt scotch from the minibar. They had his favorite, Speyside Cardhu. He'd already checked.

But Laker had the feeling Barsinian was not beyond his reach. The feeling couldn't be justified by facts, only by experience. His hunches hadn't always proved right, but often enough to win him the nickname of Lucky Laker. Which he detested. But he did believe in his luck. So, with darkness falling and the temperature dropping, he'd set off, to check out his one and only decent lead.

He gave up his seat and took his place among the straphangers. He asked a tattooed teenager with ice skates over his shoulder if he spoke English. The answer, as usual, was yes, and Laker got directions to get off at the St. Christopher's Gate stop and go straight down the road to the chocolate shop.

He clambered down from the tram and surveyed the town's ancient wall. It looked less like a wall than a pile of rocks, blackened with centuries of soot. At intervals stood castellated towers, on which men had stood on freezing nights like this one, watching for marauders to come over the horizon. Men who'd had basically the same job he did.

As he drew near the gate, a van was coming to a stop in front of it. No vehicles were allowed in Old Town. People in warm, expensive clothes climbed down from it. A bare-headed young woman whose long blond hair was swirling in the wind raised a sign that said "Jamboree," the cruise line that owned the ship in the harbor that he'd seen from his hotel window this morning. The tourists followed their guide through the gate, and Laker followed them.

They were pointing and talking excitedly in various languages, blowing puffs of steam into the cold air. Laker had to admit the scene was picturesque. Floodlit spires and turrets seemed to float in the night sky. Lining the narrow street were small buildings with blackened beams and rough stone walls. They were shops now, and in their brightly lit windows were displays of local crafts: amber jewelry, stained glass, household items carved from wood. There were also clunky wristwatches, goggles, entrenching tools, and other gear left behind by the Red Army. More inviting to Laker were the windows of bars and restaurants, fogged by the warmth inside and glowing softly. Smoke wafted from their chimneys into the cold wind, which brought Laker the scent of burning firewood. He was tempted to go in and find a seat by the hearth.

It turned out he had only to follow the tourists to reach his destination. Klein & Grossberg Chocolatier, said the spotlit wooden signboard hanging over the street. No neon signs in Old Town. The tourists broke from their pack and hurried to the windows, exclaiming with delight. Laker, looking over their shoulders, saw that each window displayed a European landmark sculpted in chocolate: the Reichstag, Notre Dame Cathedral, Big Ben. Even the Ministry of Justice, where he'd been that morning.

One window had a chocolate *Titanic,* afloat on a sea of melted chocolate. The tourists exclaimed delightedly over it. Laker hadn't thought you would want to be reminded of the *Titanic* when you were on a cruise.

He followed the tourists into the warm, bright interior. Here the chocolate was in more edible form. Tiers of shelves were stacked with boxes of various sizes, filled with bite-size candy. The boxes were that distinctive green with silver ribbon he'd seen in Barsinian's locker. Signs in Estonian, German, and English described an endless variety of chocolates and fillings. He waited at the counter where women in green smocks were rushing around, giving samples to the tourists or ringing up their purchases. When his turn came, he stepped up to face a plump, freckle-faced redhead.

He no longer bothered to ask Estonians if they spoke

English, just said, "I'm looking for those chocolates with the Vanna Tallinn liqueur in them."

She wrinkled up her freckled nose.

"Don't like them?"

"Some of us think the national liqueur tastes like rubbing alcohol."

"They're not popular?"

"Oh, they're very popular. We can't keep up with demand. We're out of them now."

"What a shame. A friend recommended them to me. He gets them here, maybe you know him. His name's Mo."

"Oh, him," she said. "He always asks for Aldona. Let me get her for you."

Aldona looked like a supermodel. Tall and slender with a full bosom, long straight blond hair, and big gray-green eyes, which she rolled when he mentioned Mo.

"Yes, he's in here all the time."

That was a little surprising, considering Barsinian was a soldier stationed on a base an hour out of town. "A good customer, then."

"He spends a lot, if that's what you mean."

"But he's obnoxious?"

Demurely she put her fingertips to her plump lips. "I don't wish to speak ill of your friend, sir."

"That's all right. The guys all know that Mo is— well, a guy."

"I wish just once he could exchange money for merchandise and be done with it. But every time he says if I give him a smile he'll buy another box. If I bend down to a low shelf so he can look down my front, he'll make it three boxes."

"When did you last see him?"

"I don't remember exactly. It's never long enough

between visits. He puts his head in the door to ask if we've made a batch of his favorites."

"He doesn't even come in when you're not here. Walks on by," said the freckled girl.

"Lucky me," said Aldona.

Laker asked a few more questions. Barsinian had told the shop clerks more than they wanted to know about him. About the man he was pretending to be, rather. He said he was a tech executive from San Francisco who dealt with a local firm that made cell phones. He proffered invitations to nearby bars and restaurants—always the most expensive ones, but that got him nowhere with Aldona.

Laker was thoughtful as he left the shop. Barsinian seemed to spend a lot of time in this area. With his olive skin, American accent, and free-spending ways, he would stand out in Old Town. People would remember him. It was worth doing a canvass.

He spent the next hour walking along the street, going into each bar and restaurant. The Estonians seemed to be aware their potato-based cuisine was on the heavy side, because Old Town's eateries offered a variety of fare: Italian, French, sushi, barbecue, vegan. All of them, even the vegan, smelled good to Laker, who was getting hungrier and hungrier.

The canvassing went the way it did everywhere in the world: tedious and frustrating. Either people were indifferent, glancing at the photo, shaking their heads, and turning away, or they were too interested. They wanted to know who the guy was and why Laker was looking for him.

He finally got a nibble, in a fashion boutique where the purses cost as much as his first car. Mo had been in, with a girl who was as pretty as Aldona but not as fastidious.

He'd spent lavishly on her. And it was only four days ago.

Laker stepped out of the boutique, zipping up his parka and putting on his gloves for the twentieth time. It was getting colder, and the dun-colored sky threatened snow. Time to turn back to St. Christopher's Gate, maybe treat himself to a taxi to the hotel and that bottle of Speyside Cardhu in the minibar? But there were lighted windows in the building across the street, and he decided to give it a try.

The signboard was in English and said, "Home Port." Hard to tell what sort of business it was. Not a shop but some sort of office. Through the windows he saw desks with computers and phones, filing cabinets, maps on the walls. The half-dozen staff members were lean and young. The men had beards and glasses, the women had braids down their backs. They all looked earnest. Laker guessed this was an NGO. Not much to interest Mo here, but he went in anyway.

A woman came up the counter as he approached. She was fair-haired and slender. In fact her cheekbones and the bridge of her nose looked like they didn't have enough flesh over them. The wide, gray eyes added to the impression of fragility.

"You folks are working late," he said.

"We stay open when there's a tour from a cruise ship on the street. But this lot will probably just gorge themselves and head back to the ship. They have no interest at all."

"Interest in what?"

"The well-being of the crew. The people who are

serving them. The people on whom their lives could depend."

Step into an NGO and you were going to get their spiel. He would have to wait to ask his questions. He tried to look interested.

That was enough encouragement for the woman. "Home Port seeks to protect the rights of sailors," she said. "On passenger ships, on cargo vessels, too. This ship that's in harbor now, it's owned by an American company, but it's registered in Panama. Because Panama has very weak laws on crew rights. Most of the crewmembers are from poor countries like the Philippines. They're far from home, maybe not too fluent in English. Many are horribly exploited, overworked, and underpaid. But they have to support their families back home. Their governments are unable or unwilling to protect them."

Laker asked a few polite questions, and learned that the woman's name was Lina, and that in her opinion, Estonia had gone too far in forgetting its socialist past. Her countrymen had embraced the tourist trade and the exploitation of workers that went with it.

Nodding somber agreement, Laker said, "Wonder if I could change the subject. Does this man look familiar to you?"

He pulled Barsinian's full-face photo, rather dog-eared by now, out of his pocket and laid it on the counter.

Lina flinched. Her already wide eyes became enormous as she stared at the photo. The blood was rushing to her pale cheeks. A bit too loudly, she said, "No. Never seen him before. Sorry."

"Oh, too bad. He's an old friend from the Army. I

heard he lived around here somewhere, but I lost his address."

"I don't think you're telling the truth."

"No," said Laker. "But neither are you. You want to try being honest with each other? See how it goes?"

"I don't know. I'm wary of Americans. You could be with the CIA or something."

"I'm not with the CIA," said Laker. Which was a perfectly honest statement. He continued in the same vein. "Whatever this man told you, his name is Mohammed Barsinian. He's a soldier in the U.S. Army, stationed at the NATO base outside town. And he's AWOL. That's why I'm looking for him."

"Oh. Oh, God." She bowed her head. Her hands were gripping the edge of the counter so hard her knuckles were turning white. "He told me his name was Mohammed. But the rest—"

"He didn't say he was American?"

"No. Syrian. All his family had been killed in the war. He'd found a boat out. He was working at a local fish-processing plant. He needed a place to stay."

"You could help him with that?"

She pointed a shaky finger at the ceiling. "We own the building. A donor bought it and gave it to us. There's a little apartment upstairs. We didn't ask Mohammed for ID, because he was an illegal immigrant. He was very grateful. He's paid us every week. In cash."

"Is he up there now?"

"No. We hear his footsteps when he is. But he works very long hours. Or that's what he said, anyway."

"When's the last time you saw him?"

"We hardly ever do. There's a separate staircase. He doesn't come in. He said he's embarrassed because when he gets off work he stinks of fish. I guess that's not true, either."

"Soldiers don't stink of fish."

"Oh God. I shouldn't have believed him." She looked up at Laker, for the first time in several minutes. "Maybe I shouldn't have believed you, either. You're going to call the police now. Make trouble for us."

"No."

"Then what do you want of us?"

"Nothing. In particular, I want you not to warn Specialist Barsinian."

"We have no way of reaching him anyway."

"Just go about your business, then. Nothing for you to worry about, except you're going to lose your rent money. Specialist Barsinian will be moving into a cell at the NATO base for a while."

He took the photograph and turned away. Lina was going to gather the other employees and give them the news, of course. He hoped he'd been able to soothe her fears. He didn't want Mohammed Barsinian to look through the window and notice anything out of the ordinary when he returned home. With luck, the NGO's staff would have closed shop and left by the time he arrived.

But Laker would still be here.

He crossed the street. The buildings along this part of it were all old two-story houses of stone and wood, standing only a couple of feet apart. He slid into a gap where he was sheltered from the wind and out of sight, but he could still see the doorway next to Home Port's windows, the one that led to the stairs to the upstairs apartment. He delved deep into his layers of clothing and pulled out his cell phone.

"Tyburn here."

"It's Laker. Barsinian's still around. He has a hideout in the Old City."

"Is he there now?"

"No. I'm watching for him. How fast can you get here?"

"Forty-five minutes, with siren and lights."

"Turn them off before you get too close. Call me when you reach St. Christopher's Gate. If we don't scare him off, we've got him."

"On our way."

Laker put the phone away. Zipped up his parka and put his gloves on. Pulled his knit cap down over his ears. It was getting even colder, and snow was beginning to fall. When conditions were this bad, you could count on a stakeout to go on for hours with nothing happening. As it got later, the street would empty, but for the moment there were still people walking by occasionally, all with hats and scarves or turned-up collars. Through the windows, he could see the Home Port staffers huddled at the back of the office. No doubt they were having an impassioned discussion about the most ethical course of action in this difficult situation. He hoped they wouldn't do anything stupid. Wished they would all go home.

Just ten minutes later, Barsinian appeared.

It was easy to spot him. The toe-inward stride that made his broad rear end swing betrayed him. By the time he stopped in front of his door, Laker was on the move. He glanced in both directions as he crossed the street, saw no pedestrians approaching through the darkness and swirling snow. He timed his approach to reach Barsinian when his hands were occupied with key and door handle.

Barsinian's head began to turn. He'd heard the squeak of dry snow under Laker's footsteps. Laker lunged. Slammed Barsinian against the door, locked an arm tight around the man's throat. Squirming, Barsinian tried to kick or elbow him.

"Specialist Mohammed Barsinian," Laker said. "You are AWOL."

Barsinian's struggles ceased. He said, "Okay. I won't try to get away. Just let me breathe."

Laker took his forearm away. He frisked Barsinian and found no weapons. Then he backed up a step. His weight was on the balls of his feet and his fists were up. As Barsinian turned, he watched the soldier's hands. But Barsinian didn't make a move, just looked at him.

"You're not from the base. I know all the MPs."

"I'm from Washington."

"Wouldn't think I'd rate that, just for being AWOL."

"They're taking inventory of the Semtex at the base armory. I expect you know what they're going to find."

"They think *I* stole Semtex? What for?"

"Why did you go AWOL?"

"Strawberry blond name of Nikola. Not the type to wait for me till my next leave. So I had to make the most of her while I had her. I just put her on the tram. Now I'm on my way back to base. My sergeant'll make me do five hundred push-ups a day for the next month. Don't you think that's punishment enough?"

"You have a talent for bullshit, Specialist," Laker said. "But it's still bullshit."

Barsinian's dumb, wheedling expression melted away, to be replaced by a lopsided, wise-ass grin. "Okay. I feel sorry for the guys taking the inventory. It'll take 'em a while to find the shortfall. I laid a fake paper trail all the way back to the manufacturer."

"But they will find it. What did you do with the Semtex?"

"Sold it, what do you think?" The grin faded as he looked at Laker narrowly. "Hey, wait a minute. You don't think—"

"It's what blew up the tram station. Local cops have established that."

Barsinian's eyes were wide, his mouth working. After a moment he found his voice. "No, man. Don't hand me over to the cops. Take me back to base. Please."

"Turn around and start walking, Specialist. Slowly. I'll be right behind you."

Barsinian obeyed. After a few steps, he said, "Where're we going?"

"St. Christopher's Gate. We'll meet the MPs there. Or I'll call the locals. Depending on how much you tell me on the way."

"I'll tell you everything. Just don't hand me to the cops. You maybe noticed, this is the whitest country in the world, man. They hate my fucking skin here. They'll flay it off me if they get the chance."

"Why did you rent that upstairs room?"

"It's a place to take dates. I hate going to hotels. You check in with a white girl and they look at you like—"

"Kind of a lavish expense."

"No, man, the bleeding hearts at the NGO gave me a deal."

"You've been spending freely, Specialist. Where's the money coming from?"

"Okay. Sometimes I boost stuff on the base, sell it in town. But never weapons or explosives, until the Semtex. It was just this one time, I swear."

"Who'd you sell it to?"

"I don't know. It was in a bar and I was shit-faced."

"You'll have to do better than that."

"Okay. It was local guys. Not foreigners. Sure as hell not Arabs."

"What'd they look like?"

Barsinian's steps slowed as if was trying to remember. Laker closed the distance between them without noticing. Swiftly and precisely, Barsinian lifted his right boot and slammed it into Laker's kneecap.

Even as the pain burned through him Laker realized what would come next and tried to step back. But the injured knee buckled and he stumbled. By now Barsinian had turned around. His right fist flew at Laker's face. Laker swayed and avoided that blow but not the next. Barsinian's left fist landed just below the breastbone, in the solar plexus. Laker's breath whooshed out of him. He tried to get his head down and fists up but was too slow. Barsinian hit him in the face twice, a left and a right, and he was out.

He came to with his face in the snow. Had the feeling he hadn't been unconscious long. There were people talking over him, hands clutching his arms, helping him get up. The world spun. Tilted. Settled down. He blinked and focused on the two faces in front of him. A man and a woman. Middle-aged. Concerned.

"The man who hit me—did you see him? Which way did he go?"

Now, at the worst possible moment, he encountered his first Estonians who did not speak English. They looked at each other, shook their heads, and shrugged. The woman spoke soothingly. Maybe offering to help him limp to their fireside and give him a glass of Vanna Tallinn liqueur.

Laker was sure he'd only been out for a few seconds and Barsinian couldn't have gotten far. He stepped away from the supporting hands and nearly lost his balance. Recovered it.

Turning slowly in a circle, he looked at the snowy ground. Ignored the dark splotches of his blood and concentrated on the footprints. It was easy to spot Barsinian's, with the toes turned inward. They did not lead toward St. Christopher's Gate, but in the other direction.

Laker followed them, ignoring the calls from his would-be saviors. He tried to run, but the snow was too deep and he was still half-dazed. The knee that had been kicked was throbbing. Barsinian knew his hideout was blown. Why the hell was he going back there? The smart thing to do would be run to the gate and flag down a taxi. Head for the train station or the airport.

The spotlight on the sign that said Home Port was still on. As Laker got closer he could see that the lights in the upstairs windows were also on. Barsinian was up there, maybe retrieving something that would help him in his flight. Cash. A fake passport.

A gun. Laker cursed himself for obeying Mason's order to leave his Beretta behind.

Lurching and grunting with pain every time his

weight came down on his injured knee, he ran toward the building. The lights were still on in the Home Port office, too, and the staffers were still huddled in their ethical discussion. One skinny bearded guy was standing, beating the air with his fist as he made his points.

Laker went blind. It was like running into a wall of light. The shock wave and the roar of the explosion hit him at the same moment, knocking him flat on his back. He lay there dazed, nearly losing consciousness. Again the wind had been knocked out of him, and as he struggled to breathe deep, heat seared his lungs. He became aware of a prickling of his skin. Snowflakes? No. Small pieces of glass embedded in his face. He opened his eyes. Good. He could see. He managed to haul himself up on one elbow.

The sturdy little building was still standing. A large hole had been blown in the roof. Water was pouring off the eaves, which confused him until he realized it was melted snow. Fires were burning in every window, reaching out into the night, gouts of flame breaking off and floating away. He could see nothing of the office, of the group of staffers, of the man who had been wagging his fist only minutes ago.

They no longer existed.

CHAPTER NINE

"I talked to Ken's parents yesterday," Stan Rahmberg said. "In Iowa. They're taking his death pretty hard. I really, really, don't want to call them back and tell them their son is under investigation."

He and Ava were sitting in his office in K Directorate, Section 14. She had come to see him as soon as she arrived for work. And promptly ruined his day. He slumped in his chair, looking more basset-hound-like than usual. The weight of the bags under his eyes seemed to drag the lids down, so that she could see their pink insides. His jowls drooped.

"I wish I hadn't found out what I did," Ava said. "But now we have to deal with it."

Rahmberg swiveled his chair away from her and looked out his window. Like most mid-level managers in the NSA, he had a view not of the outside world, but of the people he supervised. In the large room beyond the glass, a score of programmers sat at desks, looking at screens and tapping keys. Nobody was at the desk at the end of the nearest row. Its surface was bare except for the computer. Next to the blank screen sat a cardboard box, its flaps sealed.

"Ken's personal effects," Rahmberg said. "I was going to send them to Iowa, but I guess I better hold onto them. You really think he'd gone bad?"

"I don't think he sold secrets. It may have been nothing more than commercially useful information."

"Commercially useful information. But after the Morales organization got hold of it, they murdered him." Rahmberg swiveled the chair back and looked at her. "How much do you know about Morales?"

"Not much."

"He's on TV a lot. Escorting some star to a Hollywood premiere. Handing out trophies at his golf tournaments. Shaking hands with politicians at fund-raisers. Bragging about how he makes deals, breaks deals, cuts corners. Doesn't surprise me that he's mob-connected. But having Ken murdered . . ." Rahmberg shook his head. "That information must've been mighty hot."

"That's why I've come to you. Before going to Admiral Hardin, I need to have some idea what kind of information Ken had access to."

"You want to know what this section does?" Rahmberg's gaze shifted back to his subordinates toiling on the other side of the window. "We're the unsung heroes of this agency. We prevent NSA from sinking under the weight of the useless data it collects."

"I know K Directorate monitors Web traffic."

"Right. K monitors jihadist and neo-Nazi websites, obviously. But also Facebook and LinkedIn and TripAdvisor. That sea of information that sloshes around the internet all the time. It's one of the biggest big-data crunching operations going on in the world today. Most of it done by computers, of course. Flagging words like *assassination* and *sarin*. That kind of thing. But at a certain level, humans have to get involved. Flagged communications go to teams of analysts, who determine which ones are significant and send them up the chain. The rest of the stuff, meaning 99 percent, comes here for disposal."

"Why don't the analysts just press the delete key when they're done?"

"Bureaucratic indecision. You know the NSA. Everybody's worried that somebody else is second-guessing them. So we hold the data for varying periods of time, following protocols given to us by the analysts. Sometimes they want files back for review. But very, very rarely."

This time it was Ava who looked out at the employees at their rows of desks. She said, "These people have access to a lot of information, in other words."

"No. They're not supposed to open and read files. There's no need to. The analysts label the files by subject matter and date. And that's all people in this section need to know."

"But if they wanted to open a file, what would stop them?"

"I'm not looking over their shoulders all the time, if that's what you mean."

"No offense, Stan. But Ken was way too smart for a shit job like this."

Rahmberg bridled. He was about to make an angry retort but thought better of it. "Yeah," he said. "Ken was bored. Maybe a little resentful."

No maybe about it, Ava thought. She said, "Suppose

Ken came across a—what do you call it—a communication he thought the Morales organization would pay money for."

"Possible. Morales's resort chain has global interests."

"What would he do with it?"

"How would he get the text or picture or whatever it was out of here, you mean? Not easy. These computers aren't connected to a printer. They don't have ports for USB sticks. Or drives for disks."

"Email?"

"We're behind a firewall."

"One that a bright programmer like Ken couldn't find a hole in?"

"No. I can't say that."

"If he sent a communication out of here, do you think you could figure out what it was?"

"Tricky. Ken would've covered his tracks. But given enough time, I think I could do it."

Rahmberg sighed and slumped deeper in his chair. "I think I'm going to have to."

Admiral Hardin listened to Ava's report without interrupting her. Her pale eyes gazed impassively at Ava. But the Y-shaped vein down the middle of her forehead surfaced and became steadily more prominent.

When Ava finished, she said, "Who else knows about this, North?"

"Just Stan Rahmberg. I came straight from his office."

"That's a blessing, anyway. There will be no investigation of the late Kenneth Brydon. I'm instructing you to say nothing more about the matter. I'll issue the same instruction to Rahmberg."

Ava leaned forward in her chair, staring across the broad desk at Hardin in disbelief. "But Ken sold information. He was murdered."

"You have no proof. All you have is a chain in which every link is weak. Brydon gambled and got lucky. He returned the next week and was mugged. That's all."

"Detective Amighetti says—"

Hardin held up her hand, palm out. "I don't want to hear any more about Amighetti. He played you brilliantly. Turned you into his ally against your own agency."

"Aren't we on the same side?"

"You're young and naive, North. Amighetti's an ambitious cop, trying to blow up a routine crime into a media sensation. To build his reputation at the expense of a federal agency."

"He's trying to find out why Ken was killed. Bring his murderer to justice. Isn't that what we want, too?"

"Noble-sounding words. Another way to put it is you're trying to destroy the reputation of a colleague who can't defend himself."

"I'm not saying we should go public with any of this yet. Just that we should begin an internal investigation, to see if Ken took any information out of here."

"You have no idea what an internal investigation is like. Mention the mere possibility of a security breach, and S Directorate Section 2 takes over. Half a dozen assholes set up shop in an office down the hall, calling in everybody in our directorate one by one and interrogating them. While the rest of us creep by the closed door on tiptoe and await our turn. Internal investigations usually don't find what they're after. But they do find out who's smoking in the building. Cruising porno on the internet. Taking classified files to the cafeteria. A lot of useless shit. Then they go back to the Director and tell him the DD's running a slack operation."

"Even if it's disruptive, we have to find out—"

"Jesus Christ, North! You should have been out of here five minutes ago. It's always the same goddamned thing with you. When your superior makes a decision, you accept it. Get your ass out the door. If you can't learn that, I have to wonder about your future with this agency."

Ava kept silent.

"I'm going to have to write you up," Hardin went on. "It'll have to be three reprimands. For Rahmberg. For Amighetti. For going to the casino in the first place. I have to warn you, they will stay in your file and do lasting damage to your career. And there will have to be a review of your security clearance, which could lead to reassignment."

"I can take a hint. You don't have to cut the buttons off my coat. Or break my sword over your knee."

Hardin stared at her openmouthed for a moment. The vein in her forehead was pounding visibly. "This is not the moment for insolence."

"Yes, it is," Ava said, as she rose from her chair. "I quit. You'll have my letter of resignation on your desk within the hour."

CHAPTER TEN

"You look bad, Laker," said Col. Antrobus. "Which on the whole is in your favor. At least people will feel sorry for you."

His hospital room at the NATO base had no mirror, so Laker couldn't verify Antrobus's statement. But he didn't doubt it. The explosion had driven tiny glass fragments into his face. They'd all been dug out, and now his forehead and cheeks were dotted with Band-Aids. Barsinian's punches had broken his nose, which was splinted and bandaged. Antrobus's voice came to him faintly, through a distortion that rose and fell like the sound of ocean waves. He remembered that, too, from the IED blast in Baghdad. The hearing in his right ear had never fully come back. He'd hoped this time he'd be luckier with the left ear.

He also hoped that as his ears healed his balance would come back. Right now he could barely lie down without holding onto something. That was why this conference was being held at his bedside. A pile of pillows propped him up in a sitting position.

Tyburn was sitting in a chair on his left. Antrobus was pacing, looking out the window at a lot full of parked Humvees.

"Are we expecting anyone else?" Laker asked. His own voice sounded faint in his ear.

"Commissioner Telliskivi of the Tallinn police. The sergeant, soon to be corporal, at the gate was stupid enough to let him in without checking with me first. When he gets here, we'll allow him a look at you. That ought to convince him you're in no shape to be questioned."

"I want to talk to him," Laker said.

"What you want doesn't matter, You are the subject of negotiations at the highest level, Laker."

"The highest level?" Laker said. He wasn't sure he'd heard the words correctly.

"Our Ambassador is meeting with the Prime Minister as we speak."

"About me?"

"As soon as our doctors finish reviewing your brain scans and determine that your concussion did you no lasting damage, you will be released from the hospital. The question is where you go then. Back to Washington to face the Senate Intelligence committee or to jail in Tallinn to await criminal charges."

Laker was having a hard time hearing and putting together the words. But one thing was clear. Antrobus was in a merry mood. Just when he'd given up hope, a kindly fate had provided him with a scapegoat. Saving his ass suddenly looked doable.

"You just had to make the rest of us look stupid, didn't you, Laker?" he said happily. "You got out in front of everybody. Made the key decision on your own. And did you ever choose wrong."

"Beg your pardon, sir," said Tyburn. "But I think Mr. Laker's decision to call me rather than the police was entirely defensible. At that point, Barsinian was an AWOL soldier, nothing more."

Laker gave the ginger-haired Englishman a nod of thanks. It'd been a nice try. A Senate committee wasn't going to consider his decision defensible. Even he didn't.

"No use, Tyburn," said Antrobus. "Laker knew about the upstairs room."

"Barsinian told him he was using it as a love nest."

"He was using it to store the explosives he was selling to the highest bidder."

"You'll recall from my report, sir, that not until this morning did we complete our inventory and determine that a large quantity of Semtex was missing. Barsinian was very ingenious about covering his thefts."

"How's Sergeant Johnson taking the news?" Laker asked.

"Deeply shaken, as you can imagine." Tyburn said. "He can't believe how completely Barsinian had him fooled."

"Tell him not to feel too bad. He had me fooled, too."

A nurse in pale blue scrubs arrived with Commissioner Telliskivi. His goatee was as neatly trimmed as before, and the long thin face looked mournful. Antrobus moved to the door to block him from entering.

"Sorry, Commissioner. As you can see, Mr. Laker is in bad shape. In all decency, we cannot make him available for interview."

"I'm willing to talk to you, Commissioner," said Laker

Antrobus shot him an irritated look over his shoulder. "I'm afraid it's out of the question."

"I'm not proposing an interrogation, just an informal exchange of information," said Telliskivi in his gentle voice. "It's intended as a courtesy to you, Colonel. When your Ambassador finishes his meeting with the Prime Minister, you will be receiving a phone call. Which I fear will not be pleasant."

Antrobus put his hands behind him and clasped them—as if literally covering his ass, Laker thought. He backed up enough to let Telliskivi enter. Then he waved the nurse away and shut the door.

Telliskivi pulled up a chair beside Tyburn. It crossed Laker's mind that they were like anxious relatives gathering around his deathbed. He tried to dismiss the thought.

Tyburn was impatient. He said, "Can you state with certainty that Barsinian is dead?"

Telliskivi said, "Yes. He perished in the explosion."

"Thank God for that anyway," said Antrobus. "It sure took you long enough."

"This is a difficult crime scene because of the force of the blast and extent of the destruction. We found Barsinian's dog tags on a roof a hundred meters away. Some thought that suggested he'd discarded them fleeing the scene."

"But we provided you with his dental records," Tyburn said.

"Thank you. And they did establish his identity. Once we had gathered up enough of his teeth."

Laker braced himself to ask a question he didn't really want the answer to. "Was everyone in the building killed? All the Home Port people?"

"We will not be able to state that for certain for a long time. Dental records won't be enough. It will take DNA analysis of bone fragments. But I have to say, it is not promising. The Home Port staff members were dedicated activists who had many friends. So far, no one reports seeing any of them alive since the explosion."

"All six of them dead," Laker murmured. He'd been the last to see them alive. He remembered looking in the window at the cluster of young people with earnest faces, listening to the bearded man who was shaking his fist as he made his points. If only he'd warned them. If only, when he'd had his arm around Barsinian's neck, he'd choked the life out of him.

Telliskivi opened his mouth, hesitated, decided to say it. "We still have hope for one of them. Lina Opalski. The owner of a café in the next street said that she came to pick up coffee for the staff and left shortly before the explosion. But he couldn't remember how long. It's possible the explosion took place before she got back."

"But no one has seen her, either?" asked Tyburn.

Telliskivi somberly shook his head. Laker thought of the thin woman with wide pale eyes and delicate cheekbones, who looked as if a tap would shatter her. Hard to hold out any hope she'd survived.

Tyburn said, "Why do you think Barsinian went back, after he knocked Mr. Laker cold? Why didn't he flee?"

Antrobus snorted. "Obvious, Tyburn. He went back to retrieve his valuable hoard of Semtex. He still had enough to sell to the next terrorist who came along, and in his hurry he set it off by accident."

"No, Colonel," Telliskivi said. "Barsinian did not sell the Semtex. Any of it."

"What?"

"Now we come to the part of the investigation which the Prime Minister is discussing with your Ambassador." He looked at Laker with sad dark eyes. "While Mr. Laker was in the ambulance, one of our inspectors thought to examine his discarded coat. He found a photo of Specialist Barsinian. We showed it to the survivors of the tram bombing."

"The tram bombing," Antrobus said. "But Barsinian wasn't on the scene."

"He was positively identified by a woman named Johanna Janssen. He was in the tram car with her, minutes before the explosion. She got a good look at him because he picked up her baby's pacifier and gave it back to her."

"Did the child survive?" Laker asked.

"No. Nor did her father, who was also with her."

"So Barsinian was the bomber," said Antrobus. "Christ. That's the worst thing that could happen to us."

It seemed to Laker that compared to Johanna Janssen they had nothing to complain about. But he kept silent.

Antrobus was pacing in agitation. "Now we know the whole truth about Specialist Mohammed Barsinian. He was a fucking Muslim terrorist. A lone wolf who just wanted to kill as many Westerners as possible. He set off the Semtex in the upstairs room deliberately. He was impatient to go to Allah and receive his forty virgins. And kill six more Estonians at the same time."

Tyburn said, "I wouldn't be so sure—"

"A United States soldier turned suicide bomber,"

Antrobus raged on. "I can imagine what your Prime Minister is telling our Ambassador, Telliskivi. 'You brought a Muslim terrorist into our midst, *and* you provided him with the weapons to kill our citizens.'"

"The Prime Minister—" Telliskivi began, but Antrobus interrupted.

"This is your doing, Laker. You had him and you let him go. Congratulations. You've done something that wouldn't have seemed possible. You've cleared the ethnic Russians of suspicion. United them and the rest of the population. Against *us*. NATO. When this gets out, we'll have thousands of demonstrators at our gates. Demanding that NATO get out of the country."

"Possibly you are exaggerating, Colonel," said Telliskivi mildly.

"Tyburn, double the guard at the gate. Triple it. Make sure the perimeter is secure."

"Yes, sir." Tyburn got to his feet. "Will that be all, Commissioner?"

Telliskivi nodded.

"What about Laker?" asked Antrobus. "What does your Prime Minister want done with him?"

"I have no information on that."

"Oh no?" said Antrobus petulantly. "You seem to know everything else."

"I would like to report to my chief in Washington," Laker said. "Can you arrange a secure link?"

"Your chief won't talk to you," Antrobus said. "Don't you know how things are done in Washington? You won't see your chief again until he officiates at your public evisceration."

"Before the evisceration, he'll want my report."

Nobody on the base was in a hurry to accommodate Laker. Two hours passed before the secure Skype link to Washington was ready. He was feeling more clear-headed and steady on his feet as he and Tyburn walked down the path to the Communications Building. The sky was blue and cloudless, but the air felt as cold as last night. Laker was grateful for the fatigue jacket Tyburn had found for him, along with shirt and pants. The clothes he'd been wearing last night were torn, blood-stained, and saturated with smoke. Only his shoes were wearable. From the direction of the front gate, the shouts of demonstrators were audible.

Antrobus had been right about that part, anyway.

Eventually he was alone in a small room, sitting in a hard chair facing a laptop screen. Sam Mason, in shirt-sleeves and loosened tie, was sitting in his office, face unreadable. Over his shoulder, Laker could see a patch of gray sky and the Capitol dome.

"What happened, Tom?"

Laker suppressed a flinch. He knew things were bad when his boss called him by his first name. "I fucked up."

"Don't excoriate yourself. There are plenty of people here waiting to do that. Right now I need your report."

Laker was familiar with Mason's debriefing style. He demanded a plain, factual narrative. No specula-tions or excuses. Laker gave it to him, starting with the cab ride yesterday morning that had put him in the middle of a riot. By the time he finished, he was feel-ing better. Not that his recent conduct looked any less stupid to him. But he understood what was going on.

Partly, anyway. And had an idea what had to be done next.

Mason was silent. He rubbed his eye. Then he lifted the patch and rubbed underneath it. The routine gave him time to think.

"Seems to me," he said at last, "the vital question is, who the hell was Mohammed Barsinian?"

"I agree."

"The thinking here, mostly based on what our ambassador in Estonia has communicated, is that he must have been contacted by Islamic radicals who converted him to the cause. Then he waited for his chance to kill Westerners, and finally it came."

"That's consistent with what Col. Antrobus thinks."

"Antrobus sounds like an asshole. Is he?"

"Yes."

"He's probably wrong, then. What do you think?"

"The Head MP here told me that on his first hitch, Barsinian was a smart, tough, ambitious soldier, working intel in Afghanistan. Encounters prejudice, resigns. Four years later, re-ups. Now he's a laid-back, good-time guy. I'm curious about those four years."

"You think he was recruited. But not by Islamic terrorists."

"The Beetle Bailey routine was his cover. He was an agent in place, waiting for his orders to come. Barsinian was good at fooling people. His sergeant thought he was a good soldier. The girls in Tallinn thought he was a free-spending IT executive from California. The Home Port people thought he was a pitiful Syrian refugee." Laker took a deep breath. "And I thought he was whipped. Nothing on his mind but trying to talk his way out of the hole he was in."

"You let your guard down?"

"I don't even have that excuse. He just beat me. He was fast and strong."

"Put that together with the skills he displayed in carrying out the tram op—"

"Yes. He was a highly trained agent."

"Working for?"

"FSB. I think your original guess was right, boss. Moscow's decided to directly intervene in the Baltic states. It wasn't a sudden decision. In Barsinian, they had a carefully placed sleeper agent. This is the moment they chose to activate him, to drive a wedge between the Estonians and NATO."

"But you've got a problem, Laker," Mason said. "Your highly trained and disciplined FSB agent suddenly turns into a panicky amateur. Having knocked you out, he could've gotten away clean. Instead, he went back to his room and blew himself up."

Laker nodded. "There's only one way his actions make sense. He had orders to destroy Home Port."

Mason never took notes during a debrief. Didn't have to. He remembered every detail. "The NGO on the floor below the apartment. Defending the rights of sailors. Why would Moscow be interested in them?"

"I don't know. And now it's impossible to find out. The records were destroyed. All the personnel killed. Or so it seems."

"There was the woman who went for coffee. Lina Opalski. They were holding out some hope for her."

"So am I."

Mason seldom smiled, and when he did, there wasn't much to it. Just a slight curl at one corner of his mouth. "Okay, Laker. What are you proposing?"

"I'm thinking that the woman—Lina is her name— has figured out that Home Port was targeted. Meaning she's in danger. She's gone into hiding or fled. The police aren't going to find her. Maybe I can."

The smile had disappeared. Mason sighed and laid both hands flat on the desk in front of him. "I am unable to give you that assignment. I've received my orders from the Secretary for Homeland Security, who's received his from the President. You are to return to Washington. Senators are concerned about intelligence-agency overreach and bungling that have caused strains in the NATO alliance. You are to be burned at the stake, live on CNN."

"I deserve it. I was wrong about Barsinian before. But . . ."

"But you're right now?"

"I'm sure of it."

"Too late. I have no discretion to give you any order but hop on the first plane back."

"Boss, you sent me to Estonia to find out if there was direct Russian involvement in the tram attack. There was. The implication is obvious."

Mason nodded. "Moscow's advancing its timetable for sending its tanks across the border."

"Not just the Estonian border."

"No. They want all of the Baltic states back."

"So we're talking about World War III," Laker said.

Mason bowed his head in thought. For a minute that felt much longer, Laker gazed at Mason's bare and gleaming pate, crisscrossed by the black straps of the eye patch. Finally he said, "There's only one order I can give you. Come home. But I hereby order you to disobey it."

"Yes, sir."

"I can offer you no protection, no support."

"I understand. I'm on my own."

"You sure you do?" Mason's broad brow was lined with concern. "This time I won't have your back, Laker. I can't stop the CIA from going after you. Or the FBI."

"Or the NSA."

"Or the NSA. You want me to call Ava?"

"No. We have to preserve your deniability. I'll call her myself."

CHAPTER ELEVEN

The red light on Ava's landline phone was blinking when she got home, shortly after noon. She ignored it. Anybody she wanted to talk to called her cell phone. It was mostly solicitations and robocalls on the home phone.

She set down the box containing her personal possessions from the NSA and dropped wearily on the sofa. It felt strange, being home at noon. She'd worked long hours at her job, when she'd had a job, and spent most weekends at Laker's loft near the Naval Yard. So she wasn't used to seeing her apartment in daylight.

It was a very nice apartment, a roomy condo on a high floor of a 1920s building near Dupont Circle. Other junior employees of the NSA would not have been able to afford such a place, as she was guiltily aware. It had been in the North family for decades, having served as a pied-à-terre for uncles in the diplomatic corps, a capital residence for cousins representing distant states in Congress, a love nest for an aunt who was the mistress of a Cabinet member. It happened to be available, and the family had thrust Ava into it.

They'd brushed aside her protests that she wanted to live on her salary, which would only allow her to rent a small apartment in the Maryland suburbs. Not that they weren't taking her career seriously. It was just that Norths did not pay rent. They only collected it.

The intercom buzzed: someone at the street door. She went to it and pressed the button.

"Yes?"

"It's Rahmberg."

"Stan, thank you for coming. I'll buzz you in."

A couple of minutes later she opened the door to him. He looked as lugubrious as ever. She waved him to a seat and offered tea or coffee.

"Thanks, but I'll have to keep this short. I'm on my lunch hour and it's a long drive back to Fort Meade."

"Of course. I'm so sorry to put you to the trouble. But I didn't have a chance to see you before I left the NSA. There were two Marines standing over me as I cleared out my desk. Then they confiscated my passes and ID card and frog-marched me out to my car."

"I was sorry to hear what had happened to you."

"Did Admiral Hardin call you?"

"Yes, to tell me to suspend permanently any attempts to investigate Ken Brydon."

"What did she say about me?"

"That you were a prima donna who couldn't cut it at the NSA."

Ava nodded, unsurprised. "She'll expect me to spend my time shopping and dating lobbyists. That's good. It'll serve our purposes."

Rahmberg turned his weary eyes on her. "I figured when you asked me to come here, it was to discuss something you couldn't say on the phone."

"Stan, we can't let this drop. Ken Brydon stole classified information and sold it to somebody in the Morales organization. Who ordered him killed."

"You want me to continue the search till I find out what he stole."

"Yes."

"Disobeying an order from the Deputy Director."

"I'm sorry. But yes."

"And if my search is successful, you're planning to go over the Deputy Director's head."

"I'll try to cover for you, but—"

"You can't guarantee it."

"No."

Rahmberg laid a hand on the arm of the sofa and pushed himself to his feet with a heavy sigh. He said, "This is going to take a while. It won't be easy backtracking Ken. He was a resourceful guy. And of course I'll have to continue with my regular duties. If anybody suspects what I'm doing for you, we're through."

She followed him to the door and opened it for him. As he went out, she said, "Thanks, Stan. I'm sorry I had to get you involved."

"Don't thank me. I'm doing this for my country." He smiled wryly. "In my job, never thought I'd get a chance to say that line."

She hugged him, and he left. Going into the kitchen, she made herself a cup of herbal tea, which she hoped would be calming. Back in the living room, she noticed the blinking light and went to listen to the message.

It startled her so much to hear Laker's voice that his message was over before she grasped it. She rewound and hit play.

"Ava, take this tape straight to your superiors," said the voice that always sounded calm, no matter what. "I don't want you to get in trouble. You're going to hear a lot of bad stuff about me. Don't believe it. I love you. I'll always remember what you said, last time we were together."

That was all. She got up and paced several distracted circuits of the apartment while her insides seemed to coil and writhe. How she wished he hadn't said that he loved her! Nothing could drag the three little words out of him, except the knowledge that he was going into extreme danger.

And what was that last part, about always remembering what she'd said? That wasn't like Laker. Too sappy. She realized after a moment's thought that he was talking in code. The last time they were together, she'd warned him to look for a bear under the bed.

He wanted her to know that he was going up against the Russians.

She sat down in front of the television and picked up the remote. She had to find out what had happened, and the only way was CNN. She didn't dare call Sam Mason or anyone at the Gray Outfit.

If only she'd been able to talk to Laker. But he'd deliberately called her home at a time when she wouldn't be there, so she would have a tape to give to her superiors, to prove that he hadn't told her where he was. He was doing his best to keep her out of trouble at the NSA. Protect her job.

Someday, the irony might be amusing.

CHAPTER TWELVE

Early the next morning, Ava was in the waiting room of Senator Charles E. North (R-Okla.)

Like most Norths, Uncle Chuck had been born in a D.C. suburb and educated at Andover and Yale, but then he had struck out for the West to make his own fortune and prove he was his own man. Even now, safely back inside the beltway, he made sure that his waiting room demonstrated to his constituents that he was still at heart Oklahoman, with paintings of oil gushers, herds of buffalo, Cherokee warriors, settlers galloping to register their claims at the land office. There were pictures of the senator with the Sooners football team, a party of fishermen in a bass boat on Lake Latownka, and a party of camo-clad hunters in a wood. Ava had to smile at the last one. As usual when he had a rifle in his hands, Uncle Chuck looked terrified of shooting himself in the foot.

A young man wearing a dark suit and spectacles too heavy for his nose came and got her. He had the air of a senatorial staffer, weary and nervous. They went not to Uncle Chuck's office but to a small meeting room.

"The senator sends his regrets that he won't be able to see you today, Ms. North."

"Oh."

"He's on the phone to the mayor of Rosedale about that tornado that hit yesterday, and there's a delegation of tribal elders waiting in his outer office, and at any moment he's going to be called to the floor to vote on—"

"Excuse me. Does the senator know I'm not here to talk about Thomas Laker?"

The aide gave a start of surprise. His glasses slid down his nose. "You're not?"

"Senator North sits on the Intelligence Committee, which has called Laker to testify. It would be the height of impropriety for me to plead on Laker's behalf."

The staffer hesitated, fingered his glasses back into place. "You wouldn't bullshit me, Ms. North? I mean, you mention Laker and my ass is grass."

"Not a word, I promise."

"Just wait here, he'll be right in." The staffer rose, buttoned his coat, and set off to avert another crisis.

Only a few minutes later, Uncle Chuck appeared. He looked like a senator, with abundant silver hair, a forehead corduroyed with the cares of office, and a broad, bright smile. In his shirtsleeves, he showed a slight paunch, but it would be concealed when he put on his suit coat.

"My favorite niece! Come give me a hug. How long has it been?"

"The New Year's Day family get-together, at Aunt Paige's in Georgetown."

"As recently as that? Seems a lot longer. How are things at the NSA?"

"I just got fired. Or to be exact, quit before I could be fired."

That extinguished his smile. His head drooped and his shoulders slumped. He eased her into a chair and patted her shoulder before settling in the seat across the table. "Well, that's just terrible. Why don't you tell me all about it, and then I'll get on the phone and—"

"Thanks, Uncle, but no. I'm here about something much more important than my job." She told him about Ken Brydon, leaving out only Stan Rahmberg's ongoing search. She wasn't going to mention Rahmberg to anyone. Her uncle listened in grave silence. The silence continued after she was finished.

Chuck North was not alone among senators in being slow to commit himself. Ava decided to put it to him.

"What I'm asking is that you'll arrange an appointment for me with my boss," she said.

"I'm sure you don't need me to get an appointment with the director of NSA."

"I mean the Secretary of Defense."

"Oh. Well, when you're going over people's heads, why not go all the way? And my asking for this appointment for you carries the implication that if he doesn't do as you request, he'll have to explain himself to the Intelligence Committee?"

"That's the idea."

"Sound tactics. Your Grand-dad Ephraim would've been proud of you. But here's the thing, Ava. SecDef would know it's an empty threat. In my committee— hell, in this Congress, there is absolutely no chance of getting an investigation off the ground if its ultimate target would be Rodrigo Morales."

"How can that be? I know he's a media celebrity. I'm sure he makes campaign contributions to all the right people, but—"

"Both true. But not the reasons why he's untouchable. It's this Cuba deal. Practically everybody wants to see it go through." Her silence made him frown. "You don't know about it? Then let me provide a little background."

Uncle Chuck was always generous with background, when he wasn't going to give you anything else. He put his elbows on the table and leaned toward her. "Fidel is gone. Raúl is gone. There's a new government in Havana. We're not sure what to make of them yet, but none of them are named Castro, and that gives us an opportunity."

"To improve relations?"

"Yes. Hell, Ava, this is a tropical paradise, just off our shores. And who's making money off it? The Europeans. The Canadians. My friends are saying they want to get in there and start building hotels."

Ava nodded. When Uncle Chuck said "friends" in that tone, he meant campaign contributors.

"And Cuba would be more than just another stop for the cruise ships. Biggest island in the Caribbean, with ample natural resources and a rich culture. Ambitious, hard-working people. They're more like us than other Latin Americans. Hell, from the Spanish-American War to the Revolution, Cuba was practically part of the United States. They built their Capitol on purpose to look like ours." He waved in the direction of the Capitol building. "We want things to get back to normal."

"Seems you've been wanting that for a long time. But the Cuban Americans have been stopping you."

"Yes. The exiles have done well, in Florida and other states. They've got money and political influence way out of proportion to their small numbers. And most of 'em are still as mad today as when Castro kicked 'em out. They say, the embargo stays. Keep up the pressure on the new government about political prisoners and human rights. Not till they're purified of the slightest taint of Communism will we deal with them."

"Isn't Rodrigo Morales a Cuban exile?"

"The Moraleses are an old Spanish colonial family. Castro stripped them of everything before he kicked them out. Rodrigo's grandfather was personally denounced by Che Guevara as a leading exploiter of the proletariat. His great-uncle died in the Bay of Pigs. You can't beat credentials like that."

"And he's made a deal with the Cuban government?"

"Right. For a new resort hotel. Yemayá, he calls it, after one of those rickshaw fellas they have down there—"

"You mean *orishas*? Santeria gods?" Ava reflected that her uncle wouldn't have won four elections in Oklahoma if he didn't have the knack of making people forget they were talking to a Yale graduate.

"That's right, honey. You should have heard the outcry from the Cuban Americans when word leaked. Their radio stations and newspapers called him *gusano. Escoria*."

"Worm. Scum."

"Yes. What made it worse was the man he was dealing with. The Minister of the Interior, Ivan Gonçalves."

"Ivan? Odd name for a Cuban."

"He was born in the days when the Soviet Union saw Cuba as its junior partner in world socialist revolution. Subsidized the Cubans generously. Young Ivan was educated at Moscow University. Groomed for power by Fidel himself. Now he's one of the last of the old-time Commies. A dead-ender."

"And he was willing to deal with Morales?"

"Since the Soviets fell, the Cubans haven't been able to find anybody else to give them handouts. They had that crazy man Chávez in Venezuela for a while, but he died. Now the Cuban economy is in desperate shape. They blame it on our embargo. We say socialism didn't work anywhere else, why do you expect it to work in Cuba? Whichever, the Cuban people have empty bellies. And this Morales resort will be the biggest development since the fifties."

"But Uncle Chuck—you said Gonçalves is a die-hard Communist. And Morales is a total capitalist. How could they agree on a deal?"

"There's a lot of speculation," the senator said. "But that's all it is. Morales plays his cards close to the vest. Here's what I can tell you. In Cuba, construction has begun. In Miami, Morales is managing to keep the Cuban exile community mollified. And in Washington, my colleagues and their campaign contributors are thinking finally we've found the man who can open Cuba up. Nobody wants to make trouble for him."

Ava pushed back her chair and stood. "Thanks for your time, uncle."

He rose with her. "I know politics is frustrating, Ava. I just wasted your time talking to you about Cuba.

You're worried about a security breach in Fort Meade and a murder in Baltimore. Things that have nothing to do with Cuba."

I'm not so sure about that, Ava thought. But she said nothing, just kissed her uncle's cheek and went out. She was also thinking of another relative who might be useful to contact. One very different from Uncle Chuck.

CHAPTER THIRTEEN

It was one of those March days when New York seemed a lot more than two hundred miles north of Washington. On her way to Union Station to board the Metroliner, Ava had walked through a warm, gentle drizzle. She could almost sense the cherry trees around the Tidal Basin straining to burst into bloom. Here in Brooklyn, she was staggering through spatters of wind-blown sleet.

At last her destination came in view: a tall, narrow nineteenth-century townhouse with an elegantly cor-niced bay window and mansard roof. It had been built as one in a row, but the others had all fallen as the neighborhood declined, and with vacant lots on either side, it looked as forlorn as the last tooth in an old man's jaw.

It was said in the North family that cousin Tilda bought houses because she felt sorry for them. It was said with some resentment, because the neighborhoods around these houses tended to improve at a rapid clip, allowing Tilda to sell for several times more than she had bought. She'd been moving steadily eastward across Brooklyn for the last quarter-century, a well-compensated refugee from the gentrification she'd helped kick off. She didn't like to live among high-end chain stores and stuffy neighbors.

Maybe she'd already moved on from this house, Ava thought as she approached, for there was a Muslim woman in a black chador sweeping the tall stoop.

"Excuse me," Ava said. "I'm looking for Tilda North?"

The figure in the long, shapeless garment turned, and she was looking into the bright blue eyes of her cousin, who had inherited them from her namesake, their grandmother, the famed Washington hostess Matilda Brigham North.

"Ava!"

"Tilda!"

They hugged. Ava said, "I didn't know you had converted."

"Oh, this. I found it hanging from the newel post on the stairway, and I had to put on something. I was in my scanties, and the stoop had to be dealt with right away."

Ava looked around. She hadn't seen so many empty bottles and glass fragments since her last trip to the recycling center.

"There was a party last night," Tilda explained. "It got a bit out of hand. Why do men have to smash bottles, do you know? I mean, I know they were drunk on their asses, but still—"

"Don't you have staff to clean up for you?"

"They fled en masse at 3 A.M. Party got too wild for

them. Ava, can you wait a moment? I want to put on something more secular. And I suppose Reza will be wanting her chador back at some point."

"Reza? A friend?"

"We got to talking on the subway, and I invited her to the party. I thought it would broaden her horizons."

It had probably done so, if the chador had ended up hanging on a newel post. "Can I come in with you?"

"Better not. Guests are sleeping here and there, and it'd be cruel to wake them. They're going to have such terrible headaches. Not to mention, some of them will be very surprised to see who's next to them."

As her cousin slipped quietly through the door, Ava put up the hood of her parka against the sleet and set to work with the broom and dustpan.

It wouldn't be fair to say that the family regarded Tilda as their black sheep. Norths weren't stuffy people. But many of them held public office, and it made their lives difficult when the family name was dragged through the headlines of tabloid newspapers or disreputable websites.

And no North had been dragged as frequently as Tilda.

She'd been kicked out of so many boarding schools that eventually none could be found to take her. She finished her education at Frederick Douglass High in Virginia. When in office, Norths strongly supported public education, but none of them actually went to public schools. In a way that was hard to explain, it made matters even more embarrassing for them that she was such a success at Douglass High, becoming head cheerleader and homecoming queen.

At graduation, she was three months pregnant, and promptly married her boyfriend, a stock car racing driver named Dwayne Truehart. The Norths gave a collective shudder, and consoled themselves that at least it would now be the name Truehart she'd be dragging through the headlines. But Tilda had kept the family name, and done additional homage to it by naming her son Dakota. Two years later, she named his sister Carolina.

By that time, Dwayne had departed. Since Tilda did not marry again, the family felt sorry for her children. But they'd turned out rather well. Dakota North had just dropped out of Stanford to head a hi-tech start-up, and Carolina North was a fast-rising player on the pro tennis circuit.

Tilda had started her working career as a wedding planner. She lived for parties anyway and was very good at it. Mounting a ceremony in Beverly Hills had led to a job producing reality-TV shows. One had become a runaway hit, causing many a North to reach for the remote or leave the room if everybody else insisted on watching.

In one way, Tilda was a typical North. By the age of forty, she'd made so much money that it was time to move on. But instead of dedicating herself to public service in the usual North way, she dedicated herself to having a good time.

The door opened and Tilda reappeared in sweater and jeans, gently shutting it behind her. Approaching fifty, she remained youthful looking, a slender figure with a head of artfully dyed blond hair and the family features of straight nose and stubborn chin. She was wearing a gold Patek Philippe watch on her right wrist and a plastic medical alert bracelet on her left. She had a rare blood type. Tilda wasn't much on precautions as a general thing, but she'd been wearing a bracelet every time Ava had seen her. She had them in every color of the rainbow. This one was forest green to match her sweater.

"Oh, thanks," she said. "The stoop looks much better. How are you?"

"Not so good. I suppose you've heard the family gossip?"

"I never listen to gossip unless it's about me. What happened?"

"I quit the NSA before they could fire me."

"Congratulations, Ava. Jobs are so overrated. All they do is keep you from making real money. What do you plan to do now?"

"Well, I thought I'd just kick back and enjoy my trust fund for a while."

Tilda raised her eyebrows. She said, "I expect you've hardly touched it so far. How can I help?"

"I remembered you generally head down to Miami Beach this time of year."

"Oh, yes. The family always says I'm way too old to go on spring break, don't they?"

"I want to go with you."

"To do what?"

"Parasail by day, party by night."

"Hmm. Ava?"

"Yes?"

"Before we go any further, I have to tell you that I don't believe a word you're saying."

Ava was brought up short. Her plan called for carrying out an elaborate and daring deception. This was an unpromising start. "How come you don't believe me, coz?"

"Because I know you, coz. Your idea of a vacation is building houses for Habitat for Humanity in Detroit or conducting bison counts in Montana. You couldn't be frivolous if you tried—though you'd try *very hard*. Start again. Why do you want to go to Miami?"

"I'm hoping you can maneuver me into the social orbit of Rodrigo Morales."

"You want to get up close and personal with Ruy? I assure you, he's better seen from a distance. Better still on television."

"All the same, I'd like to meet him."

"Why?"

Ava hesitated. "How good are you at keeping secrets, coz?"

"Terrible. Don't tell me."

"Then let's just say I'm curious about Morales's business activities. I want to observe and ask questions."

Tilda folded her arms tightly and hunched her shoulders. She gazed into the drifting sleet, looking uncharacteristically somber. Finally she said, "No."

"You won't help me?"

"I won't introduce you to Ruy Morales."

"Why not?"

"He's a dangerous man."

Ava laughed. "You mean, he's broken so many hearts? I know about the three marriages and the countless scandals. I'm not planning to have an affair with him."

"I don't mean that at all." Tilda turned her head and

looked into Ava's eyes. "I mean, people have disappeared, when they've tried to do the kind of thing you're trying to do. Can't the NSA send someone else?"

"Coz, I really am out of the NSA."

"Oh! I thought that was part of your cover or whatever it's called. So this is your own idea. They shitcan you, and you're going to risk your life for them. You are such a North."

"Morales needs to be checked out, and nobody else seems willing to do it. When I tell you what he's done—what I think he's done—"

Tilda put up a hand. "No. As you say, it's better I don't know, if I'm going to help you. And I do mean if. I haven't decided yet."

"Why do you say he's dangerous?"

"He has an oversize ego and an uncontrollable temper. He's not particularly smart, contrary to his reputation as a brilliant dealmaker. But he has other people to do the thinking for him."

"Carlucci?"

"Ah. You've heard about Carlucci."

"I've seen him. A haircut like Shakespeare, and a face somewhere between Richard III and Iago."

"Better watch that sort of thing, if you're going to meet Ruy. He hates well-read women."

"Does that mean you'll introduce me to him?"

Tilda twirled her med-alert bracelet while she thought about it. At last she said, "If I don't, you'll go blundering around Miami Beach on your own, and we can't have that."

"Thanks, coz."

"But there's a lot more to it than an introduction. If

you expect Ruy Morales to give you more than one glance, you're going to need a lot of work."

"You mean, what they call a makeover? I've never had one."

"That's obvious. Honestly, coz, I've never known a beautiful woman who did less to earn it than you. We're going to my spa for a few days."

They stood. Tilda looked her up and down. "And I can promise you, you won't be wearing that civil service dark blue pantsuit again."

Ava smiled. "It was out. I wore it yesterday to visit Uncle Chuck in the Senate Office Building."

"You asked Chuck for help? And of course he did nothing for you."

"How did you know?"

"That's what he's been doing for the country for the last twenty years."

CHAPTER FOURTEEN

The sign stuck in the ground in front of Laker's bench said, in French, "Please don't walk on the grass. It's winter and the lawn is resting."

The lawn would have to wake up soon. Winter was ending. Though the fountain was dry and the rows of pollarded trees stood leafless, the daffodils were blooming and the sun felt warm on his face. Another couple of weeks and it'd be April in Paris.

He was in the Place des Vosges, a small park surrounded by row houses in mellow, ruddy brick and gray stone. They were more than four centuries old and none the worse for wear. Nearby stood an equestrian statue of King Louis XIII. It had a post supporting the horse's belly, so it looked to Laker as if the king were riding a merry-go-round horse.

Spending hour after hour sitting on a park bench, you had to take amusement where you could find it.

He felt confident that he was not conspicuous, because there were plenty of people in the square: children running around and shouting in the playground, lovers strolling arm in arm, old folks walking little dogs. Two soldiers pushed through the gate in the low fence surrounding the square. They were young women with their hair scraped back from grim, watchful faces. Maroon berets, muddy-green camo uniforms, automatic rifles slung from their shoulders. Security had been tightened all over Europe because of the terrorist attacks in Estonia.

As they walked slowly up the path toward him, Laker let his gaze drift back to King Louis. Someone—probably Colonel Antrobus—had leaked his name. Television and newspapers were full of speculation and indignation about Thomas Laker, the shady American operative who'd failed to prevent Mohammed Barsinian, Muslim terrorist in a NATO uniform, from killing six people. Then, instead of facing the consequences, Laker'd disappeared.

At least they didn't have a good picture of him. Sam Mason worked hard to keep photos of his agents out of circulation. The picture that kept popping up on television and the papers was almost twenty years old, showing Laker in his shoulder pads and Notre Dame football jersey.

Now, sitting on the bench, he was wearing a baseball cap and sunglasses. He hadn't shaved in several days. His beard had a lot more gray in it than the hair on his head, so that he looked years older than he was. Heavier, too, in a loose fleece pullover.

The soldiers walked by him without a glance.

A few minutes later, the woman he was watching for appeared. Her name was Simone Lascelles, and she had long, dark hair she left to dangle down her back and a bony, angular face. She stepped from the shadows of the gallery that ran around the square and shepherded her charges across the street. They were a boy and girl whose ages Laker estimated at eleven and twelve. Offspring of one of the wealthy families who lived on the Place des Vosges, they were jaded beyond their years. They had their cell phones in their hands and were texting with both thumbs. They looked resentful when Simone confiscated their phones and pushed them into the playground. Sitting on the swings, they planted their feet on the ground and refused to swing.

Simone backed away from them and took out her cigarettes and lighter. She needed a break. Laker got up and approached her unhurriedly. He put his hands in his pockets and bent forward, hunching his shoulders. It was something he did to lessen his height and make himself less intimidating. Ava had told him it didn't work. When he was a few paces away, he called, *"Mademoiselle, un moment, s'il vous plait."*

She looked at him with wariness, even hostility. Maybe she was afraid he was going to bum a cigarette. They were expensive in Europe. He let her wonder while he closed the distance. Then he said softly, in English, "I want to talk to Lina."

She flinched violently. Lost the cigarette as her mouth fell open. Dropped both kids' cell phones.

"I don't know what you're talking about," she said, several seconds too late.

He bent and picked up the phones. She accepted them with stiff, clumsy fingers.

Laker said, "Your friend Lina."

"She's dead."

"No. You're hiding her."

THE HAVANA GAME 119

Simone fell back a step. She wanted to run away. But then she remembered the children. She looked at them, still slumped motionless on their swings, and back at him.

"I don't mean you any harm," he said. "Or Lina, either. But you have to put me in touch with her."

"You're not police. I know who you are. Laker." It came out *Lakaire*.

He nodded. Didn't seem there was any point denying it.

"Suppose I run screaming toward them?"

She looked over his shoulder. Laker turned. The two soldiers had reached the far end of the square and were heading slowly back in their direction.

He faced Simone again. "Lina needs to talk to me. For her own good."

"I knew Lina at university, years ago. But I haven't seen her in a long time. Haven't heard from her since the explosion. If she survived, I know nothing about it."

"I know you're helping her, Simone."

She glanced at the children again. They were on their feet, watching. They'd picked up on their governess's fear of the tall, strange man.

"There's a passionate debate going on, on the Facebook page of Greenpeace," Laker said. "People writing in from all corners of NGO-land. Somebody attacked Lina for naïveté. Said she shouldn't have spoken to that American agent at all. Not trusted him for a minute. You defended your friend. Said she was right to believe the American because he was telling the truth. Mohammed Barsinian wasn't the Syrian refugee he pretended to be. He was—"

"I remember what I wrote. So what? Everybody knows now what Barsinian was."

"You wrote, 'The American said to Lina, "Let's try being honest," and he was.' Those were my exact words."

"So you knew I'd spoken to Lina." Simone squeezed her eyes tight shut. *"Mon dieu! Comme j'étais bête."*

"Easy mistake to make."

"We've been so careful. We even made the decision not to tell her parents she's alive. It was so hard to leave them to suffer."

"It's worth it. Lina was right. Being thought dead is the only way for her to be safe. People are after her."

"You know all that?"

"I have to talk to her. Tell me where she's hiding."

She shook her head vehemently, causing her long hair to swing from side to side. "No! Why am I even listening to you? You almost got Lina killed."

She was expecting him to deny it. Argue with her. But he said, "I made a mistake. Please give me a chance to make up for it."

Simone gave him a long look. Made up her mind. "All right. But I'm not going to tell you where she is. You will go to the Café Bec Rouge tomorrow night, seven o'clock. It's in the Twentieth. Lina will meet you. Or she won't."

Laker knew these were the best terms he was going to get. He said, "Thank you."

He arrived on time and sat down at one of the sidewalk tables. The café was located near the top of one of the steepest hills in the Twentieth Arondissement.

He could look out across the city's scattered lights, pick out the floodlit Arc de Triomphe, the glittering needle of the Eiffel Tower. Tourist Paris was a long way from the Twentieth.

This was a wide street, lined with parked cars and featureless modern apartment buildings. Traffic was light, pedestrians few. The only other customers sitting out here in the chilly wind were the smokers, who had no choice. Next to his table was one of those heaters the Parisian cafés used, a steel stanchion with a kerosene fire, topped by a shield to reflect the heat down. He slid his chair closer to it.

Lina Opalski was out there in the darkness some- where, watching him, making up her mind whether to talk to him. There was nothing he could do but wait and sip espresso. He was finishing his second cup when she dropped into the chair across from him.

Her thin frame was draped in a long, loose raincoat, probably not her own. She looked as if she'd lost weight. The wide, pale eyes and fragile bone structure of her face were more noticeable now. She was tense and tired. She didn't meet Laker's eye.

"Simone said you know why I fled."

"Your fears are justified. The people who sent Mo- hammed Barsinian to kill your friends may have sent others to look for you."

She took a deep breath and let it out, slumping into the folds of the oversize raincoat. "It's a relief to hear someone else say it. There've been times when I doubted myself. Thought the reason I ran away was that I'm paranoid."

"You're not paranoid."

She said nothing, preoccupied by her own thoughts.

Laker didn't push her. The waiter came out to ask for her order. She only shook her head. He went back inside.

Eventually her head came up and the pale eyes met his. "I've been alone too much the last few days. Had too much time to think. Sitting in somebody else's apartment, watching television. Mostly news programs. What the people back home are saying about us. My dead friends and me. At first we were innocent victims of a terrorist. We were accorded a certain amount of pity and respect. But soon enough it came out that Mohammed had fooled us into giving him shelter. A lot of people hardened their hearts. Even said we got what we deserved."

"Barsinian was very persuasive, playing his various roles. He fooled me, too."

She went on as if she hadn't heard him. "What depressed me most were the interviews with people on the street in Tallinn. This was the first my fellow countrymen had ever heard of Home Port. And they didn't think it was doing any good at all. We wouldn't be missed. Just another NGO, wasting money on the problems of poor people far away."

"Your work did matter a great deal. To the wrong people, in the wrong way."

"You mean, we managed to do something that made us worth killing." Her mouth twisted in a bitter smile. "I suppose that's a comfort. Who sent Barsinian?"

"The Russians."

She gave him a startled look. Then her gaze drifted away. She was searching her memory.

"We have only one open case involving Russia,"

she said at last. "It'd come into the office recently. We hadn't done much with it. A routine case."

"Tell me about it."

"We were contacted by a Mrs. Lamon in Manila. She said she'd just received a text message telling her that her son had been killed in an accident. He was a sailor working on a cargo ship called *Comercio Marinero*. The message said the ship's next port was Vladivostok, Russia. The man who sent it said he was also a Filipino, working on the same ship. The sender's name meant nothing to her. It was probably a borrowed cell phone. Crewmen typically aren't allowed their own phones. But the message itself was signed, with the name Ramón Milaflores. "

"And this Mrs. Lamon wanted you to investigate. How much credibility did you give to the message she'd received?"

"We took it very seriously. You have to understand, one-fourth of the sailors on the world's merchant ships are Filipino."

"As many as that?"

"They're willing to work hard for very little money. Manning agencies recruit poor men in Manila, provide them in lots to shipping lines all over the world. That way the shippers avoid dealing with unionized sailors. The Filipinos are far from home, with no one to look out for their rights. So they stick together. If this sailor hadn't informed Mrs. Lamon, she might not have found out for weeks that her son was dead."

"Killed in an accident, you said. But you felt that it should be investigated."

"Yes. The email didn't give any details. But merchant sailors are often overworked. Kept in bad living conditions. Ordered to ignore safety procedures. When accidents happen, the shipping line is supposed to file a report. But there are ways for them to avoid their obligations."

"For instance?"

"The *Comercio Marinero* is owned by Compania Ecuadoriana de Navegación Interoceánica SA of Guayaquil, Ecuador. Abbreviated CENI. A pretentious name for a small, second-rate outfit. Their ships are registered in Liberia, because Liberia has weak laws. Reporting accidents aboard is optional. So we started pressing the authorities for an investigation into the accident."

"Which authorities?"

"The port authority in Vladivostok, the minister of marine in Moscow."

"Any replies?"

"No. We're just an NGO. We have to pester officials with emails, calls, and letters for weeks before we get any response. And in this case we weren't optimistic. We didn't have enough information on the accident. Like where the ship was when it happened. We expected the Russians to stall us for weeks, demanding clarifications, denying responsibility."

"That wasn't what happened."

Lina shook her head, slowly and sadly. "What do you think I should do? Go home?"

"No. We have to assume you're still in danger. Stay in hiding. Don't contact anyone."

"Until?"

"Until you hear from me."

"What are you going to do?"

"Moscow doesn't want anyone to investigate the accident aboard this freighter. So I will."

"You're going to Vladivostok."

"Apparently that's where the ship is now."

"You realize that's on the other side of Russia?"

"I realize."

"Laker, what do I do . . . if I never hear from you again?"

He smiled bleakly.

"I'm sorry," she added.

"It's a fair question. But it's one of many that I don't have an answer to."

CHAPTER FIFTEEN

"I can't understand, coz, why you give up the pleasures of a northern spring—hearing the song of the first robin, seeing the crocuses poking through the snow—for *this*," Ava said. "It's like D.C. in August."

"Sweating is good for your complexion, coz," Tilda said. "It cleanses the pores."

They were sitting in a golf cart parked on a manicured fairway, at the edge of a grove of pine trees. Temperature and humidity were about ninety. The sun blazed down from a milky sky. Tilda had her cell phone to her ear and was waiting for another bulletin from a caddy whom she'd tipped generously to keep them informed about the progress of Rodrigo Morales's foursome, who were playing the next hole.

This was their second day of pretending to play golf while shadowing Morales around the golf course at his country club, Finca de Palmas, halfway between Miami and Palm Beach. Like all his properties, it reflected his obsession with Cuba. The clubhouse, visible in the distance, was a more sprawling version of Hemingway's Finca Vigia: pale yellow stucco with rows of tall windows and a columned entry porch.

"When I asked for your help," Ava said, "I thought you'd just take me along to a party and introduce me to Morales."

"At parties he gets mobbed. We want him to notice you."

"But I hadn't imagined you'd get so deeply involved. I shouldn't be staying at your house. If I'm doing something reckless, I should be the only one to pay for it."

Tilda's Patek Philippe emitted a tone.

"Noon, at last," she said, pulling from the cupholder a beaded stainless steel container. "Vodka tonic. Care for a sip?"

"Do you have any water?"

"I never did see the point of putting water in bottles and carrying it around. I mean, it's just water."

Ava mopped her brow with her sleeve. "Morales spends a lot of time playing golf. I suppose he does it to make contacts, wheel and deal?"

"There's only one reason Ruy does anything: to win. Only he's not winning today." She adjusted the phone at her ear. Another report from her spy was coming in. "The third player has holed his ball. Ruy just got on the green. Let's move up. This could be our chance."

Tilda stepped on the pedal, and the cart moved softly over the dense emerald grass. "One of three things happens when Ruy falls behind. The other guys will start playing badly enough for him to catch up or he'll cheat or he'll throw a tantrum."

The cart went up a gentle slope between two sand

traps. At the top a little cluster of carts was parked. Players were standing around, backs to them. Tilda pulled up at the rear.

"What's with all these people?" Ava asked.

"They're waiting. Ruy's foursome has been stuck on this hole for a long time, mostly because Ruy went into the water hazard. Then the trees. Then the rough. But nobody's going to play through. You don't try that on Ruy. Here, have a look."

She handed over a pair of binoculars. Leaning over so she could see through a gap between people, Ava spotted Morales, in white shirt, maroon slacks, and visor. He was alone, the other players having retreated to their cart and the shade of its awning. As he studied the lay of his ball, she studied his face. Only the tight, almost prissy set of his full lips spoiled his handsomeness. He was taking his time plotting the ball's course to the hole, pacing and smoking a long cigar.

Finally he went over to his caddy and exchanged cigar for putter. He spat on the green and addressed the ball, shifting his feet, waggling his hips. At last he made his stroke. As the ball went on its way he tried to guide it with motions of his head, hands, and hips. Eventually he started jumping up and down.

All apparently in vain. He raised his putter in both hands and bent it in a loop. "Childish, but you have to give him points for strength," chuckled Tilda, in response to Ava's report. "That's a titanium shaft."

Murmurs and chuckles went the rounds of the spectators in front of them. After their long wait, they felt entitled to some entertainment. Morales threw down the putter. One of the other players got out of the cart and went over to pat his shoulder. Ruy shook off the hand and backed away shouting so loudly Ava could almost hear him.

"I can only see people's backs," Tilda said. "What's going on now?"

"He's berating one of the other players."

"Probably for distracting him. People aren't supposed to breathe when Ruy's putting."

Morales took a roundhouse swing at the other player, who ducked it and ran for the cart. He jumped in and the cart sped away. Ruy snatched the bent club away from his caddy, who had picked it up, and threw it after the cart. The crowd in front of Ava guffawed and applauded.

"Now's your chance," Tilda said. "Here, I have a fresh shirt for you."

"You expect me to change here?"

"Nobody's looking at you. Wherever Ruy is, everybody looks at him."

Ava pulled her sweaty polo shirt over her head. She emerged from its folds to find her cousin leaning over her, about to apply an ice cube from her drink to Ava's bra.

"What are you doing?"

"Pointy nipples will get Ruy's attention."

"Absolutely not, coz. Give me that shirt."

Tilda handed it over and stepped out of the cart as Ava pulled the shirt over her head. "Get over there. Ruy hates to walk."

Ava switched seats, handed Tilda her vodka tonic, and set off, maneuvering around the jolly crowd. After a few minutes, she passed the caddy, trudging along with the bag of clubs slung over his shoulder, bent putter in one hand, dead cigar in the other. Morales was a hundred paces ahead, stamping along the fairway with head down and arms swinging.

She pulled up beside him and said, "Can I give you a lift?"

He looked over at her, and his glower melted at once into a smile. Well, a leer. He ran his eye over her, which made her feel as if she were being licked by an over-friendly dog. Her skin would be sticky afterward. At least his expression rewarded the efforts of the staffs at her cousin's favorite boutique and spa. She was wearing a golf skirt of a length more appropriate for skating. Her long legs were waxed to perfect smooth-ness and tanned to a rich hue of caramel. Her sleeveless V-necked top revealed more tan skin. A pale redhead, Ava generally stayed out of the sun, but Tilda had liter-ally pushed her down on the tanning bed. Her teeth, to which dental veneer had been applied, must be blind-ing Morales with their whiteness. To increase the ef-fect, she raised eyebrows whose point and arch had been enhanced with dying and waxing. The techni-cians at the spa had also lengthened and thickened her eyelashes. Every time she blinked she could feel the added weight.

Morales's step was lighter as he came around the cart and got in beside her. He smelled unpleasantly of sweat and cigar. She gave him a minute to thank her or introduce himself, but neither was forthcoming, so she said, "I'm going back to the clubhouse."

"No, make it the pool pavilion. I have a lunch meet-ing." He glanced at his watch. "Let's get going. I'm late."

Ava obeyed. She supposed that was what people did.

"Haven't seen you around the club before," he said.

"I've just come down with my cousin."

"Who is?"

"Tilda North."

"Oh! Is your name North, too?"

"Yes. First name Ava."

"I know Senator Chuck North. Terrific guy. Big help to me in opening my Tulsa hotel. And Secretary Allegra North. Very helpful to me in cutting through the red tape at her department. And Ella North-Beckham, the media consultant. Keeps trying to persuade me to run for office. Says a Florida senatorial seat is mine for the taking, and that'll be only the beginning."

This went on as the green-and-white striped pool pavilion came in sight. Morales seemed to be trying to show her that he knew more of her relatives than she did.

At last she stopped the cart at the pavilion entrance and Morales got out. He turned to give her another head-to-toe scan. "Come for a swim. I'll buy you a suit . . . if you let me pick it out."

He actually waggled his eyebrows. Ava cringed. "But you have a meeting."

"It'll only be three, four hours. Just relax poolside. Tell 'em to put your drinks on my tab."

So much for her status as a North. He couldn't even be bothered to ply her with drinks before bedding her. He expected her to get drunk on her own. "Sorry, my cousin's waiting back at the clubhouse."

"Come on."

"Sorry."

The plump-lipped mouth went pouty again. But only for a minute. Then he said, "Tell you what. There's a big charity do at my house tomorrow. Bring your cousin. I'll tell the guys at the gate to let you in."

Without waiting for a reply, he turned away.

"I'd have to call today a disappointment," said Tilda.

"Don't tell me you think I should've waited for him poolside."

"No, of course not. He'd have mauled you. And once Ruy sleeps with a woman, he loses all interest in her. You'll have to keep resisting him."

"Don't worry about it."

"But it is frustrating to miss the big charity do. I happen to know what the occasion is. You could have found out a lot."

"Coz, didn't you hear me? We're invited. He's going to tell his guards to expect us."

"Ruy never remembers to do things like that. And we won't be able to talk our way in. This is the benefit for Saved from the Deep, the charity that helps newly arrived migrants from Cuba. The event of the year for the Cuban-American exile community. Security is always ultra-tight."

"Oh," said Ava. "I would've liked to get into that."

"Missed opportunity, I'm afraid."

It was evening, and they were sipping cocktails in the living room of Tilda's house. She'd always hated The Hive, as she called the family mansion in Palm Beach, because it had so many bedrooms, containing so many Norths. She had her own place in South Miami

Beach, an art deco house of pale stucco highlighted by pink and azure panels and curvaceous balconies. The slats of the Venetian blinds of the living room's wide windows were open, striping the opposite wall with golden light from the setting sun. Ceiling fans revolved lazily over the cousins' heads.

A car with a powerful engine could be heard coming down the street. The noise stopped abruptly. Tilda got up and looked out.

"He's parked right in front of the house," she said. "But I don't know the car."

"It's a Lancia, an old one, I think from the '50s." Ava had recognized the triangular shield on the slotted grille. She wasn't much interested in cars, but keeping company with Laker, she couldn't help picking up a thing or two.

"It's handsome," Tilda said.

The door opened and the driver got out. It was Arturo Carlucci. He tossed his flat driving cap on the seat. The sun shone on his bald head. As he walked up the front path, he was taking off his calfskin driving gloves. He did it with deliberation, tugging on each fingertip in turn. He passed from their view. The doorbell rang. Tilda gave Ava a wide-eyed look. Saying nothing, she turned and went into the front hall. Ava didn't follow. She was rooted to the spot.

"Good evening, Ms. North. Nice to see you again." The voice was soft, unaccented.

"Hello," said Tilda, sounding strained.

"I won't ask to come in. Just dropping off something for you. And your cousin. Is she here?"

Ava lurched unwillingly into motion. Walked into the hall to stand beside Tilda. Carlucci smiled at her.

Below his smooth hairless pate, his forehead was deeply scored. There were crow's-feet at the corners of his eyes, radiating across his temples and halfway down his lean cheeks. Parentheses from his nostrils to the corners of his mouth. She'd never seen a face marked by so many wrinkles.

She noticed that the left sidepiece of his sunglasses was taped to his face with a Band-Aid and remembered that the ear on that side had no top to rest it on.

"Pleased to make your acquaintance, Ms. North."

She managed a nod.

"Mr. Morales mentioned inviting you to the party tomorrow. I thought you should have invitations." He took two stiff envelopes from the pocket of his white linen shirt.

"Very kind of you," said Tilda, who still didn't sound like herself, as he handed her one envelope.

"You'll have to show these at the gatehouse, and they'll have to have your names on them. Sorry." He unhurriedly took out a stout fountain pen, a Mont Blanc, and unscrewed its cap. "May I have your first name, Ms. North? Ruy forgot. Sorry again."

"Ava."

"Start with an E, or an A?"

"A."

He wrote the name on the envelope, in a large, or-nate hand. "Anything else? I mean, a 'Rep.' before, or an 'Esq.' after?"

"No."

"With a North, there's usually something else."

"I'm just a civil servant. Or was. Now I'm looking for some fun in the sun." She gave a nervous laugh.

"You've come to the right place. Look forward to seeing you both tomorrow."

He handed her the envelope, nodded, and walked away.

Tilda shut the door and leaned her back against it. "He's going to have his people in D.C. check you out."

"If they dig deep enough, they'll find out my paychecks came from the Department of Defense."

"Not the NSA?"

"No way. That information is very closely held."

Tilda was tapping the invitation envelope nervously on her thumbnail.

"Cheer up, coz," Ava said. "Now we can get in Morales's house."

"Just so we can get out of it."

CHAPTER SIXTEEN

Rodrigo Morales's house in north Miami Beach was a sprawling mansion of white stucco, with a long row of round arches along the front and a red tile roof. It faced the bay and the downtown Miami skyline. Palm trees, tall, graceful, evenly spaced, enhanced the extensive grounds. The black iron fence was maybe a little too high, security having trumped esthetics, and the twisty spikes topping the bars looked downright menacing. Ava had plenty of time to admire the property. They were the last in a line of cars, inching along the fence toward the gates.

Tilda had a beautiful car. Laker would have loved it. It was a well-preserved 1963 Studebaker Avanti convertible. Its gleaming paintwork was deep bronze, with a tan pinstripe picking up the tan interior and wire wheels. The top was down despite the hot sun. Tilda said she enjoyed the wind in her hair, and made fun of Ava, who wore a broad-brimmed hat whenever she was outdoors.

When they got close enough to the gate, Ava saw

that no cars were being allowed in. Valets were taking them away, while guards checked the invitations and IDs of guests and ran handheld metal detectors over them.

"Is all the security unusual?" she asked.

"It's like this at every big gathering of the exile community," Tilda replied.

"Are they worried about saboteurs from Havana?"

"No. About each other. There are factions and feuds. Insults are hurled via the radio or the internet. Sometimes it escalates to threats and brawls. Sometimes bombs are thrown. Literally. Miami was a combat zone in the '80s and '90s. Then it calmed down. But with the Castros gone, quarrels are heating up again between the hard-liners and the *dialogueros*—the people who want to negotiate with the current Havana regime."

Ava remembered what Uncle Chuck had told her. "The Moraleses were always hard-liners. But now Ruy's a *dialoguero*. How's he managing that?"

Tilda laughed. "Everybody wonders."

So, Ava thought, Morales was walking a tightrope over the yawning gap in the Miami exile community. The success of his billion-dollar resort project in Cuba was on the line. If Ken Brydon had discovered some secret that could hurt him with one side or the other, that might have been reason enough to murder him.

Tilda looked over and her eyebrows arched above her sunglasses as she guessed Ava's thoughts. She waved a hand at the Morales mansion.

"Are you going to sneak inside and search the place?"

"That would take an army."

"What are you going to do, then?"

"Use my eyes and ears."

Reaching the gates at last, they left the car and passed through security. Guards were stationed along the driveway to direct them to the backyard, where the party was taking place. It was more informally landscaped, with bougainvillea, jacaranda, and other lush tropical plants.

They passed a spreading live oak tree. From its limbs hung piñatas, being whacked with sticks by enthusiastic children as their parents stood around sipping drinks and shouting encouragement in English and Spanish.

"I thought piñatas were Mexican," Ava said.

"All kids love them. Dakota and Carolina certainly did. I always had them for their birthdays." Tilda smiled at the memory.

Looking more closely at the nearest piñata, Ava saw that its bulbous form was in green army fatigues, and had a bearded face. "That's Fidel Castro."

"And that's Raúl."

"Seems like the third one is attracting the most whacks. Is it Che Guevara?"

As they drew closer, she saw that the piñata was wearing a gray business suit. It had a handsome, grinning face and a head of chestnut hair. "Oh my God—it's JFK! What do they have against him?"

"He failed to send the U.S. Air Force to cover the Bay of Pigs invasion. And he nixed various CIA plans to assassinate Fidel with exploding cigars and such."

A lusty blow cracked JFK at the waistline. His halves parted to gush treats on the delighted children.

Loudspeakers on poles were playing "Guantanamera." The tune was abruptly cut off, and a booming voice welcomed guests to the fund-raiser. It was coming from a tiny gray-headed man standing on a faraway platform, facing sun-bathed rows of chairs. The more dutiful guests trooped over and sat down, while the others remained in the shade of the mimosa trees, drinking their mojitos and daiquiris.

"Oh, don't those look good?" said Tilda. "Let's head for the bar."

As they waited in line, Rodrigo Morales was introduced. He mounted the podium. He was one of the few men wearing a suit in the sultry Miami afternoon, a well-tailored tan gabardine. As he raised his arms to acknowledge the applause, dark sweat stains in his armpits were revealed. He stood, smiling and bowing, even though the applause was quickly dying down. Tilda whispered that this crowd, mostly hard-liners, was dubious about Ruy.

He began by giving his family credentials. The wind was against Ava, and only snatches came to her: "My grandfather endured beatings from Castroite thugs . . . our *casa* confiscated, our family heirlooms lost . . . starting over from nothing in Miami . . . rebuilding his fortune, supporting his family . . . never neglecting the long struggle to stop agents of Soviet imperialism from taking over the Western Hemisphere."

Tilda handed her a tall cold daiquiri. "Do we have to listen to this? I hate listening to speeches as much of the rest of the Norths love giving them."

"Yes. Come along, coz."

By the time they found seats, Morales had moved on to himself. He told how he had kept the Caribbean soccer tournament from using the Orange Bowl stadium last year. During the applause, Tilda whispered an explanation: Cuba had the best team, and the exiles would have been forced to witness a Commie victory.

Then Morales boasted of organizing a boycott that drove out of business a music venue that had hosted a Cuban singer.

"But she's a chart topper, internationally adored," Ava whispered. "What did she do wrong?"

"She was here on tour—why didn't she defect? Unforgivable."

Morales went on in the same vein for some time. And with some effect. The applause went on a little longer as he stepped down from the platform. Aides were standing by to hand him a bottle of water and a towel to mop his brow. Several audience members had come around to talk to him. Their expressions were adamant. As the group moved toward the house, Ava stood and handed her daiquiri to Tilda.

"Where are you going?"

"If they're holding a meeting, I want to be in on it."

"Be careful."

Before the servant holding the door could close it, Ava hurried in. The air-conditioning was delicious. She trotted down the corridor, bringing up the rear of the group trailing Morales. At least she was dressed well enough to blend in to the crowd, in a sleeveless white silk sundress from Prada, imprinted with a giant red hibiscus bloom. She tugged her broad-brimmed hat a bit lower over her eyes.

Quickening her pace, she drew level with a grayheaded woman in white slacks and striped top. They smiled at each other. Ava said what a nice party this was, in Spanish. It wasn't one of her stronger languages, but adequate for party chat. She and the woman were still talking as they passed between the uniformed guards on either side of a doorway.

To Ava's relief, her new friend took a seat on the opposite side of the room from Morales. Ava sat beside her, giving her hat brim another tug. The window curtains were drawn against the strong sun, and she was grateful for the dimness. The guests, about a dozen of them, mostly male and mostly older, were settling into comfortable armchairs and sofas. Morales sank into a button-tufted leather chair and put his feet up on an ottoman. He cut and lit a long cigar. No one else was smoking, but there were no objections. It was his house.

Once the servants had distributed drinks and the door had closed behind the last of them, Morales spoke. "Alfonso."

An old man with white whiskers and a yellowing seersucker jacket spoke up from the opposite sofa. "Yes?"

"When the FBI wanted to wiretap you after that string of bombings of *dialoguero* radio stations, the judge refused to sign a court order. And whose judge was that?"

"Your father's judge, Ruy."

"Diego."

"Yes?" said a younger man sitting in an armchair.

"When the police arrested your uncle for firing a bazooka at an East German freighter bound for Havana, whose prosecuting attorney refused to indict him?"

"Your father's prosecuting attorney, Ruy," said a younger man in an armchair.

Morales nodded. "That's why it bothers me when I read criticism from you two in the papers."

"We are only raising questions about your new project in Cuba," said Diego.

"And that's only because you're so secretive about it." Alfonso got up and gestured at the mahogany coffee table, which was bare. "We were hoping to see a model of the resort. Some pictures of the construction site."

Morales exhaled smoke. "All in good time. We're still almost a year from the grand opening."

The old man resumed his seat, looking dissatisfied. Diego said, "I hope that when you go to Cuba, you at least bring up human rights and political prisoners. Are you pressing the government—"

"I do not go to Cuba. They come here."

"But don't you have to check on progress at the site?"

"I'm a dealmaker, not a construction foreman."

The woman beside Ava spoke up. Ava ducked her head as all eyes turned in their direction. "You should invite the Havana papers to tour the site. Make it an occasion to talk to the government about freedom of the press."

"Freedom of the press is a wonderful thing. But I don't want my competitors reading about the resort just yet."

The woman sat back, muttering under her breath.

The old man was on his feet again. "In other words you are getting no concessions at all from the government in Havana. Nothing in return for building them a hotel that will provide them with a steady stream of revenue for years to come."

"Arturo, shall we tell them?" said Morales. He was looking into the far corner of the room. Ava turned to see that Carlucci was standing in the dimness, leaning his back against the wall. She quickly turned her face away.

"You have already let too many people in on the terms of the deal, Ruy," he said.

"But we're among friends."

"If it gets back to Gonçalves, he won't like it."

"He'll just have to lump it."

They were both smiling. Ava sensed that the exchange had been rehearsed. It was meant to flatter the guests. Morales put down his cigar and swung his feet to the floor. "That steady stream of revenue going to the government? It will be a trickle."

"What?" said the woman beside Ava.

"We have already negotiated the tax rate the resort will pay. I'd better not reveal the figure, but it's very modest."

"What does that matter?" asked the old man. "The Cuban government will own the resort."

"I will own the resort."

"The old man shook his head. "I don't believe it. Gonçalves is a doctrinaire Communist. He's dead set against private ownership. From the moment I heard you were negotiating with him—"

"I remember what you said," Morales interrupted. He rose to his feet. Swept the group with a benign look. "My friends, for sixty years we have been fighting the Havana government. With propaganda. Economic sanctions. Even with force. And where has it gotten us? Our native land is still wretched, imprisoned, poor. Now there is a new government in Havana—"

"With a lot of the same old faces," said the woman beside Ava. "Especially Gonçalves."

"Ruy outsmarted him." It was Carlucci again, speaking up from his dark corner. "No one can get the better of Ruy in a deal."

"The Cuban economy is in terrible shape. People are practically starving," Morales said. "Gonçalves is desperate for jobs. Most foreign companies that build in Cuba bring in their own workers, from Canada or Europe or Asia or wherever. Gonçalves demanded that I recruit a one-hundred-percent Cuban workforce. I said yes."

Morales raised his forefinger. Looked about the room. Made them wait.

"*If* he would let me have 100 percent ownership of the resort. He gave in."

Carlucci was now sauntering into the center of the room. "You see the beauty of it, ladies and gentlemen? The nose of the capitalist camel, under the Communist tent. Gonçalves has unknowingly traded an immediate economic boon for the long-term weakening of the regime. More foreign corporations will demand ownership. The government won't be able to refuse."

"A new, free Cuba will be born." Morales finished.

Carlucci raised his glass. "To the future of Cuba."

Ava glanced about the room. Most people were smiling. The old man still looked doubtful, and the woman beside her was muttering again. But neither could refuse to raise a glass to that toast.

Morales stood beaming and nodding as the guests drank, as if he was the one being toasted.

* * *

"You're sure Carlucci didn't see you?" Tilda asked.

"Pretty sure. As soon as the meeting ended I slipped out. He was busy talking to people in the front of the room."

This seemed to satisfy Tilda, who was slumped in the passenger seat, head on one side. She might even have dozed off.

They were driving down Alton Road with the top down. The sun had set behind the downtown Miami skyscrapers across Biscayne Bay. Ava was at the Avanti's wheel, because Tilda'd had a few too many daiquiris. Ava had found her dancing the mambo with an elderly but impressively flexible gentleman.

"Sounds like Ruy handled the meeting well," said Tilda. So she wasn't napping.

"I have to admit I was impressed. And surprised," Ava said. "Morales seemed like such a jerk when he was coming on to me. But in that room today, he was very articulate and persuasive."

"Probably following Carlucci's script." Tilda chuckled. "If this Yemayá resort is the sharp tip of the wedge that's going to open up Cuba, there'll be fortunes to be made. Carlucci and Ruy are playing for high stakes."

"Yes." Ava was thinking that if Ken Brydon had somehow gotten in their way, the two men wouldn't have hesitated to kill him.

"The reason I asked if Carlucci saw you," Tilda said, "is that I think we're being followed."

Ava's insides writhed. She sat up straight and grasped the wheel tight, searching her rearview mirror.

"Are you sure?"

"No. But I've had a certain amount of experience

spotting tails. You know, when leaving the houses of—um—certain prominent men by dawn's early light, and watching out for paparazzi and celebrity stalkers."

"I don't doubt your expertise, coz." She realized that Tilda had been slumping because she was watching the side mirror.

"It's one of those pricey German cars with ice-blue headlights. I can't see what color or make it is because it's too far back. But it's stayed behind us through our last five turns."

"That's it," Ava said. "I'm moving to a hotel tonight. I can't involve you in this."

"Too late, coz. I'm already involved. You're staying with me."

Ava didn't reply. She was trying to spot the car with blue headlights in her mirror. Couldn't. She returned her gaze to the road ahead.

Her thoughts turned to Laker. She had no idea where he was or what he was doing. But she knew what he'd say if he were here, because he'd said it in the past, at other times when she was getting out of her depth. "You're plenty smart, Ava. But you're not a field agent."

CHAPTER SEVENTEEN

The plane hit an air pocket and dropped like a shot duck. Laker's bottom lifted off the cushion and his seat belt cut into his hips. They settled at a lower altitude where the air was even rougher. Russian planes were old and noisy; creaking and clunking filled the cabin. The engines didn't sound right, either. Laker and his neighbor, a burly man whose eyes had blue irises and bloodshot whites, exchanged a glance. He was hunched forward, riding his seat like a galloping horse. People were talking loudly and fearfully. Somebody was crying.

It was no use waiting for a reassuring announcement from the pilot. The intercom had failed early in the flight. Eventually the flight attendant—the only one—appeared at the front of the cabin. She was a squat, formidable woman with a wide, thin mouth that never smiled. She shouted that they were going to make an emergency landing.

She didn't say where. Laker hoped it would be an airport.

He looked out the window. It had a swirling tracery of fine scratches, like an ice rink in need of a Zamboni. He could see white land, gray sky. That was all. But his ears told him the plane was descending. The deaf one was acutely sensitive to pressure. The landing gear whirred and clunked into place. Good. They weren't going to belly-flop in the snow.

The wing dipped as the plane turned, revealing a landing strip and a cluster of small buildings. He glanced at his neighbor. The man was gazing at the lighted windows of the buildings as an exhausted swimmer looks to shore. Laker gave him an encouraging smile. He didn't respond.

The plane came around into an approach. Nearing the runway it yawed left and right as the pilot fought the crosswinds. Then it dropped, bounced, skidded. The pilot got it under control and reversed thrust to slow down. The engines' roar was only a little louder than the passengers' cheering and clapping.

Nearing the end of the runway, they passed the snow-covered wreck of a plane that hadn't been so lucky. It looked as if it had been stepped on by a giant foot. They taxied to the terminal and stopped. The flight attendant stood impassively by the door as they disembarked. Some passengers asked her how long the delay would be. She didn't answer.

There was no jetway, just a flight of stairs and a short but painfully cold walk across the tarmac to the terminal. The place was bare bones: just a coffee shop and a lounge with threadbare sofas and a television set. Laker chose a seat as far from the television as possible. Keeping his hat and coat on, he bent his head over a book and pretended to read.

When he reboarded, he would have to pass through security again. Every time was a risk.

His passport wasn't the problem. As always when he left the U.S., he'd taken an emergency passport with him. This one was American, in the name of Edward McLean of Lowell, Massachusetts. He'd obtained it through his own State Department connections, and even the Gray Outfit didn't know about it.

The risk was that the official he handed the passport to would recognize the photo. Laker had seen himself in newspapers and on television screens across Russia. Luckily the Russian media had only the same old photo the European media had, of the young football player in his Notre Dame jersey.

He was fairly confident that Moscow hadn't put out an alert. For him to travel all the way across Russia was so reckless, so foolhardy, that the FSB wouldn't believe he'd attempt it. He could hardly believe he was doing it himself. If he was caught, it would be sheer bad luck.

Which wouldn't be a comfort. He had no idea what the Russians would do with him.

According to Russian media, Washington had sent shady operative Thomas Laker to snatch the NATO soldier and Muslim terrorist Barsinian from the grasp of Estonian justice. He'd failed. Now Washington claimed to be making every effort to apprehend the fugitive Laker. But the Americans were not to be trusted.

The layover stretched on and on. The first announcement said that the plane to Vladivostok was being repaired and would soon be on its way. Then there was a lengthy silence, followed by an announcement that certain key parts would have to be flown in from Moscow. The usual Russian pattern, Laker had noticed, was an optimistic declaration, followed by a pessimistic declaration, followed by an improvisation by the people on the spot.

So he was not surprised to look out the window and see the pilot, co-pilot, and even the unsmiling flight attendant climb into a vehicle and head for the wrecked plane at the end of the runway. They were going to try to scavenge the needed parts. Laker wondered how long the wreck had been exposed to the weather. Decided to put that out of his mind.

It was the middle of the night when they were summoned to reboard. The official to whom Laker handed his passport barely glanced at it. He passed through the metal detector and out into the cold. The flight attendant was waiting at the top of the stairs. Her mood hadn't improved.

His seatmate's attitude, by contrast, had greatly improved. The bloodshot eyes were merry. He grinned, leaned toward Laker, and said, "Screwdriver."

"What?"

He opened his bag to display two bottles, one of vodka, one of orange juice. "You drink with me. To smooth flight," he said, offering a plastic cup.

"That's illegal, you know," Laker said. Russia was one of the hardest-drinking countries in the world, but it had strict laws against in-flight liquor. He nodded toward the flight attendant. "She'll confiscate your bottle."

"She not care."

"I wouldn't try her. Really."

The man was already pouring a drink. "You drink

with me," he said. "You no drink, you bring us bad luck. We need good luck."

He thrust the cup toward Laker and glared at him. "Drink!"

This was going to be tricky. If Laker drank and was caught, he could be handed over to the police in Vladivostok. But if his seatmate started a fight, they'd both be arrested.

The flight attendant had keen eyes. She was standing in the aisle, looming over them. "Give me that cup! And put those bottles away!"

The man said no, backing up his refusal with a quaint Russian expression referring to the flight attendant's private parts.

She snatched the bottle of orange juice from him and poured it over his head. Laker braced for an explosion, but the man only sat there, blinking and sputtering. Maybe the cold drenching sobered him. Or maybe he was thinking, better to lose the juice than the vodka. The flight attendant dropped the empty bottle in his lap and stalked away.

Laker was fastening his seat belt. The pilot was announcing, over the repaired intercom, that Vladivostok was four hours away.

A mere hop, by Siberian standards.

CHAPTER EIGHTEEN

Laker caught a cab to the harbor. He doubted that the *Comercio Marinero* was still here, but it was worth a try. The cab dropped him in front of the Port Authority building. But instead of entering, he picked up his suitcase and crossed the road. Having traversed the vast Eurasian continent, he felt compelled to walk the last few feet to the waterfront.

He'd never been to Vladivostok before. He'd heard it called the Russian San Francisco, partly because of its relatively mild climate. Winter's grip was clearly easing. The only piles of snow in sight were small and dirty. There hadn't been a fresh snowfall in a while. The sun was shining in a partly cloudy sky. The temperature was in the forties. All sorts of vessels were moored in the piers that lined Golden Horn bay. To his left was the naval base with its sleek gray destroyers and cruisers as well as a white hospital ship with a red cross. To his right was the commercial port. He noted the high, boxy shape of a car carrier. An enormous oil tanker. A number of container ships. The nearest one was being unloaded. Tall cranes were lifting the big boxes from its decks, swinging them slowly over the pier and lowering them precisely onto railroad flatcars.

There were ferries and sailboats, and even a hot-dogging Russian in a wetsuit, roaring around on a Jet Ski. His gaze traveled to the far shore of the bay, where a new-looking cable suspension bridge marked the passage from the harbor to the Pacific.

Laker felt a pang. He was an ocean and a continent away from his home. And his beloved. It was night-time in Washington, D.C. Ava would be asleep in her comfortable apartment near Dupont Circle. He wondered what kind of day she'd had at the office. He hoped he'd managed to keep her out of trouble with the NSA. Couldn't risk contacting her again.

Laker turned away from the bay. And from his debilitating thoughts. There was work to do.

The Port Authority was a late-nineteenth-century building, pale blue with white pilasters and some sort of shield or coat of arms in stucco over the door. Flagpoles flew the horizontally striped red, white, and blue flag of the Russian Federation.

Laker entered. In the West, he could've found out online if the *Comercio Marinero* was still in port. But in Russia routine information could still be hard to come by, and anyway he had no internet access. He'd dumped his smartphone, which could give away his location, long ago.

He stepped into a high-ceilinged, echoing hall. At the far end was a wooden counter, behind which four officials were sitting. Each had a long line in front of him or her. Laker joined the nearest one and prepared to be patient. Waiting in line still made up a large part of life in Russia.

Some of the people around him wore suits, but most were in jeans or overalls. There were a lot of Chinese; the border wasn't far away. Also people he guessed were from other East Asian countries. Indians and even Africans. This was Russia's main Pacific port, and it drew travelers from all over. Laker was glad of that. He wouldn't be conspicuous. He spoke Russian, but not well enough to pass for a native.

The line inched forward. Laker nudged his suitcase along with his foot. Eventually he was able to get a good look at the official behind the counter. In Russia much depended on the mood of the functionary you were dealing with. This one didn't look promising.

He was a man in his seventies, in shirtsleeves with his tie loosened. He had a high forehead and a long Roman nose with steel-framed reading glasses perched on the very tip of it. The glasses, and his long gray sideburns, combined to make him seem like a character in a Russian historical movie. Laker could imagine him with a dueling pistol in hand, gazing contemptuously at the opponent he was about to shoot dead. Too bad he had only this long line of supplicants wanting information to sneer at.

He listened indifferently as the man in front of Laker asked his question, then turned to his computer and tapped keys leisurely. While it worked, he stroked one of his sideburns. When the answer popped up, he relayed it to the man. The man asked another question, but the clerk only shrugged and looked over his head at Laker. Apparently answers were one to a customer.

Laker stepped up to the counter and made his query.

The clerk worked the computer and read off its screen, "The *Comercio Marinero* was at Berth 17 of Grozny Pier. It sailed two days ago."

"Bound for where?"

"I don't know."

"Can you find out?"

"It's not worth looking. Such information quickly goes out of date. Freighters are diverted to unscheduled ports if cargo is there to be picked up." The long explanation seemed to exhaust him. He slumped on his stool.

"How about its previous port of call, before Vladivostok?"

The clerk looked over Laker's shoulder at the next person in line. Laker planted his feet, straightened up and squared his shoulders. Ava said that he was good at looming.

He did manage to motivate the clerk to tap more keys. "No information," he said.

"How can that—"

"You're holding up the line!" the clerk interrupted, loudly enough for everyone to hear. "Now move along."

Arguing with officials could get you arrested in Russia, so Laker picked up his suitcase and walked away. As he was going out the door, he heard a chorus of loud groans. It had come from the people in line behind him. The clerk was rising from his stool, placing a "Closed" sign on the counter. Break time.

Out on the sidewalk, he set down the suitcase to button his coat. At least he'd learned the ship wasn't here anymore. He had time to find a hotel and think about his next move.

"Turn into the alley up ahead."

The words had been spoken softly by a man passing him. He recognized a bushy sideburn of the supercilious clerk. Without pausing, he walked to the corner of the building and around it. Laker followed.

The clerk was shaking out a cigarette for himself. He offered the pack to Laker, who shook his head.

"The previous port of call should have been there," the clerk said. "Somebody deleted it."

"Could you find out some other way?"

"I have worked at the Port Authority for almost fifty years. There is little I do not know about its workings."

Laker said, "I'm willing to pay."

The clerk smiled haughtily. Money was beneath him. "You speak good Russian, but you're a foreigner. I hear a lot of accents in my office. I would guess . . . American?"

Laker confirmed it. He'd already worked out his cover story, which was about half true. "My name is Edward McLean. I work for an NGO in Boston called Aid to Sailors—"

The clerk interrupted. "Our president warns us to be wary of foreigners from NGOs. He says we should assume they're spies."

"Do I look like a spy?"

The clerk looked him up and down. "No. You look like a big, dumb, well-meaning American."

He chuckled. Laker joined in.

"My name is Porfiry. I tell you what, Edward. Go to the Great Patriotic War Memorial at six o'clock this evening. Maybe I will show up, and maybe I will have information."

"If you do, what will you want in return?"

Porfiry didn't answer. He hung his cigarette on his lower lip and walked away, holding his distinguished-looking head high. Laker didn't know what to make of him.

Laker walked uphill toward the city center. He wasn't looking for a cab. In an unfamiliar city, a field agent had to get a feel for the streets. You never knew when you might have to flee for your life through them.

There was an opening in the sidewalk ahead, half-surrounded by a railing, with stairs going down. A subway station? He descended. It was a narrow, bustling corridor, lined with shop windows on both sides. No train platforms, though. It was just a mall. He supposed that in winter people liked to do their shopping underground.

As he climbed back to street level, a young man leaning on the railing glanced idly at him. Then glanced back. Then turned and walked quickly away. Laker's stomach muscles fluttered.

The next moment he thought that his face must have reminded the kid of his school principal. Or his girl-friend's father. That was all. Laker was just being paranoid.

But paranoia was a field agent's best friend.

Laker couldn't ignore the possibility that somebody was going to see through his beard and match his face with the one in the pictures on television and in the papers of the fugitive American agent.

Nor could he ignore the possibility that his photo had been snapped in one of the airports he'd passed through and sent to Moscow. His own government was

John Lutz

taking pictures of travelers and running them through facial recognition software, seeking matches with pictures of persons of interest. No doubt the Russians were doing the same.

Laker set down his suitcase. Time to consider unpleasant possibilities and countermeasures.

He was in the old city center now, surrounded by buildings in various shades of pastel stucco, rising to mansard roofs and cupolas that reminded him of Paris. Some of the buildings were hotels. A few even bore the familiar signs of Western chains. It would be convenient and comfortable to check into one of them.

But if the FSB figured out that he was in Vladivostok, these hotels would be the first places they would look for him.

Overhead wires ran along the streets. That meant trams. He walked along until he came to a knot of people waiting on the curb, and joined them. After a few minutes the tram came along. He boarded and took a seat, gazing at the passing scene. Once the streets started looking shabby, he got off.

Choosing a direction at random, he set off. The suitcase was beginning to feel heavy when he spotted a hotel sign across the street. It was on a brick building three stories high. Behind dirty, cracked windows he could see crooked paper shades.

Just the kind of place he was looking for. It would take a while for the FSB or police to get around to this fleabag. He might even be able to avoid surrendering his passport by offering a bribe.

He entered between dusty artificial plants and crossed a linoleum floor to the counter. It was enclosed in wired glass, and business was conducted through slots. Nobody was in sight, but he could hear a television. There were a lot of notices pasted to the glass, things guests were forbidden to do, and things management wasn't responsible for. Fleabag hotels were the same all over. It was enough to make Laker homesick.

A rap on the glass brought a short, bald man with thick glasses to the counter. He was happy to rent Laker a bedroom and access to the communal bathroom, but stonily refused to let him keep his passport, for any consideration. Laker watched gloomily as the man locked it away in a desk drawer, along with the cash in advance for three nights' stay Laker'd just given him.

The stairs were so narrow Laker had to hold his suitcase against his chest. He went along a dim corridor until he reached his room, Number 8. The door of the room across the corridor was open. A man was lying on the bed reading. Spotting Laker, he said, "Oh, hello, let me help you with that key."

"I can manage."

But the man had already tossed the book aside and was sitting on the edge of the bed, sliding his shoes into loafers without using his hands. His eager friendliness reminded Laker of the fellow freshmen who'd welcomed him to his dorm at Notre Dame. This man wasn't much older than a college kid, Laker saw, as he practically bounded across the hall. He was smiling, showing crooked but very white teeth. He took the room key, which was fastened to a bulky knob so guests wouldn't carry it away with them, from Laker's hands and started to unlock the door.

"These locks are terrible," he explained. "Cheap and stiff. Takes practice to open them." He was a skinny kid, wearing a T-shirt and hip-hop jeans, with a low crotch and back pockets just above the knees. The ginger hair at the back of his head had been fashioned into elaborate curlicues by some artist with electric clippers.

"There!" he said, throwing open the door and waving Laker in. The greenish brown carpet looked as if it would emit some malodorous liquid when stepped on, but he ventured in anyway, flicking the switch to turn on the bare, dusty bulb hanging from the ceiling. Glancing at the cracks and damp-stains, he hoped it wouldn't rain hard while he was here. He laid his suitcase on the bed, causing the mattress to sag deeply in the middle.

"Well, welcome to our flophouse." The kid put out his hand. His bare forearm was tattooed in swirls that echoed the curlicues of his haircut. "My name is Yuri."

"Edward." They shook.

"You're . . . German?"

"American."

"Really? Americans don't usually speak such good Russian." He switched to English. "Mind if we talk your language? I don't get as much chance to practice as I'd like."

"No, that's okay," Laker said. But he was wondering if it was. Russians were typically wary of foreigners, especially Americans. A friendly Russian who wanted to speak English could be trying to play you in some way.

"You're here on business?" Yuri asked. "If so, they should give you a more generous expense account."

"No, I'm waiting for a ship."

"Cruise ship?"

"Any freighter that takes passengers will do."

"But where are you bound?"

"Wherever it's going."

"Ah, a traveler. And are you writing about your travels?"

"What makes you think I'm a writer?"

"Your eyes. You're very observant. Want to see the sights of Vladivostok? I can show you around. War Memorial. Tsar Nicholas' Arch. Yul Brynner statue."

"Yul Brynner statue?"

Yuri planted his feet wide apart and folded his arms, like Brynner playing the King of Siam. "He was born here. In Vladivostok at the wrong end of the Trans-Siberian Express. But that didn't stop him. He made it to Moscow. Paris. Hollywood."

Yuri's eyes went dreamy. He had a similar trip in mind for himself. Laker asked, "Are you a tour guide?"

"No. I write for the newspaper. *The Lord of the East Times*. You've seen it?"

"I just got here."

"We cover shipping news. Sports. City council meetings. Just local stuff, never anything national. Or anything important." He grinned widely, showing the crooked teeth again. "That's how journalists in Russia stay out of trouble."

Russians didn't ordinarily criticize the government, even indirectly, when talking to strangers. Laker's suspicions returned. He said, "Well, I need to unpack."

Yuri took the hint. He left Laker to it, after a second handshake and a parting piece of advice, that the Chinese restaurant on the corner was the only decent place to eat in the area.

*   *   *

On one point, anyway, Yuri proved trustworthy. The Chinese place was good. Laker had Szechuan chicken as a late lunch. Then, as the shadows lengthened and the air grew chillier, he made his way back to the waterfront. He wanted to be early for the rendezvous with Porfiry.

He asked a passerby the way to the Great Patriotic War Memorial. She told him to just keep walking along the waterfront and he'd see it. Eventually he did. It was a replica of a submarine, mounted on brackets by the side of the road, like a boy's plastic model on a shelf. Only when he got closer did he grasp the size of the thing. It was a real submarine. He asked another passerby and was told that it was S-56, which had fought the Nazis in the Atlantic.

Laker slowed his pace. It was rush hour, and traffic was heavy but moving. Pedestrians on the streets were walking briskly, probably eager to get home. He was watching for idlers around the submarine who could be waiting for him. It was possible that Porfiry had called the police, told them about the foreigner asking questions.

But he saw no suspicious loiterers, and anyway he didn't think Porfiry would get involved with the police. More likely, he just wouldn't show up.

Right on time, though, Porfiry emerged from the darkness. He had an overcoat with a fur collar and an astrakhan hat. It set off his sideburns handsomely. He gave Laker no greeting but a long look.

"You're surprised. You thought I wouldn't show up?"

Laker couldn't see any reason not to give him the honest answer. "No."

Porfiry gave his thin smile. He didn't have his reading glasses on, but he kept his nose in the air anyway. He said, "Let's walk."

Laker moved around to his other side and they set off past the submarine. Porfiry noticed the maneuver. "Why did you do that?"

"I'm mostly deaf in my right ear."

"What happened?"

Again Laker saw no reason not to tell him. "IED blast."

"You were fighting in Afghanistan?"

"Iraq."

This seemed to interest Porfiry, but he didn't explain why.

Laker said, "Were you able to find out the ship's previous port of call?"

Porfiry gave a rather self-satisfied shrug. "It was easy enough to track down the hard-copy backup. Before Vladivostok, the *Comercio Marinero* was in Magadan."

He gave Laker a sideways look, which Laker could only return blankly. He'd never heard of Magadan.

"Something unusual about that?" he asked.

"Magadan is north up the coast, in Siberia. Its port is closed from October to May. To get in in March, the *Comercio Marinero* would have had to follow an ice-breaker."

Porfiry dug out his pack and lit a cigarette. He was able to do it with his gloves on. Impressive.

"Magadan is a place with an evil history," he went on. "Stalin built it as a transit hub for the gulags. Thousands of prisoners passed through on their way to serve their sentences. For many, a one-way journey. For twenty years, it was the headquarters of Dalstroy. You've heard of Dalstroy?"

Laker nodded. "A very profitable gold-mining operation. The miners were prisoners condemned to hard labor."

"Yes. They talk about blood diamonds in Africa. This was blood gold. Much of it passed through Magadan. Are you investigating a bloody deed there, friend Edward?"

"In a sense. I work for an NGO concerned with sailors' welfare. There was an accident aboard the *Comercio Marinero* while it was in Magadan. A sailor was killed."

"You have tried the usual channels and found nothing, of course. And here you are. There may be paperwork in Magadan. I know nothing about that. But there should be other paperwork on that ship here in Vladivostok. The bills of lading."

"What are those?"

"Forms that the agent of the railway line gives to the ship's cargo officer. So many containers of computer components or whatever, bound for some port or other. The cargo officer signs them, and makes sure that copies are filed with the Port Authority."

"Bills of lading," Laker repeated. They would tell him what the *Comercio Marinero* was carrying, and where she was going. He said, "You're sure they're in your files?"

"Quite sure. They're necessary for customs and insurance. Money matters. You might lose an accident report, but bills of lading are sacred."

"You could get me those papers."

"Possibly."

"Will you?"

"I'm thinking about it." They walked on, passing a big piece of metal with the fateful date 1941 and nothing else. Mounted steps leading to a small church with a single gold onion dome. On a wall ahead, Laker saw a relief of sailor and soldiers. Grim faces, heroic poses. There were also metal tablets fixed to the wall, with names in Cyrillic. He looked up and down. The wall was long. A lot of tablets.

"The dead of the Great Patriotic War." He pointed at one name. "Here is my father. Killed in the Baltic Sea in 1943, when his destroyer was sunk by German bombers. Without him the war years were hard for us. We nearly starved. My mother was bitter. She said Stalin was a fool to let Hitler get the better of him, and my father was a greater fool to go to the other side of the country and die for Stalin. It was a good thing she said this only to me."

Laker felt that Porfiry was enjoying having a listener. He nodded and waited.

"I was a dutiful son," Porfiry went on. "I got a job at the Port Authority and supported her all her life. Now she's gone, and I'm still there."

He tossed his cigarette butt away. "I suppose to a man like you, a former soldier, an NGO worker who travels to the ends of the earth to do his good deeds—you probably think I haven't done much with my life."

"I don't think that," Laker replied. "What do you think?"

Porfiry's nose went up. "Given myself away, haven't I? Yes. For a man my age, there's nothing left but retire, sicken, and die. Only I can't bring myself to retire, much as they want me to. I'm hanging on, hoping for a chance . . . to do something. You understand?"

Laker understood that it must be tough to go through life bearing such a noble visage and haughty air, while suspecting, deep down, that you'd done nothing to earn them. But he sensed that Porfiry wasn't interested in what he had to say. He'd talk himself into helping Laker. Or he wouldn't.

The bell of the nearby church sounded the quarter hour. Porfiry jumped. He looked at his watch. "I have to go or I'll miss my ferry."

Laker was willing to bet that hadn't happened often in fifty years. He walked down the steps with the old man. At the bottom of the steps, Porfiry turned to him. "If I decide to help you, and if I'm able to find the papers you want, how do I let you know?"

Laker pointed. "The curb. Under the bow of the submarine. Chalk an X if you want to meet here that night 6 P.M. A cross if you want to make it the night after."

Porfiry laughed. "An NGO do-gooder. Pretending to be a spy. I'll bet you read that in a le Carré novel."

He walked away with his nose in the air, one gloved finger stroking a sideburn. Soon he'd be on his usual ferry, headed home. Laker wasn't going to hold his breath awaiting help from Porfiry.

CHAPTER NINETEEN

Vladivostok's train station was imposing and exotic-looking, as befit the starting point of the Trans-Siberian Express. On its facade, pointed turrets flanked round arches resting on bulbous pillars. Laker joined the morning crowds rushing into the entrances beneath the arches. He felt sleepy and itchy after a restless night. The flophouse was infested with bedbugs. Naturally.

In a high-ceilinged, echoing hall, he skipped the long lines at the ticket windows and bought his ticket to Magadan from a machine. It was twenty minutes till his train left. He sat on a bench and waited, alternating yawning and scratching with glances at the clock.

Suddenly he straightened up, fully awake and alert, bugbites forgotten. Something in the scene before him had touched a tripwire. He didn't know what.

Slowly he scanned the crowded hall for someone who did not fit in. Saw commuters carrying briefcases or laptops. A group of sailors in blue uniforms. A young woman with a baby strapped to her chest and a toddler holding her hand. An Orthodox priest with beard, black robes, and a large silver cross on his chest. A group of tourists, led by a guide holding a sign in the air, followed by a heavily laden luggage cart. They were probably bound for the Express.

Nothing unusual so far. Laker's eyes narrowed as he focused on the line of the ticket windows across the hall. A stocky young man with buzz-cut dark hair and a folder under his arm cut in front of the first person in line, a tall woman in a red coat, and spoke to the clerk behind the counter. The woman waited patiently, without protest. She smelled cop.

So did Laker.

He watched as the man made his way along the wall, speaking to each ticket clerk, handing him a piece of paper from the folder. Then he went into a snack bar. Through its glass wall, Laker saw him repeat the routine with the cashier.

When the man strode toward the doors to the street, Laker rose and followed unhurriedly. Before stepping out he pulled down his hat and turned up his collar.

He was in time to see the man getting into a Toyota sedan parked in the station forecourt. On its door was painted полиция. Police.

Reentering the station, Laker walked to the glass wall of the snack bar. The cashier was busy with a tape dispenser, taping a photo to the counter next to his cash register. When he took his hands away, Laker saw the familiar picture of himself in his football jersey.

Laker didn't hesitate. Didn't hurry, either. He turned and walked out of the station, tossing his train ticket into a refuse bin. Crossing the street, he boarded a tram. There was no time to waste but he couldn't risk a cab. The cops had probably worked their way along the taxi queue by the curb, handing his picture to every driver.

They were probably looking for him in the big downtown hotels already. They'd get around to his flophouse eventually. Before they did, he wanted to retrieve his passport. Obtaining a forgery in a town where he had no contacts would be time-consuming and dangerous.

The tram let him off a block from his hotel. He approached warily, in case the police were here already, but saw no signs of them. At least he hadn't been bugbitten in vain.

He entered the bleak lobby. It was empty and his room key on its doorknob was still lying on the counter where he'd left it. He listened for the television in the back office, heard nothing. The desk clerk probably hadn't come in yet.

The glass panel over the counter was thick, but the wooden door next to it looked flimsy. Laker lifted his foot and slammed it into the door, which flew open and swung against the wall. As it bounced back he caught it and stepped through. He'd seen the clerk put his passport in the top drawer when he'd checked in. The desk was sturdier than the door. He'd have to pick the lock. He picked up a paperclip from the desk, straightened it, and set to work.

The lock didn't resist for long. He opened the drawer. There were several passports but only one was blue. Snatching it up, he turned and went out the door.

Yuri was standing in the lobby. Between Laker and the door. He was barefoot and in his underwear; the splintering of the door must've awakened him. He raised his ginger eyebrows. "Can I help you, Edward?"

"Get out of the way. I'm in a hurry."

"So I see."

"Yuri, I don't want to hurt you."

The young man stepped aside. As Laker rushed by, he saw Yuri picking up his key from the counter. "I'll bring your suitcase to you," he called after Laker. "The Eagle's Nest. Noon."

The day warmed up as the sun rose higher. At noon there were a lot of people at the Eagle's Nest. It was a hill topped by a statue of two men in monks' robes standing with a cross. The railing in front of it was fringed with padlocks. The fad for lovers to declare their undying bond by writing their names on a padlock and fastening it on some monument had started in Paris and by now had reached even Vladivostok. Several couples were placing their locks when Laker arrived. It was the sort of spring day that made young people feel amorous.

He took a seat on one of the long benches. Many people were sitting and looking at the views of downtown, the blue bay with its two silvery bridges, the green hills beyond. He'd thought it over long and hard before deciding to come to the rendezvous. His suitcase contained only a couple of changes of clothes, nothing that could help the police. It wasn't worth the risk that the meeting would prove a trap. But Laker didn't believe Yuri would set him up. It was just a feeling; he had no reason to trust the young man. He went back and forth on it. Finally, half an hour ago, he'd picked up a copy of the *Lord of the East Times* and spotted Yuri's byline on several stories. He'd told the truth about that, anyway. It was enough for Laker to meet him.

Five minutes late, Yuri arrived. The suitcase made him easy to spot in the crowd climbing the broad path from downtown. He was wearing a light jacket and his hip-hop jeans. He loped over to Laker and dropped the suitcase in front of him.

"Thanks."

"Consider it professional courtesy. From the *Lord of the East Times* to *The New York Times*. Or whoever you work for."

"What makes you think I'm a reporter?"

"Takes one to know one, isn't that the saying?" He dropped on the bench beside Laker. "And the police being after you only confirms it. You're working on a story they want kept secret. If they catch you, they'll strip you of your press pass and put you on a plane back to America."

If only, Laker thought. He decided to play along with Yuri. "You're right. I'm a reporter. Did the police come to the hotel?"

"I don't know. I left shortly after you did, for my office. From there I called my friend in the police. Asked what was up. He said they were looking for Thomas Laker, an American spy." Yuri grinned, showing his wayward teeth. "That's what they always do with a Western journalist they don't like. Call him a spy. My friend said I was not to publish anything until further notice. They don't want you to know they're looking for you. They're hoping to catch you unawares."

Laker nodded. It sounded plausible. "Did your friend tell you how they know I'm in Vladivostok?"

"Yes, he's very good about telling me things I can't publish. Somebody saw you in the street. He recognized you from a photo on television."

Somebody in the street. Just the unlucky break he'd been afraid of. Maybe it'd even been that teenager on the steps from the underground mall, who'd taken a second look and hurried away.

It could have been worse, though. They didn't have his Edward McLean alias. His passport was still good. For a while, anyway.

Yuri had been watching him intently while he'd been thinking. Now he said, "Is Thomas Laker your real name?"

"No. My real name is Lester Comingore, and I'm on the *Washington Post*."

Yuri grinned again, nodding. The name was familiar to him, as Laker had hoped. He'd chosen carefully from among his many acquaintances in the Washington press corps. Les was a world-renowned investigative reporter, known for his unconventional methods and willingness to take risks. He avoided appearing on television because he didn't want his face to become known.

"What are you working on, Mr. Comingore?"

"Call me Les." Laker figured Comingore wouldn't mind. "There was an accident aboard a freighter. A Filipino sailor was killed. It's being covered up."

Yuri was disappointed. "Not much of a story. You couldn't sell that anywhere but Manila."

"The coverup is serious. An NGO was looking into the accident. Moscow ordered it hit."

"Of course. Home Port, in Tallinn, Estonia It was passed off as a Muslim extremist bombing. You were there, as Laker. You've chased this story a long way. What else have you got on it?"

The kid was well-informed and quick on the uptake. Laker told him what he'd found out about the *Comercio Marinero*. When he got to the part about going to Magadan, Yuri interrupted.

"You can't go. Now they've found out where you are, they'll figure out why you're here. They'll be looking for you in Magadan. And it's a small place. No, I'll have to go."

"You realize how dangerous that would be?"

Yuri shook his head. "Not so dangerous. I'll tell them I'm working on a story about the ties of commerce and friendship that unite Russia's two great Pacific ports. The prosperous future we share. It's the kind of crap I usually write. I'll be very convincing."

"You figure you can just bring up the accident and they'll answer your questions?"

"I probably won't even have to bring it up. Russians love to gossip. They know they can tell me anything. Even if I felt suicidal enough to put it in a story, my editors would never publish it."

"Why go to Magadan, then?"

Yuri swiveled to face him. He was unsmiling and intense now. "To earn your gratitude, Les. You publish the story in the West. Without mentioning my name in it, of course. But you'll tell your friends about me. At the *Washington Post*. At other media. I need contacts."

"For when you emigrate?"

"That's the plan."

Laker thought it over. Failed to come up with a better idea. "All right. Just be careful. You want to meet here tomorrow?"

"Not enough time. Make it the day after. Noon." He put out his hand and they shook. "Thanks for the chance, Les. You won't regret this."

Laker watched the kid walk away. He hoped he wouldn't regret it. Hoped, too, that he'd be able to keep his various names straight. His aliases were multiplying.

CHAPTER TWENTY

Two days later, when Laker returned, the scene at the Eagle's Nest looked very different. Winter was taking another crack at Vladivostok. Gray, snow-laden clouds covered the sky. The wind had a sharp edge. He put up the hood of his parka as he climbed the hill.

The parka was new, replacing his wool topcoat. He'd also bought heavy, dark-framed spectacles with plain glass lenses and dyed his beard black. He wondered if Yuri would recognize him.

The last forty-eight hours had passed slowly. A spy spent most of his time waiting and lying low, Laker's boss Sam Mason liked to say. You had to be good at these two things or you'd end up in a foreign jail. Or worse.

The police were looking for him in the sort of places foreigners frequented, so Laker avoided these. He killed time in university libraries, movie theaters, late-night jazz clubs, Laundromats. Provided you didn't vandalize the machines or lie down on the floor and go to sleep, you could hang around a Laundromat all day.

He checked the curb at the war memorial a couple of times, but Porfiry had left no chalk marks. Laker wasn't surprised.

He reached the top of the hill. There were fewer people here, and most of them were striding toward their destinations without pausing to take in the view. One couple, whose ardor must be keeping them warm, were up on the monument with the statue of the monks, fastening a padlock to the rail. A tourist with a backpack was struggling against the wind to open a map and find his way. A businessman with a briefcase had stopped to take a call on his cell phone.

Only one man was sitting on the bench overlooking the city, shoulders hunched and hands in his pockets. When Laker got close enough, he could see the curlicue haircut. It was Yuri. Laker rounded the bench and sat down beside him.

"Any luck?"

Yuri turned to him. The pupils were dilated, the gaze unfocused. "Sorry, Laker. This is what they had to do to make me betray you."

He pulled his hand from his pocket. It was red and swollen, the cuticles exposed and bleeding. All his fingernails had been pulled out.

Laker jumped up. The businessman was running toward him. He'd dropped his briefcase and phone. His right hand was in his pocket. "Stop! Put your hands on your head!" he shouted in English.

Instead Laker ran at him. They collided just as the man's gun hand cleared his pocket. He dropped the pistol as they both went sprawling. Laker recovered first. He kicked the man in the head and picked up the pistol.

The tourist's map was sailing away on the wind. Already he'd dropped into a shooting crouch. His arms came up, the left hand cupped under the right, which held the gun.

Apparently Laker had missed his chance to surrender and wasn't going to get another one. He and the tourist fired at the same moment. The tourist missed. Laker didn't.

The tourist crumpled to lie awkwardly upon his backpack, blood pouring from the bullet wound in his throat. Laker was running already. On the monument, the man and woman were pulling out their weapons. Machine pistols, HKs or something similar.

Laker made it to the path and the partial cover of a grove of bare trees before he heard the rattle of automatic fire. The bullets didn't even clip any twigs near him; they were missing by a mile. He kept running downhill, slipping the pistol into his coat pocket.

As soon as he reached the downtown streets, he stopped running. Took off his glasses and pulled the hood of his parka over the wool cap on his head so that he wouldn't look like the description that the agents on the hilltop were now telephoning to their backups in town. Tried his best to blend in among the pedestrians on the sidewalk despite his height.

He wasn't hearing sirens. That could only mean that the local police had been ordered to stand down, leave the field clear for operatives who'd been sent from Moscow. He could take it for granted that they were now being told to shoot him on sight.

Ahead of him a car swerved to the curb. All its doors opened and men piled out. He swung around. Another car was mounting the sidewalk, scattering pedestrians. His retreat was blocked. But between him and the car was an opening in the pavement and steps down to an underground mall. Laker ran to it. The doors of the car were opening. A man got out and propped his elbows on its roof to aim, got off one shot before Laker plunged down the steps. It hit somebody. He heard screams behind him.

The fluorescent-lit corridor of the mall was brighter than the street. The crowd was thicker, with people taking refuge from the weather to shop or idle before windows. They didn't seem to be aware of what was going on above them. Piped-in music covered the noise. Most of them were bare-headed so Laker pushed back his hood.

He plunged into the crowd, slipping among them as quickly as he could without causing a commotion. He knew from his previous visit that the underground mall was only this one corridor, with two exits. He had to get to the other one before it was blocked.

The stairs came into view. Feet appeared and descended them. There were three men, right hands in their coat pockets, faces grim and alert, eyes scanning the people in the corridor.

He didn't bother to look over his shoulder. Of course his pursuers were coming up behind him. He was trapped. He went into the store entrance on his right.

It was a small furniture store, only a couple of customers in it. This was no good. Even if his pursuers hadn't seen him go in this store, they had secured both street entrances and would begin a shop-by-shop search. There was a sofa he could hide behind, but that would buy him only seconds. He was trapped and outnumbered.

He looked at the sofa again. How had it gotten here? How had all the merchandise gotten here? Not by being carried down the stairs.

He went up to the salesman at the cash register, a stout young man with eyes as black and shiny as his hair. "Where's your back door?"

"What?"

Laker drew his pistol and put the muzzle against the tip of the man's nose. His black eyes bulged with fear.

"The faster you show me the back door, the faster I'm out of here."

The salesman turned and led him through a curtained entrance to a small stockroom. There was a door in the opposite wall. The salesman's hand came out of his pocket with his keys. They rattled as the hand shook. He slid the key in the lock, turned it. Laker pushed him aside and flung the door wide.

The corridor was narrow and dim. Its walls were bare concrete. Laker ran swiftly and quietly in his soft-soled shoes. It wasn't long before he heard rapid footfalls behind him.

The corridor zigged and zagged, because some stores were smaller than others. As he came around a turn, a door opened right in front of him. He brought up short as a woman stepped out, gave him a blank look, and dumped an armful of flattened cardboard boxes on the floor. She stepped back, and the door swung shut. Jumping over the pile of boxes, he got up on his toes and sprinted.

Rounding the next turn he heard an exclamation, a heavy thud, a curse. His leading pursuer hadn't seen the boxes in the faint light. He'd slipped and fallen. That bought Laker a few paces.

He lost them soon enough. The corridor ahead was nearly blocked by a large trolley piled high with boxes. He had to turn sideways to squeeze past the cart. A blond man in overalls was pushing it. He said indifferently, "Big load. Sorry, pal."

"Me, too," said Laker, and punched him in the chin. He dropped, unconscious. Grabbing the trolley's handles, Laker angled it to block the whole corridor, swiveled its back wheels to jam them.

He had a straight stretch of a hundred paces ahead and he covered it at a sprint. He was around the next turn when he heard the thuds. His pursuers were pushing boxes off the trolley to make an opening they could clamber through. That would take a little while.

The corridor ended in big double doors. He pushed them open and was on a loading dock. Stacks of boxes. A big dumpster, reeking of restaurant garbage. And the back of a truck yawning open, as its driver took out crates and stacked them on a dolly.

Laker put the gun in his face. "Give me your keys."

The driver raised his hands, though Laker hadn't told him to. He said, "They're in the ignition."

Laker jumped down from the dock. The truck's door was open, and he climbed in. Grasped the keys and turned. The engine roared to life. He let out the clutch and went through the gears. As the truck climbed the ramp, crates slid out the back and crashed onto the cement.

Reaching the top of the ramp, he was at street level. He merged into traffic. Large, wet snowflakes were falling on the windshield. The skies had darkened so much that the streetlights were on. Laker turned on his wipers and headlights. Glanced at his mirrors and saw no pursuing vehicles.

Taking deep breaths, he relaxed his grip on the steering wheel. It would take his pursuers a while to get the truck's description and license number from the driver and circulate it.

Enough time for him to drive miles away before he abandoned the truck.

Chapter Twenty-one

Porfiry paused in the doorway of the Port Authority. His head reared back. Apparently, in his window-less, warm office, he hadn't realized that it'd been snow-ing all afternoon. He settled his astrakhan hat a bit lower on his ears before plunging into the swirling snow.

On the opposite side of the street, Laker followed him. It was quitting time and the sidewalks were full of people. He could move closer. He crossed the street and quickened his pace until he had a clear view over bobbing heads and shoulders of the astrakhan hat.

Two policemen armed with an automatic rifles walked by. The police were back on the hunt. The FSB must've admitted they needed help, after this afternoon's screw-up. Though there'd been no choice, Laker felt bad about the man he'd shot dead at the Eagle's Nest. Felt worse about Yuri. No use hoping he was still alive. The FSB didn't care for trials. His usefulness over, he'd gotten a bullet in the back of the head.

They reached the ferry dock. A small, round-bowed vessel was waiting. Porfiry showed his pass and went over the gangplank. Laker paid his money and followed. Porify went into the warm, bright cabin and sat down on a bench. Took out his reading glasses and perched them on the edge of his nose. Opened his *Lord of the East Times*.

Laker waited on deck as the lines were cast off, the gangplank retracted. The engine noise picked up as the ferry got underway. Then he opened the door of the cabin and went in.

He was only a step away when Profiry looked up. He flinched so violently that his glasses fell off. Uncrossed his legs to get up. But Laker was already looming over him.

"Let's step out on deck, Porifry."

"No. I won't talk to you. Go away."

"Fine," said Laker loudly, in English. "We'll talk here."

Porfiry's cheeks turned as gray as his sideburns. He followed Laker out on deck.

No one else was braving the cold. Snowflakes dropped steadily into the black waters of the bay. Porfiry faced him. "That trouble in the city center this afternoon. That was you?"

"Yes."

"You lied to me."

"Yes."

Porfiry turned away. He didn't seem to grasp that there was no way of getting away from Laker. He moved slowly toward the bow, his hands feeling his way in front of him, like a sleepwalker in a nightmare.

Laker grabbed him, spun him around, pushed him against the rail, got in his face. He pointed toward the bridge that marked the passage into the Pacific. Its silver cables and A-frames were glittering in floodlight, the red lights atop the tall A-frames blinking. "The ship is out there somewhere. I have to know where it's bound and what it's carrying."

"I have nothing for you. Go away."

"I'm running out of time, and you're all I've got."

"Why did you have to choose *me*?" Porfiry whined.

"You chose me, remember? You were . . . intrigued by the possibility you might help me. It was interesting to muse about. Sorry, my friend. You're going to have to deliver on your promises."

"I've done too much for you already."

"I don't agree," Laker said. "But the FSB will, if they should happen to catch us together."

Porfiry threw a panicky look over the side. Maybe he was thinking of jumping.

"We're going back to the Port Authority," Laker told him. "You're going to look for those bills of lading you told me about."

"It's no use."

"I'm not giving you a choice."

"I've already tried!" Porfiry wailed. "All the information about *Comercio Marinero* has been deleted from the computer system. The hard copies have been taken from the files. I've never heard of such a thing. Very powerful people want that ship's cargo and destination kept secret. Since I realized that, I've been so afraid. I can't take anymore! Get away from me!"

"No. Because you know something else."

"I can't help you."

"There's something you decided not to tell me. I saw it in your eyes."

"Go away!"

"I'm sticking by your side. There will be police on the pier. You're not going home tonight, Porfiry."

The Russian's eyes were closed and his head was lolling, as if he had a fever. Laker didn't enjoy terrorizing a timid old man, but there was no other way.

"All right," Porfiry said at last. "There was one item of information they could not delete, because it is in my head. The shipping agent who handles all vessels of the CENI line is Arkady Resnikov. His office is in the Bakunin Building. He'll have copies of the *Comercio*'s bills of lading."

"How do I know you're telling me the truth?"

"Because I'm too scared to lie. Please let me go."

Laker released his fistfuls of Porfiry's overcoat. The Russian sagged against the rail, panting puffs of steam into the frigid air. The best thing Laker could do for him was walk away. He did, without bothering to warn him not to tip off the police anonymously. All Porfiry wanted now was to crawl back into his safe, dull life and stay there till he died.

The cab dropped him on a handsome street with a canal running down the middle. It was lined with old, well-kept office buildings. The Bakunin Building had elaborate carved stonework, with a round-arched portal leading to its front door. Laker hadn't heard of the occupation of ship's agent before. It seemed to pay pretty well. The snow had tailed off, with only a few flakes drifting under the street lamps. It was lying deep enough on the sidewalk to make him wish he had boots. He was going to have wet socks on the plane.

Or the interrogation room, or wherever he ended up spending the rest of the night.

The lights were on in the lobby, and the front door was open. A man sitting at the front desk looked up as Laker entered. Laker ignored him as he headed for the elevators, hoping the building was big enough that the man didn't know all the tenants' faces.

"Wait!"

He stopped. The man, who had a block of chin embedded in a fatty neck, tapped an open book on the desk in front of him.

"Sign in."

Laker scrawled in Cyrillic and walked on.

"Wait!"

Laker ignored him. Footfalls behind him echoed off the lobby's marble walls. The clerk got in front of him. His head came up to Laker's sternum.

"Your pass."

"Look, I'll be back down in a minute. I left my briefcase in my office."

"I must check your pass against your signature."

"Oh. Okay, then," Laker said.

He hit the man on his protruding chin. Harder than he intended. The man's head flew back. His body went limp and crumpled. Laker caught him and dragged him back behind the desk, where he couldn't be seen from the street.

The directory said that Arkady Resnikov's office was 612. The top floor. The elevator went all the way up without a stop. Its doors slid open on a corridor lined with wooden doors that had frosted-glass windows. No lights were showing in the ones he passed.

Nor in the window with 612/Аркады Ресников

painted on it. Laker broke it with his shoe. That made a lot of noise. Couldn't be helped. He put his wet shoe back on, reached in and unlocked the door.

He crossed a small anteroom with a secretary's desk. The inner office door was open. He entered and flicked the light switch. There was a computer on the desk, its screen black. It was bound to be password protected, so he was relieved to see a gray-green metal filing cabinet against the wall. Resnikov, like Porfiry, believed in hard-copy backup. He pulled the handle of the top drawer: locked.

Not an insurmountable problem. He pulled a chair over, tipped the cabinet forward to lean against it. Bent to reach under the cabinet and grasp the tip of the bar-lock. He pulled this down, releasing the drawers.

While he was working, a siren was drawing steadily closer. Maybe a coincidence. Or maybe someone had entered the lobby and found the unconscious man.

He tried *Comercio Marinero* first and came up blank. But CENA, SA was on the label of a hanging file, and one manila folder was dedicated to the ship he was after.

It was promisingly thick. He pulled it.

No time to go through it here. The siren was approaching. It cut off as he crossed the anteroom. He ran to the window at the end of the corridor. Six stories below, a police car with flashing lights was stopping in front of the building. Across the street, an army truck pulled up. Soldiers clambered out of the back. Laker considered: they didn't know where he was, and it was a big building. He ran back along the corridor, found the door to the stairs.

He descended quickly, noiselessly in his soft-soled

shoes, passing the fifth, fourth, third floors. No noise from below. With luck he could make it all the way to the lobby and find a back door.

No. Luck wasn't with him. From below came a racket of footsteps and shouts. They were on the way up. He opened the second floor door and ran down the corridor to the window at the end. Unlocking it, he hauled up the sash. It looked a long way down to the sidewalk. He'd forgotten that Russians didn't count the ground floor. He'd have to hope the snow would cushion his fall.

He swung one foot and then the other through. Sat on the window ledge to stuff the folder in his waistband. Put both hands down and pushed off. He made a good landing, flexing his legs and rolling as he hit. His knees and ankles hurt, but when he got on his feet, they could take the weight.

But the folder had gotten dislodged. Papers were fluttering all around him. He grabbed the folder and began snatching papers from the air and the sidewalk.

Light hit him from above. He looked up through flashlight beams at figures leaning out the window he'd jumped from. He ran. Heard shots. One was close enough to kick up a fountain of snow to his left. Then he was around the corner and away.

Traffic on the highway to the airport was moving slowly. In the back of the taxi, Laker peered at the papers he'd managed to salvage. Most were limp with moisture, their ink blurred. They were headed with dates from other years and pertained to earlier journeys of the *Comercio Marinero*. The container ship had been plying the routes between Vladivostok and Latin American ports for a long time. Finally he came up with a current bill of lading. A single form with boxes neatly filled out, laying out the information just as Porfiry had promised. At Vladivostok, the ship had taken on eight containers of generators and associated electrical equipment, bound for Puerto Chiapas, Mexico. Laker would easily beat the ship there.

If there had ever been a bill of lading for the cargo taken on at Magadan, he didn't have it.

At the airport, he discarded the papers and checked the departure board. The next international flight was leaving in an hour, for Tokyo. He bought a ticket and headed for the gate.

Before joining the line of passengers waiting to have their passports stamped, he went into the men's room and shaved off his beard. The picture in the Edward McLean passport showed him without a beard. He could only hope the Russians hadn't penetrated that alias yet.

When he was second in line, he could see over the edge of the passport control officer's counter. There was a picture taped to his desk. Even from five feet away and upside down, Laker could see it was the shot of him in his football jersey. He was clean-shaven in that picture, too.

He glanced around. Two sets of soldiers with automatic rifles were within sight. He'd seen plenty more in the terminal. He'd discarded his pistol hours ago.

The woman at the counter picked up her bag and walked away. The officer beckoned Laker.

His heart pounding, he stepped up and handed over his passport. The official opened it to the photo of Edward McLean. Glanced at it, then up at Laker. No sign of interest. So far so good. Laker willed him not to look at the photo taped to the desk.

He looked at it. Then back at Laker. Their eyes met and held. The official's were as blank as Laker's. He stamped the passport and handed it back.

Laker was literally sick with relief. He hurried to the nearest men's room and into a cubicle, where he lost his lunch. Then he went to the mirror. It showed him the face of a man who in the last few hours had brow-beaten a frightened old clerk. Enticed an eager young journalist to his death. Killed an enemy agent. A man who had been disowned by his own country and knew the long odds against him on his solitary mission. Knew also that he'd probably never see the woman he loved again.

The man in the photo the passport control officer'd looked at had just made the key interception and been cheered by thousands as he'd run it back for a touchdown. He was looking forward to a shower, a beer, and a date with a pretty cheerleader. Beyond that, to years of playing a game he loved and becoming rich and famous.

No wonder the officer hadn't made the match. The features were the same, but it wasn't the same man.

Laker dashed cold water on his face and walked down the corridor to his plane.

CHAPTER TWENTY-TWO

Behind Tilda North's house in South Miami Beach, there was just enough room for a small pool and a narrow strip of patio. In late afternoon, Tilda was lying on a beach towel, sunbathing topless. Ava was sitting in the shade in a caftan, listening to the radio.

"You know, coz?" Tilda said. "In my entire life, I'd never listened to as much NPR as I have since you came to stay with me."

Ava switched off the radio. "Sorry."

"I don't mind. I understand that you have the usual North addiction to news. But I do have one question."

"What's that?"

"Why do you freeze like a deer in the headlights whenever the name Thomas Laker is mentioned?"

When Ava didn't reply, Tilda propped herself on an elbow and slid her sunglasses down to give her cousin an inquisitive look.

"Do you know Mr. Laker?"

"Yes."

"How well?"

"We've been dating for a while."

"Really? What sort of man is he?"

"I don't know what you mean."

"I mean, is he the sort to let a terrorist get away and kill six people, then scarper?"

"That's all bullshit."

"How do you know?"

"Because he told me."

Tilda laughed. "You mean, you *trust* him? Most of the guys I'm dating, I wouldn't trust them to feed the cat."

Ava was annoyed to see tears falling into the lap of her caftan. She turned away and covered her face.

When she looked up, Tilda was sitting beside her. She'd taken off her sunglasses and put on her bra. "Ava, I'm sorry. I had no idea. Please forgive your frivolous cousin. You're in love with Thomas Laker?"

"Yes." Ava fought down her sobs and wiped her eyes.

"What was this latest report? I didn't quite hear."

"There are rumors in Moscow that Laker has popped up somewhere in the Russian hinterland. That he murdered a heroic officer of the law, then disappeared again. The Kremlin denies it all."

"What do you think? Is that all bullshit, too?"

"Last thing he told me was, the Russians were up to something big, and he was trying to find out what. But that was a long time ago. I hope the rumors are true. Because then at least he's alive."

The tears were starting again. She felt her cousin's arm around her shoulders. "Oh, Ava. Have a good cry. I'll leave you to it. I know Norths hate having witnesses to their weaker moments. Then shower and change. I'll be waiting for you in the kitchen with G and Ts."

An hour later, Ava was on her second G and T and feeling better. They were in the kitchen, where Ava was making salad at the counter and Tilda was grilling tilapia at the island. They were discussing a story in the business section of today's *Miami Herald,* which quoted people in the real-estate development and travel industries saying that Rodrigo Morales, while promoting his Yemayá Resort heavily, was being suspiciously vague about how construction at the site was going.

The phone on the wall rang, once. Without looking up from the grill, Tilda said, "Go ahead. I can wait."

"What?"

"This is the person who calls you every couple of days. Hangs up after one ring. And you go call him back on that cheap cell phone you bought with cash at Walgreen's."

"Sorry, coz. It's someone at the NSA who's helping me."

"I didn't ask."

Ava went to the living room, whose walls were striped with orange light from the sunset through the Venetian blinds. She took her untraceable burner out of her purse and keyed in the number of Stan Rahmberg's cell. She wasn't feeling hopeful. So far he'd had nothing to report, except that Ken Brydon had done a brilliant job of covering his tracks.

This time, though, he said hello in a voice breathless with excitement.

"You're getting somewhere?" she asked.

"Yes. The trick he pulled to get the info out of here was incredibly slick. What he did was—"

"It's all right, you don't have to explain." She was too impatient to sit through five minutes of geek talk. "Just as long as you're sure that this is it."

"Oh, I'm sure. But I can't figure out why it's significant. Why he thought Morales would pay big money for it."

"What is it?"

"A thread from a discussion group called The Bubbler. The members are dive shop owners and dive boat skippers around the Caribbean. The thread starts with a guy called Mike Nelson saying, don't go to Rainbow Reef anymore. It's not worth the trouble. Other people respond, asking him why. Apparently it's a coral reef, a popular place to take divers. Mike Nelson says it's degraded. Then somebody else says it's the rise in sea temperature that's degrading reefs the world over, and another guy says that's caused by global warming, and still another guy says global warming is a hoax, and soon everybody's flaming each other. Nobody mentions Rainbow Reef again. You know how online discussions go."

"Yes. The next question is, where is this Rainbow Reef?"

"I poked around on Google. There are a lot of dive sites called Rainbow Reef. One of them is off a town called San Ferdinand, on the north coast of Cuba."

"You're on to something, Stan. I'm sure of it. I have to find this Mr. Nelson."

There was a brief pause, then Rahmberg laughed.

"What?"

"Sorry, Ava. I forget sometimes how young you are. Mike Nelson was the frogman hero of a '50s TV series called *Sea Hunt*. It's just a username."

"Oh."

"I was able to hack into the billing section of the website that hosts The Bubbler. Mike Nelson is Larry Berman, owner of a dive shop called Plunge, located in Key West."

"That's great, Stan."

"So you're going to Key West?"

"Tomorrow morning. It's a short flight."

They managed to end the call without either of them saying what both were thinking. That harmless as it seemed, this was the information that had gotten Ken Brydon killed.

The propeller plane flew low over the sunlit blue sea, paralleling the course of the highway that linked the Florida Keys, then made a steep descent into the smallest airport she'd ever seen. It wasn't equipped with jetways. She and the other passengers stepped out in fierce heat and enervating humidity. They walked down the stairway and across the cement. In the terminal, the air-conditioning practically froze the beads of sweat on her forehead.

Her cabdriver took the scenic route, without bothering to ask if she was willing to pay extra for it. They drove past beaches studded with leaning coconut palms and tourist-thronged streets lined with houses painted yellow, pink, and turquoise, dead-ending at a big striped buoy that said, "Southernmost point in the United States. 90 miles to Cuba." At Plunge, they told her that Larry was leading a dive tour and gave her directions to the marina. When she arrived, the concrete dock was busy. A dozen or so divers were carting or carrying

John Lutz

their gear to the boat. Ava's idea of a scuba diver was a Navy SEAL, but these folks tended to middle age and rotundity. Perhaps they liked the feeling of weightlessness that they got in the water. The boat was a simple affair, just a hull with benches down the sides, an awning overhead, and a cluster of metal air tanks in the middle.

Larry Berman was in the stern, adjusting the twin outboard motors as his young employees helped the divers board and stow their gear. He was a big man in his forties, wearing a Marlins ballcap to shade his lined and reddened face. His tropical print shirt was missing buttons and gapped to reveal a graying mat of black hair around his pierced belly button.

Once she got his attention, she said, "I'd like to talk to you about your posts concerning Rainbow Reef."

He frowned. "How'd you find those?"

"Oh, just poking around online. I'm interested in coral reefs. My name is Marlo Jenks, and I'm in the marine biology department at FSU." Laker had told her once that if you couldn't think of any other excuse for asking questions, pretend to be a professor. People never asked a professor for ID.

"You're not some kind of activist, are you? I don't want to end up in the newspapers."

"I only write for academic journals, and I won't use your name."

That seemed to satisfy Berman. He suggested that they meet at Jimmy Buffett's bar when he got back. But she was impatient and asked if she could ride along. He told her to have a seat.

All the divers were aboard. The youngsters cast off as Berman took the wheel and steered them away from the pier. Apparently the dive site wasn't far offshore, because the divers began struggling into their wetsuits and buoyancy control vests, crossing their legs to don their flippers.

Ava welcomed the sea breeze and the gentle rocking of the boat. But the face of the man next to her turned greenish pale. He slid to his knees, then laid himself down full length on the deck.

"Are you all right?"

"Seasick."

"Want me to ask them to take you back?"

"No. It's like this every time. I just have to get under the waves."

Berman slowed and guided the boat over to a buoy. He stopped the engines. As the youngsters tied boat to buoy, he gave a safety lecture that would have put Ava off scuba-diving immediately, if she'd ever been on it. Then he wished the customers a pleasant dive. In their tanks, weight belts, and fins, they could barely get up from the benches and waddle to the stern, where one by one they stepped off and disappeared with a splash. The seasick man had gone first.

Both youngsters hopped in the water to cool off. She and Berman were alone on the boat. Sitting on the bench next to her, he said, "Listen, this is—um—kind of delicate."

"I understand. You could get in trouble with the authorities in Cuba and the U.S. for getting that close to the Cuban coast, even if you didn't land. Don't worry, I won't tell."

Berman smiled as he rubbed white sunblock on the bridge of his red nose. "It used to be worth the risk. Customers would pay plenty to dive at Rainbow Reef.

Florida didn't have a reef to match it. The variety of corals and fish. The colors. The clear water. It's all 'cause Cuba's economy has been in the toilet for decades. There was practically no development. Kept the offshore waters pristine. But I guess you know all about that."

Ava didn't, but she nodded.

"It had to end sometime, of course. When I saw the dredgers in San Ferdinand harbor, I knew the jig was about up. It was just a fishing village. Then they started building that big resort on the beach just up the coast—"

"Yemayá?"

"That's the one. They figured they were going to need a harbor deep enough for cruise ships anyway. So they built themselves a basic container-shipping port. That way they could bring all the construction materials almost straight to the site."

"And the reef?"

"It's a quarter mile offshore, and for a while it was okay. I kept bringing parties in, even though it got a lot riskier."

"How so?"

"Cuban shore patrol did not want anybody near that harbor. I had gunboats pulling alongside, armed sailors boarding, threatening to impound my boat and put everybody aboard in jail."

"Why?"

"They said they didn't want decadent capitalist spear fishermen poaching the livelihoods of the poor fishermen of San Ferdinand. Usual Commie bullshit. They were never that worried about us diving on the reef before that port was put in."

"Why did they want to keep people away from the port?"

"I don't know. Doesn't really matter anymore. About a month ago, I snuck some divers in, and they went down to Rainbow Reef. Came back real pissed off, demanding their money back. Told me it looked like the surface of the moon. Corals dead, no fish, water murky."

"What do you think happened?"

"Probably a chemical spill from one of the freighters in the harbor. Kind of thing that always happens around a port, sooner or later. That's when I posted the message, telling other dive operators Rainbow Reef wasn't worth the hassle anymore. Nothing to see."

A few feet from the stern, a diver splashed to the surface, coughing.

"Looks like somebody forgot to keep his regulator in his mouth. 'Scuse me," Berman said as he got to his feet. Leaving Ava to her thoughts.

CHAPTER TWENTY-THREE

The next morning, Ava found her cousin reading the *Miami Herald* in bed. Tilda claimed to read only the society page and the comics, but in fact she read the business section as thoroughly as the rest of the Norths did.

"Mind if I come in?" Ava asked from the door. "I'm afraid I'm kind of sweaty."

"Not at all, coz. I'm glad the home gym is getting some use. Sit down and pour yourself some coffee."

Ava pulled a chair up to the bedside and picked up a cup and the coffeepot from the night table, where it rested next to framed photos of Dakota and Carolina.

"There's some interesting news," Tilda said. "Rodrigo Morales has noted that the travel media are terribly excited about his resort in Cuba, so he's going to gratify their curiosity at a cocktail party tomorrow evening, in his flagship hotel in downtown Miami. Representatives of the Havana government will be there, possibly even Minister of the Interior Gonçalves."

"Tomorrow evening," Ava repeated.

"Yes. I doubt we'll be invited. But it's easy to crash these big media events. What shall we wear?" Tilda took off her reading glasses and gave her cousin a second look. "Oh, dear, Ava, you've got that North expression. As if you've just formed some resolve."

"I have, actually. I'll be going to this media event alone. And right after breakfast, I'm moving to a hotel."

"Don't start that again."

"What I'm doing—trying to do—is about to become more dangerous. I'm not going to involve you any further."

"I'm not scared." Tilda laughed. "How can I be, when I don't know what's going on?"

Ava considered. "That's true," she said. "Let me tell you what's going on, so you can be scared."

Tilda threw her covers off and perched on the edge of the bed, facing Ava. "Finally," she said. "I'm all ears."

Ava told her about Ken Brydon's murder, ending with what Berman had told her yesterday.

Tilda was silent for a moment, thinking it over. Then she said, "Of course I'm sorry for Mr. Berman's scuba customers, having their vacations spoiled," she said. "But what about the Cuban fishermen? They live terribly close to the edge. Have you read *The Old Man and the Sea*?"

"Coz! You proudly boast that you've never read a work of literature."

"I've read a few of the short ones. But you see what I'm getting at? Corals are where fish breed. If some chemical spill has turned the waters off San Ferdinand into a dead zone, the fishing may never recover. What are the people going to eat?"

Ava nodded. "I think Morales has been keeping the bad news from the Havana government. That's why he killed Ken Brydon."

"Ruy and Carlucci are entirely capable of committing murder to protect a lucrative deal. But that's not proof. What's your next step?"

"It's obvious." Ava tapped the newspaper. "Members of the Havana government will be there tomorrow night."

"Possibly even Minister Gonçalves."

"I'll tell him or whoever's there. See what the reaction is. If he's shocked, then we can be pretty sure that's why Ken was killed. If he shrugs me off because he already knows, then we've been barking up the wrong tree."

"Seems to me you're playing a delicate game, coz. Promise me you won't let Ruy see you talking to the Cubans. I've observed this phenomenon before. Attacks of patriotic insanity run in the North family. They decide they want to get into Arlington National Cemetery by the shortest route."

"That's why I'm going alone tomorrow night."

Tilda shook her head decisively. "It's why I'm going with you."

As Tilda predicted, they had no trouble getting into the media event. They showed photo ID, stepped through a metal detector, and joined the throng in the enormous ballroom. Tilda was wearing a white dress from Dolce

& Gabanna, printed with a large vase overflowing with flowers of every imaginable color. Her MedicAlert bracelet was fuchsia. Ava was more understated in a strappy black silk frock trimmed with lace from Prada.

Most of the other guests, being media people, were heading straight for the bar, but Ava and Tilda walked slowly along the walls, looking at the big black-and-white photos. It was a cavalcade of celebrities in 1950s Havana: Frank Sinatra at the microphone, Fulgencio Batista in his blue sash of office, Meyer Lansky and Lucky Luciano in straw hats, strolling the Malecón, Desi Arnaz at his big drum, no doubt thumping out "Babalu."

"Looking for your namesake?"

It was Morales, smiling at Ava, looking relaxed and handsome. He had dressed for the occasion in a white dinner jacket with a wine-red cummerbund. He nodded to Tilda as he stepped up beside Ava.

"Sorry?"

"I said looking for your namesake?"

Ava was still confused. She had been named for her great-aunt, the first woman pediatrician in Virginia. Morales pointed at the next picture on the wall. It was of Ava Gardner, posing on the rampart of Morro Castle with Spencer Tracy.

"Oh," said Ava. "Isn't she beautiful?"

"I'll say. Legend has it she liked to swim in Hemingway's pool at Finca Vigía. In her birthday suit. Wish I had a picture of that."

One thought led to another, and Morales ran his eye unhurriedly over Ava's body, collarbone to ankle. To distract him she said, "And who are the men on the veranda?"

"The courtyard," Morales corrected. "That's the Morales house in Old Havana. The men are my grandfather and his brothers."

They moved closer to the photograph, which showed three men in white suits with gleaming black hair, sitting on wicker chairs placed amid potted tropical plants on a gleaming tile floor, in front of a tall arched doorway. All were smoking long cigars with evident enjoyment. Morales pointed at each in turn. "Abuelo Francisco, who eleven years after this photo was taken would be beaten by Castroite thugs, driven into exile with nothing but the clothes on his back. He founded the family fortune in Miami. Tío Pablo, who spent his life serving the exile community as a state senator in Tallahassee. And Tío Antonio, whom I never knew, because he was killed at the Bay of Pigs."

Morales shook his head and turned away to regain his composure. After a moment he snapped his fingers and a waiter approached with a tray of champagne glasses.

"Let me show you Yemayá," he said, as he handed glasses to Ava and Tilda.

On a dais in the center of the room, under a glass dome, was a meticulously executed scale model of the resort complex. Rain-forested hills above, beach and blue sea below, and at the center an eight-story building with projecting wings topped by twin lanterns with round-arched windows and finials.

"Architecture inspired by the Hotel Nacional in Havana," Morales said.

"Inspired?" Tilda murmured in Ava's other ear. "I'd call it outright plagiarism."

"The pool complex, the tennis club, the spa, the

beach pavilion," Morales said, pointing out each feature. "And less than five miles away, we'll have our own port facility."

"San Ferdinand," Ava said.

"Yeah, that's right. So the cruise ships can moor practically at my doorstep. I won't have to share them with Havana."

"It looks great, Ruy," Ava said. "But aren't you supposed to be giving a progress report tonight? Shouldn't there be pictures of the construction site?"

He shrugged. "Who wants to look at mud and rebar?"

"But at least you're going to give a detailed report about how things are going?"

"I flew over in my helicopter a month or so ago. The site's looking fine."

"You flew over in a helicopter."

"Look, I'm not the kind of guy who takes core samples and plants stakes myself. I make deals. Other people take care of the details."

She remembered something he'd said at his previous parties, that the representatives of the Cuban government had come to him to make this deal. "Ruy, have you ever been to Cuba?"

The full lips jutted in the famous pout. "Hey, I wanna go . . . and I don't wanna go." He unwrapped his forefinger from his champagne glass and pointed at the photos on the wall. "Havana doesn't look like that anymore. It's poor. Slums everywhere. All the beautiful buildings crumbling. Probably even Casa Morales. What can you expect after sixty years of Commie rule? I know it's gonna break my heart, first time I see Havana. But then I'll dry my tears, roll up my sleeves, get to work restoring it to what it was in 1957."

Morales drained his glass, handed it off to a passing waiter, and turned away. "Excuse me."

As Ava watched him go, Tilda stepped up beside her. "My my, what a speech."

"*Can't repeat the past?*" Ava quoted. "*Why of course you can!*"

"He reminds you of Gatsby?"

"Coz! There's another work of literature you've read."

"Another short one. I wouldn't call him Gatsby, though. A one-night stand with Daisy would've been enough for Ruy."

On their right, a foursome of guests who'd been chatting broke up, to reveal Arturo Carlucci standing behind them. He was wearing a charcoal suit and silver tie. His bald head glittered under the chandeliers. The long dark hair curled out over the bump of his right ear, lay flat on the left side. He looked over the shoulder of the man he was talking to. At Tilda, then at Ava.

Tilda shivered and whispered, "*God*. At least when Ruy undresses you with his eyes, he stops at the skin. Carlucci flays you down to the bone."

Ava said nothing. She was busy returning Carlucci's gaze. Only when he looked away did she take a sip of champagne. Tilda linked arms with her and walked her away. "Do *not* get into staring contests with that guy, okay? He's—" she broke off as a thought struck her. "Your friend Brydon—was it Carlucci who—"

"We don't know. But Brydon was killed by a thrust through his back that pierced his heart. A long, thin blade. When Carlucci was starting out with the Jersey mob, he was famous for his prowess with a stiletto."

Tilda drained her glass, took Ava's, and drained that too. "Why did I have to ask?" she moaned.

There was a stir of talk among the people around them. Ava looked up to see that everyone was looking toward the door. A lone man was standing on the threshold, looking as if he didn't really want to enter.

"Who's that?" Tilda asked. "He looks like he's just come from the funeral of his favorite child."

Ava recognized him from pictures. "Ivan Gonçalves, Minister of the Interior."

The new Cuban government had banned Castroite army fatigues, and Gonçalves was wearing a black suit, white shirt, and black tie. The suit was baggy on his tall, thin, stooped frame. The fraying of the shirt cuffs was visible even at a distance. Gonçalves had a fine head of gray hair, full beard, craggy face, and glittering black eyes. He would have looked distinguished, except that his shoulders were bowed and he was hanging his head. His complexion reminded her of that of the seasick man aboard the dive boat in Key West. He would obviously have preferred to be anywhere else this evening.

"Ivan Diegovich!"

It was Morales, sweeping down on his guest with hand outstretched.

Gonçalves stiffly extended his own hand, saying, "I do not use a patronymic."

"You ought to. A lover of all things Russian like yourself." Morales was aware of the wide circle of onlookers and was playing to them. Dropping Gonçalves's hand, he pushed back his French cuff and consulted his gold watch. "Say, didn't I tell you it was *hora británica* tonight?"

Gonçalves looked blank, and Morales repeated the Spanish phrase.

"Oh. *Hora británica,*" Gonçalves said, giving the R a few more rolls and redistributing the emphasis. Morales spoke Spanish with an American accent.

"Yeah. In Havana that means only twenty minutes late. And you're half an hour late. What was the problem, you caught a slow elevator?"

"I did not stay here. I've come straight from the airport."

"I can tell. You look like you haven't had a decent meal in months. You know the joke, right? The three biggest victories of the Cuban Revolution were education, medicine, and women's rights, and the three biggest defeats were breakfast, lunch, and dinner."

"Yes. I know the joke," said Gonçalves stonily, over the laughter of the circle of spectators.

"Well, come on, I'm taking you over to the buffet table." He put his arm around Gonçalves's shoulder. Gonçalves cringed.

"Excuse me," he said. "I will rejoin you in a moment."

"Sure. The men's room is first door on your left," Morales called after him. Once Gonçalves had gone out the door, he added, "We got a product in capitalist Miami a man your age could use. Called Depends."

The spectators laughed delightedly. Morales, satisfied, reached for another glass of champagne.

"Lays it on thick, doesn't he?" Ava whispered.

"Oh, that's just the way Ruy treats his partners. If you've made a deal with him, he's made a fool of you."

"I'm going to talk to him. This is my chance."

"Careful, coz."

In the corridor, she waited until Gonçalves came out, dabbing his brow with a handkerchief. Oddly, considering he was an old Commie, he had the air of an aged and faded aristocrat. Not just any aristocrat, she thought. Don Quixote, with his hollow cheeks and beaky nose and deep, dark eyes.

"Señor Gonçalves?"

He waved the handkerchief to make her go away. "I can find my own way back."

"I don't work for Morales." She stepped in front of him. "I have something important to tell you."

"And you are?"

"It doesn't matter. Just listen. The coral reef off San Ferdinand—"

"The port, yes."

"Do you know about this?"

"What?"

"It's been blanched. Nothing alive down there."

He stared at her. It was news to him. "How did this happen?"

"About a month ago, there was a toxic chemical spill. From one of the ships unloading in the harbor."

Gonçalves put up a long bony hand to stop her. As if he couldn't take in anymore. Then his mouth set, his eyes glittered, his very nose seemed to sharpen into a blade. He was like Don Quixote spotting the windmills. Without a word, he brushed past her, stalking back into the ballroom.

Ava made herself wait. Following him closely into the ballroom would give the game away. She counted to sixty and returned.

Nobody was looking her way. All eyes were on the two men confronting each other. They were speaking Spanish, loudly and angrily. Gonçalves had pulled himself up to his full height. His shoulders blocked her view of Morales, of whom she could see only gesticulating arms in white dinner jacket sleeves. Carlucci was at his side. He seemed displeased that everyone was witnessing the argument. Soon he had Morales and Gonçalves walking across the room, ringed by flunkies. They were heading for a pair of French windows.

The ballroom, like all Morales's properties, had architecture inspired by old Havana. There were tall French windows all around, with long draperies framing them, leading out to wrought-iron balconies. She'd noticed as she and Tilda drove up that these rows of balconies went all the way up.

Before her cousin could arrive to tell her to be careful again, Ava walked briskly out of the ballroom, found the stairs, and climbed them at a run to the next floor, then headed for what she judged would be the balcony above the one where Morales and Gonçalves were talking.

She had to cross another ballroom. Giant yellow cats and blue squirrels hung from the ceiling. Spectators in similar costumes and dye jobs ringed long tables where young people sat intensely over pads and cards and laptops. It was a Pokémon competition. No one glanced at Ava as she rounded the tables and went to the window and out.

It was a small balcony, more for appearance than use, with a wrought-iron railing. The downtown skyscrapers around her glittered with lights. The bay was only darkness, but for the lights of an occasional boat. At first she couldn't hear anything but the swish of traffic three floors below and thought she was on the wrong balcony. She dropped to her knees and leaned close to the wrought-iron uprights.

Now she could hear Morales saying, "I knew nothing about this." He sounded as if he'd said it several times already. "You want me to get my project supervisor on the phone? He shoulda told me, and he didn't."

"No. I've seen you get your underlings to lie for you before."

"All right. I knew about the toxic spill. Satisfied?"

"Why did you not inform me?"

"I was going to. Once the hotel was finished."

"It is inexcusable to delay!"

"I knew you were gonna be a pain in the ass about it."

"You must compensate the people for their loss!"

"You mean the snorkelers and scuba divers? 'Course I will. They're my guests. We'll sink a ship as an undersea attraction. A pirate ship. The one from the latest *Pirates of the Caribbean* movie. Disney'll be happy to unload it cheap, and the publicity will—"

Morales was free-associating and enjoying himself. The old Cuban cut him off. "I'm talking about the people of San Ferdinand."

"What about them?"

"They are fishermen. The reef is one place the fish breed. Another is the mangrove swamp, which you destroyed when you were deepening the harbor. This is a death blow to the village of San Ferdinand!"

"Are you crazy? San Ferdinand is gonna be fine. It's entering its golden age, as the cruise ship port for Yemayá. There are gonna be plenty of jobs, driving shuttle buses, carrying luggage, selling souvenirs—"

"Why not diving for coins that passengers on the ships will throw?"

"I'm tired of you bustin' my chops, old man!" It was easier for Ava to hear, because he was raising his voice. "You keep dragging me through arguments you've already lost. This project is providing jobs, and your people need them."

"What sort of jobs? Socialism teaches the dignity of labor. Do you respect that? No! It will be the Special Period in Time of Peace, as El Líder called it, all over again. When the weakling Gorbachev and the drunk-ard Yeltsin destroyed the Soviet Union—"

"I know all about it. The subsidy from Moscow stopped coming, and you couldn't hack it on your own."

"El Líder had no choice but to encourage the people to turn their homes into hotels and restaurants. Invite the tourists in and allow them to use their dollars. Soon Cuba had two economies, dollars and pesos. The people working for the tourists got rich while those working for their own fellow citizens languished. My father was a surgeon. He made less than a cabdriver. My uncle was a professor. He made less than a bellboy."

"You're boring me, *camerón*."

"I'm going back tonight. To organize the people of San Ferdinand."

"No. You're not gonna turn out a handful of your fellow dead-enders with 'socialism or death' placards and Che T-shirts. You're not gonna open an official inquiry. You're not gonna alert Greenpeace and the Sierra Club. Because all these things will be bad for business. And you need—"

A sound interrupted Morales. Ava didn't realize it was the door opening until she heard Carlucci's voice. It was softer, harder for her to understand what he was saying.

"Ruy . . . Ruy, step back. Please. We don't want an accident here. You know, somebody falling off the balcony, getting run over. Step back. Good."

A pause. Then Carlucci went on. "Now, we have a problem. An immediate problem. A *mutual* problem. The room's full of travel writers. We want them to write about how everything is going according to plan at Yemayá. Which for them is kind of a dull story. They'd much rather write about strains and tensions and so forth between you two gentlemen. So, Ruy, Ivan, you're going to go back in there and make nice."

Gonçalves said something she could not make out, because Morales was talking at the same time. Carlucci cut them off.

"You'll both make speeches. They don't have to be long. Or clever. Just say everything is fine. There are no disagreements. Got it?"

The other two were mumbling again. It sounded like assent. At the sound of the doors opening again, Ava rose to her feet and went back in.

Tilda was waiting for her at the foot of the steps. She stared wide-eyed as her cousin descended, but waited to speak until she was close enough to whisper.

"We have to get out of here."

"It's okay, nobody saw me talking to Gonçalves."

"Coz—"

"We'll go in a minute! I just have to hear what they say."

By the time they got back to the ballroom, Gonçalves was already finishing his speech. He'd kept it brief, all right. He was stepping back from the microphone, patting his lip with a handkerchief like a man who has just vomited. The two were standing on the dais, with a big computer-generated photo of the resort on the wall behind them. Tilda kept Ava at the back of the crowd.

It was Ruy's turn. His face was flushed to the same color as his cummerbund. HIs mouth was in full pout. "I can only underline what my . . . friend Ivan just said," he began. "Things are fine."

He'd run dry. Carlucci, standing behind him, looked concerned. But then Morales thought of something to say. The hard, glittering eyes softened into pools of chocolate. A sly grin spread across his face.

"Listen, let me level with you folks. You're wondering what Ivan and I were talking about out there. You want me to tell you? I will. We were talking about my family's cross."

Carlucci and Gonçalves exchanged a look, united in puzzlement, if nothing else.

"I told him about the darkest day the Moraleses ever knew. My grandfather had just come back from turning in his Cadillac. The government made him get a tune-up first. We knew they were going to confiscate everything before they expelled us. So we gave our prized possessions, paintings, jewelry, table silver, to friends who were staying on. They'd keep them for us till we returned—which would be in only a few weeks, we thought. By now, of course, all our family heirlooms are long gone. And you know, ladies and gentlemen, my friend Ivan totally sympathized. He had tears in his eyes."

The room was hushed. Gonçalves kept his face blank. His shoulders were sagging so that deep vertical folds showed in the too-large suit. His head was bowed, gray locks straggling across his forehead that he didn't brush back.

Morales went on. "But there was one family heirloom that was too precious to entrust to anybody. Our Toledo cross. Solid silver. Our ancestors brought it from Spain. It always stood in the place of honor in the house. Men of the family kissed it before they went to war. Women prayed before it before they got married. Or went to the convent. Every child said his Pater Noster in Latin before his first Holy Communion. We couldn't smuggle it out, couldn't entrust it to anyone. So Abuelo Francisco buried it. He raised a tile in our veranda and put it in, in a lead box. All by himself, so the servants wouldn't know."

Morales folded his hands in front of his crotch. "Well, I got kind of worked up, talking about that. And you know what my friend Ivan said to me?"

Morales stepped over to him, put his arm around the sagging shoulders of the older man, who cringed helplessly.

"He said, Ruy, you should have that cross back. I'll see to it personally. Soon as he gets back to Havana, he's going to throw a police cordon around Casa Morales. Kick out whatever lowlifes are living there. Bring in the best archeologists from the university. If that cross is still there, he'll find it. His personal pledge to me. Because this is not just a partnership. It's a friendship."

He flashed a grin around the room as the applause began.

"Was that all bullshit?' Tilda whispered.

"It's not what was said on the balcony."

"He sure knows how to play a crowd. Look at them."

Photographers were stepping forward with their cameras, amateurs holding their smartphones over their heads. Reporters were scribbling in their notebooks. Morales was forcing Gonçalves to shake hands with him. Ava felt sorry for the old man. When Morales got you down, he couldn't help grinding your face in the mud.

Tilda was pulling on her arm. "I've already called for our car. Let's go."

They walked quickly down the stairs to the lobby. The Avanti was waiting at the door. Tilda tipped the car valet generously, and they got in. Tilda waited only to raise the convertible top before driving away.

"We're not going home." She sounded tense, unlike herself. "We're going to a hotel in Palm Beach—or no, I'm too well-known there. We're going to a motel in Orlando."

"Tilda, I told you, nobody saw me with Gonçalves."

"They didn't have to. You think they're not going to be able to connect the dots? What they killed Brydon to prevent from happening—you just made it happen. It won't take them long to figure out who you are and what you're up to."

The words sobered Ava. She was silent. Wondering if Orlando was safe. If anywhere was.

CHAPTER TWENTY-FOUR

Despite his poor Spanish, Laker was able to make the cabdriver understand that he wanted him to pull over. He'd spotted just the type of place he was looking for.

The street, only a mile from the Mexico City airport, was a humble one, lined with small shopfronts. The windows of the shop that interested him were almost completely covered by posters and stickers in fluorescent colors, advertising cheap rates for the services it offered. After paying the driver, Laker went in. The little place was packed with people. Some were standing in line at the counter to receive and cash remittances from their relatives working in the United States. Others were waiting at another counter to place long-distance phone calls. Laker went to a third counter.

With terse words he didn't understand, and a gesture he did, the clerk directed him to the one computer in a row that wasn't being used. They were all old ones, cased in battered tan plastic, with CRTs a foot and a half long. But Laker's came to life when he put pesos in the slot. He tapped keys. The letters were worn off half of them.

He'd discovered this site during his layover at Tokyo airport. Theoretically, it could tell you the location of any ship at sea. The catch was, its receivers could only pick up their transponders when they were close to land. Entering *M/V Comercio Marinero*, he got only "Out of Range." So he had time to prepare. He just didn't know how much.

Or what he was going to do.

The screen went black. After a moment's hesitation, he fed in more pesos, and went to the site of the State Department, United States of America.

He'd been awake for most of the long flight from Tokyo to Mexico City, trying to make a plan. It wasn't going to be possible for him to seize the ship single-handed, search the hold for the container loaded at Magadan, and open it. That left him with two options, neither of them good.

The first was to sink the ship. In the Middle East, Laker had trained with Navy Seals, and it was just possible he would be able to improvise an explosive charge and fix it to the hull of the ship while it was docked. But he was no demolition expert. The explosion might kill dockworkers or sailors. Or himself.

The second was to go the official route. Have American diplomats persuade the Mexican government to seize the ship legally, search it, interrogate its crew. But if Laker walked into the American embassy, he'd never get a chance to make his case. He was a fugitive, a suspected rogue agent. They'd tie him, gag him, and put him on a military plane back to Washington.

While the *Comercio Marinero* steamed out of Puerto Chiapas and disappeared over the horizon.

There was one hope. Laker had been a CIA agent for fifteen years before being recruited by the Outfit. He'd served in many stations in the Middle East and Europe as well as Langley. If there was anybody he knew in the Mexico City station, anybody he could trust, he'd make a gingerly approach to that person, try to convince him that *Comercio Marinero* had to be stopped.

He kept clicking on the State Department site until he came to the Mexico City page. The CIA didn't try to conceal the names of its officers who were attached to foreign embassies. It just listed them under vague and innocuous titles. Finding the personnel roster, Laker scanned it.

The third assistant attaché for cultural affairs was Theresa V. Lydecker. It was a name he knew well.

Only too well.

At sundown, Laker was sitting among the many people idling and chatting on the benches lining the path leading to the Palacio de Bellas Artes. It was the grandest building in a city that was fond of grandeur, an immense white marble edifice with pillars and pilasters and a cornice decorated with statues of angels and muses, topped by triple stained-glass domes.

Laker was watching the semi-circular columned portico within which were the main doors. He was hoping Theresa V. Lydecker would eventually emerge from them. Over lunch, he'd read in a newspaper that the Ministry of Culture was holding a cocktail reception in the Palacio to welcome the dancers of the American Ballet Theatre, who'd be giving a series of performances over the next week. Laker was betting that Terry's cover would require her to attend.

The reception was a stroke of luck. Otherwise, he would've had to watch for her outside the embassy. Perimeter security was bound to be tight, and he'd have run a high risk of being spotted.

But was Terry being stationed here a stroke of luck? That remained to be seen.

They'd met at The Farm, the CIA's training facility in rural Virginia. All recruits to the Agency were cocky—it went with the territory—but Laker and Terry stood out. Everybody knew Laker had turned down offers from NFL teams to serve his country, and he hadn't been averse to basking in their admiration. Terry was beautiful and fearless. She excelled in small-arms marksmanship, unarmed combat, and all the other deadly skills they were learning. She and Laker were like the football team captain and the homecoming queen: everybody expected them to have a romance, and they did.

A fling, anyway. Laker soon tired of arguing with Terry and broke it off. He wasn't much interested in listening to women back then, though he'd had two good ears.

Terry became a legend at The Farm, and not just because she aced all the courses. In one fieldwork exercise, the students were dropped off at a shopping mall. They were to find hapless strangers and persuade them to drive them to Baltimore. Terry went into the mall and disappeared for a week. She said she'd persuaded a man to drive her to Las Vegas, since Baltimore was too easy. She left no one in doubt of how she'd persuaded him. Maybe the point of the stunt was to get back at Laker. Instead, it almost got Terry washed out of the CIA.

Their paths had crossed only once since, when they were both working out of Lahore station five years later. Pakistan, then as now, was one of America's most dubious allies. Terry was running a valuable asset in the Ministry of Defense in Islamabad. He called her in the middle of the night, saying that his superiors were on to him. He had to be pulled out. Terry wanted to drive to Islamabad at once. Laker and the station chief tried to persuade her the asset was panicking and imagining things. She'd only make matters worse if she went to Islamabad.

She went anyway. The asset ended up in prison. Terry was demoted to a desk at Langley.

Since he'd gone to the Outfit, he'd heard nothing about her. He wondered if age and hard experience had had the same effect on her as they'd had on him, made her less cocksure, more patient.

He doubted it.

The wait stretched on and on. The light was fading. But he had no trouble recognizing Terry when she stepped between the pillars of the portico. If her hair was dyed now, she'd dyed it the same honey-blond it had been in her youth. She was wearing high heels, a short red skirt, and a print blouse. A small, elegant leather handbag hung by a strap from her shoulder. Laker didn't doubt that it contained her Glock.

It would be a bad move to startle her. When she was thirty paces away, he rose from the bench and advanced into the light cast by a street lamp. Then he stood still, keeping his hands well away from his pockets.

He saw the hitch in her stride as she recognized him. She scanned left and right, then walked right up to him, stopping just beyond his reach. Her face, with high, rounded brows over heavy-lidded blue eyes, a short nose, and a wide mouth, was as beautiful as ever.

"You've got a hell of a nerve, Tom Laker," she said.

He said nothing.

"You think I'll cut you some slack. Just because we slept together a few times before I kicked you out."

Terry's memory always worked to her advantage. He said, "I'm making no assumptions."

"Good. Because the only way I'll help you is advise you to turn yourself in. You fucked up big-time in Tallinn, Laker. Either that or you made some kind of deal with that asshole Barsinian. Sooner or later, you'll have to face the consequences."

"I know that. But there's something else going on, something bigger. All I ask is that you give me a hearing."

The low-lidded eyes surveyed him for a long moment. Then she smiled. "I have the feeling this is going to be a long story. And these shoes are pinching. There's a good café across the street. Let's go."

"Thanks, Terry. And don't worry, I won't try anything."

"I'm not worried. Not because I trust you. Because I can take you down, anytime I want."

Laker didn't argue. He and Terry walked abreast, arm's length apart, across Avenue Juárez. Terry chose a sidewalk table, despite the traffic fumes. One of those odd, stubby coatracks they have in Mexican cafés stood by the table. It was four feet tall and bristling with prongs. Terry hung her purse on it and hitched up the strap so that her Glock would be in easy reach. The waiter approached and they ordered tequila. Herradura was good enough for Laker. Terry insisted on Don Julio 1942.

She eased off her shoes without taking her hooded gaze off Laker. "Let's hear it."

"There were no complicated secret negotiations between Barsinian and me. We fought and he won."

"The great Laker, top operative of the agency whose name none dare speak, beaten by a slightly overweight Army enlisted man?"

"Barsinian was a highly trained agent of the FSB."

He was expecting her to scoff. But Terry only looked thoughtful. She said, "Word from Langley is, the head of the agency whose name none dare speak called the DCI recently."

"What did he say?"

"That the DCI had shit for brains. Mason said his people had been checking the story Barsinian told the Army about what he'd been doing between his hitches and it didn't hold up. When he was supposedly in Tehran visiting relatives, he was really in Moscow being trained by the FSB. Or so Mason claims."

Laker sipped his drink. He felt warmed by more than the tequila.

Terry read his face. "Yeah. Your boss is still in your corner. In the eyes of the CIA, you are a long way from rehabilitated. But I'm willing to listen."

Laker told her about the *Comercio Marineo*. When he was finished, Terry summoned the waiter and ordered another tequila. Laker shook his head.

"Okay, I'll bite," Terry said. "What's in the container from Magadan?"

"I don't know."

"But you guess . . . ?"

"Munitions. Small arms and explosives, for the ethnic Russians in the Baltic."

"Why send them the wrong way around the world in an Ecuadorean freighter?"

"To obscure that they're coming from Russia."

"Seems like a very questionable plan to me."

"It's working so far. I'm the only who suspects."

"And you don't know much," said Terry, with a tart smile. "So what's the rest of the plan?"

"Fighting intensifies in the Baltic states. Moscow says somebody has to restore order. And orders the tanks to roll."

"NATO isn't too popular in the Baltic right now, thanks to you. But the treaties are still in effect. An attack on one member is an attack on all, including the U.S. You think the Russians are willing to start World War III?"

"I don't know."

Terry's glass arrived. She emptied it in one swallow. "There is only one reason why you're not lying facedown on the ground while I'm cuffing your wrists."

"And that is?"

"We've been getting disturbing intel out of northwest Russia. Army units concentrating along the borders. Air and naval assets shifting to nearby bases. We thought they were running a bluff, but—"

"Maybe they're not."

She folded her arms under her breasts and cocked her head. "What do you want from me?"

"I want you to set up a meet with your station chief. And the ambassador. Only those two, and on neutral ground."

"Neutral ground? I thought you said you were willing to face the consequences of your actions."

"I am."

"So when do you surrender?"

"After you seize the ship."

"What if the station chief and the ambassador refuse to go along with your plan?"

"Then I'll stop the ship myself."

Terry gave her slow smile. "You know, Laker? You can still do it."

"What?"

"Make my panties wet." Turning, she signaled the waiter and pointed at her empty glass. "Okay. I'm going to let you walk out of here. We meet again, 5 P.M. tomorrow. Someplace very open, very public. Say the monument to the martyrs in Chapultepec Park."

"You'll have the station chief and ambassador with you?"

"No, Laker. The first step is I poke around a little and decide whether I believe you."

"We don't have much time. We don't know when the freighter will arrive in Puerto Chiapas."

The waiter returned with her third shot. She waited until he left, then said, "Don't rush me. Right now, I trust you enough to let you go, and no more. So go."

At five the next day, he was walking slowly up a broad path toward the memorial to the Niños Héroes. Six tall white marble columns adorned with black eagles commemorated six cadets who'd died defending Chapultepec castle, on the hill behind the monument, in 1847. It was an especially sad monument for an American, since they'd been fighting American troops.

There were a lot of people enjoying the green, spacious park on this sunny afternoon. Some were sitting on the steps of the monument. As he drew closer, he saw that one of them was Terry.

She looked as relaxed and comfortable as the people around her, sitting with her legs straight out in front of her, crossed at the ankles. She was wearing skintight designer jeans and red ankle boots, with a black top that bared one shoulder and hung loose around her waist. Her Glock could be hidden under it or in the red leather shoulder bag, matching the boots, that rested on the marble step next to her hip.

As he approached, she lifted her sunglasses to rest on her piled-up golden-brown hair. "You're getting sloppy, Laker. A slow, straight down the middle approach. What if I had ten agents planted around the perimeter? You must actually trust me."

"I don't have much choice." Laker sat beside her on the step.

"That's true. I've had an interesting phone conversation with Señor Pablo Esquierdo."

"Who is?"

"The *Comercio Marinero*'s agent in Puerto Chiapas."

"That was a rash thing to do, Terry. You may have made him suspicious."

"Not a chance. I speak Spanish like a native—a *Mexican* native. I said I was Señora Montoya, of the local Carrier plant—"

"And if he calls back?"

"He'll get a secretary who'll say, 'Carrier. Señora Montoya's office, can I help you?' C'mon, Laker. This is not my first time at the rodeo. I asked him if he had capacity for five containers of HVAC equipment, bound for Guayaquil. Which I picked because it's the headquarters of CENI Shipping and the *Comercio Marinero*'s home port."

"Is that where the ship's bound?"

"Yep. My guess was good. Next stop after Puerto Chiapas. But he said the ship isn't taking on any cargo at Chiapas. It's going to the shipyard for a refit."

"That's no reason to turn down a paying customer. The bills of lading from Vladivostok say that it's unloading nine containers at Chiapas. So it would have room. Why would a cargo ship turn down cargo?"

"I couldn't press him without arousing suspicion. He was trying to interest me in another ship that could take my HVAC equipment. But I did manage to find out a few things about the *Comercio*. It has a crew of nineteen. Four officers, all European, fifteen sailors, all Filipino. The captain is a Pole, named Jozef Korzeniowski. He joined the ship in Magadan."

"I wonder if he has Russian connections."

"CIA has a file on him. Classified highly enough I'd have to fill out a Need to Know in order to access it, unfortunately. It's possible he's the only one who knows about this secret cargo. Your munitions or whatever it is. I've been asking people about box boats—"

"What?"

"Container ships. Typically the containers arrive sealed, on a train or a truck, and they just load them onto the ship. The paperwork says what's supposed to be in them, but nobody looks inside. If they're reefers—refrigerated containers, for perishables—the crew has to wire them up. Otherwise, they don't have anything to do with them. They're stacked in the hold or on deck and sit there till the next port, where stevedores unload them. In fact, my source said, the crew is discouraged from going near the containers. The shipping lines are afraid of pilfering."

"The sailors are second-class citizens, especially if they're Filipino."

"Yeah. Bottom line, Laker? I still am not ready to buy into your munitions for the Baltic theory. But you've done enough to establish the probability the Russians loaded something they don't want the world to know about in Magadan. And the chance that Captain Korzeniowski will not head for Guayaquil is one the U.S. cannot afford to take. We need to know what's in the container."

Laker let out a sigh of relief. "Did the agent say when the ship was expected in Puerto Chiapas?"

She glanced at her watch. "Approximately twenty-four hours from now."

With Terry, relief was generally short-lived. "For Christ's sake! I need to meet with the station chief and the ambassador as soon as possible. You know how slowly official wheels grind."

"I'll make the call."

She rose, taking her cell phone out of her purse. He made to get up.

"No, stay there. I don't want you listening in and giving me advice I don't need."

So Laker sat where he was and watched Terry pace as she waited for her boss to come on the line. Her long-legged, hip-swinging gait was pleasurable to watch. Practically every man who passed gave her a lingering look.

The station chief must have come on the line. She was talking. Gesticulating. Abruptly she fell silent. The look on her face alarmed Laker. She ended the call. He got to his feet as she ran back to him.

"They won't meet with me?" he said.

She didn't pause and he fell in beside her. "We have to *move*. They're coming for us."

"Drop the phone. They can track it."

A kid was approaching on a bike. Terry smiled at him and said something in Spanish to make him stop. She tossed the phone to him. The kid stood there, astonished.

"Vamos!" Terry called. Turning to Laker, she said, "My boss is an asshole. No brains and no balls. He wouldn't even hear me out."

"Maybe we can go over his head to the ambassador."

"No, Laker. Anything that comes from you is fruit of the poison tree. They're after us. They'll tase us and put us on a plane to D.C."

Striding quickly, they were nearing the boulevard that bordered the park. Another kid was idling beside one of the cars parked along the curb. Terry spoke to him and handed him some pesos. Laker figured she'd hired him to watch the car. It'd been a sound precaution: the car was a little red Mercedes-Benz SUV. As they got in, Laker said, "Can they track your car?"

"Yep. We'll leave it at the subway station."

"I'm sorry, Terry. You threw me a line and I pulled you in."

"Never mind. What matters is, the asshole cut me off before I could even give him the details."

"So they won't be waiting for us at Puerto Chiapas."

"Nope. We'll be on our own to stop the ship." Terry smiled grimly as she maneuvered the car out of the space. "However the fuck we're going to do that."

CHAPTER TWENTY-FIVE

Laker was standing atop one of the big rocks that made up the breakwater between the harbor entrance and the beach at Puerto Chiapas. It was a beautiful afternoon. The sea was calm, the sky cloudless. The sun, low in the west, was a smear of blindingly bright yellow. He was squinting at the horizon. Thought he could see a bump. Definitely a ship. Probably the *Comercio*.

Hearing a horn honk behind him, he turned. Terry was waving from their car, parked on the palm-tree lined beachfront street. He trotted toward her.

The car was a battered old Honda. Terry had rented it, with a large advance cash payment, from a man she'd met in the market square. Then they'd driven into the hills to visit mines and quarries, hoping they could find someone to illegally sell them TNT for a bomb to fasten to the ship's side. They'd had no luck.

Terry said they could force their way onto the bridge and take the captain hostage. She had her Glock. Laker said Korzeniowski had probably prepared for that possibility.

Laker and Terry were at their wits' end. And exhausted by their night's journey. Puerto Chiapas was a small town at the end of a series of worsening roads served by slow buses. With time running out, she'd set off to survey the port facility while he watched for the ship. Since neither of them had a phone to access the website that gave ship coordinates, there was only the old-fashioned way.

"She's inbound," Laker said as he got in the car.

Terry turned to him. The hooded blue eyes were bright and the full pink lips were smiling. She had an idea. Even before he knew what it was, Laker felt his heart lift.

"We'll be ready," she said. She twisted the key and with a series of coughs the car started up. Bucking over broken pavement, swerving around other cars, mule carts, and stray dogs, she crossed the town to the wide road that led to the port.

They stopped at the back of a line of trucks, waiting to clear security and enter the port through a gate in a high chain-link fence topped with barbed wire. Terry turned off the road, then turned again. The Honda slid down into a shallow arroyo.

As the car bounced and shook, she said, "There's a stretch up here that isn't covered by cameras."

"Have we got wire cutters?"

"I picked some up."

"Nothing else we'll need?"

"Just my gun."

They left the car in the arroyo where it was out of sight and scrambled up the bank. Laker went at the chain link with the long-handled, short-bladed clippers. He peeled the section of fence back for Terry and stepped through after her, dropping the clippers.

Now they were standing on a wide stretch of asphalt, among parked trucks, front-loaders and other vehicles, and stacks of containers. A freighter was moored to the dock under a set of gantry cranes, which were unloading it. There were a lot of men, some working, more standing around, in hard hats and yellow vests, who paid no attention to them. He followed Terry to a kiosk at the water's edge. It had a flagpole, flying the Mexican flag, and two men were sitting in it. Next to it was a dock, where a motorboat was tied up. It was a flashy little rig, with a blue and yellow paint job, sirens and searchlights. Tires were strapped to the sides at intervals to serve as fenders. On the bow was painted the word PILOTO.

"So that's your plan," Laker said.

Terry jerked a thumb at the men in the kiosk. "They'll be getting the call from *Comercio Marinero* any minute. But they're not going out. We are. I'll drive the boat and you'll board the ship."

"Terry, how am I supposed to pass myself off as a pilot? I've got no clue how to guide the ship to the pier."

"You're not going to. You're going to run it aground."

"Oh," Laker said.

"I'll explain it all, but first we've got to take care of these guys. We have to be on the radio when the call comes in." She pulled the Glock from her belt and jacked a round into the chamber. "You ready?"

She went in first. Pushing open the door, she leveled her pistol on the man standing at the chart table. Shifted it to the man sitting at the radio. Terry told them in Spanish not to move and they'd come out of this okay.

The men seemed unable to move anyway. Both stared fixedly at the gun. One was middle-aged, with glasses and a gray moustache. The other was young and skinny. Laker had enough Spanish to order them to lie on the floor. Where there were boats, there was rope, and he found a supply of mooring line neatly coiled in the corner. He knelt and tied the men, hands and feet.

Terry was poking around in a cabinet. She found a light blue epauletted shirt and cap, which she dropped on the chair next to Laker.

He noticed that the shirt was the same as the ones the men were wearing. "Okay, I'll look the part," he said. "But I don't speak Spanish well enough to pass as a native."

"You don't speak Spanish well, period. But it doesn't matter. English is the lingua franca of shipping. And you'll be talking to a Polish captain, European mates. They won't notice anything off about your accent." She bent over the radio and adjusted dials. Static thinned and a jabber of voices came through. "Not the *Comercio*," she said.

Finished with his knots, Laker stood, peeled off his sweaty shirt, and put on the uniform shirt. He could barely fasten the buttons.

"Mexicans don't come in your size," Terry said. She was standing over the chart table now. With her fore-finger she traced a course into the harbor. "After the entrance channel, there's this dogleg to the freight pier. You'll direct the helmsman to cut the turn too tight, and the ship will run over this sandbar here. It'll be stuck fast. They'll wait for the tide to turn and hope it will lift them, but it won't. Then they'll bring lighters alongside and unload containers onto them. It'll take hours and hours. Days, even."

"Buying us the time we need." Laker smiled at her. "This'll work, Terry."

She smiled back. Turning back to the cabinet, she whipped off her black top. Terry still didn't bother with a bra. She put on a blue uniform shirt, yellow vest, belt with flashlight and utility knife.

The radio gushed static and a new voice came on. Terry sat down and put on the headset. After a moment, she turned to him and nodded. It was the *Comercio Marinero*. A brief exchange and she shucked the headset and rose. "They're approaching the harbor mouth. Let's go."

The men on the floor had their heads turned away. It was a silent plea: we won't be able to describe you. Please let us live. They'd feel better once he and Terry were away, Laker thought. But they wouldn't be able to wriggle free of their bonds in time to interfere with the plan.

Terry jumped to the dock, then boarded the boat. She started the motor as Laker cast off. Gulls rose from the water, grudgingly getting out of their way as they motored slowly into the main channel, passing the freighter the cranes were unloading. Traffic in the harbor was light, just a few pleasure boats bound for the marina. Terry opened up the throttles and the bow rose.

Laker sat on a bench at the stern. He lifted the lid next to him, took out a life vest, and put it on.

A few minutes later, they left the harbor. The boat bobbed with the waves, but gently. The sea was calm. The bottom rim of the sun was just touching the horizon, casting a long yellow streak toward them across the blue water. They didn't need GPS coordinates to locate the *Comercio*. It was the only ship in sight.

As they closed the distance, Laker rose to stand beside Terry at the wheel and get a better look at the ship he'd chased half-way across the world. It was a typical, small-sized cargo vessel, about 120 meters long. The bow wave was only a low curl of white water, because the ship was moving very slowly. Containers were stacked on the flat area aft of the bow. Only a few stacks, and not tall; the ship wasn't fully laden. At the end was the sterncastle containing the crew quarters and the bridge, which was topped with communication masts and disks.

Terry slowed down and flashed her navigation lights. She got on the radio as she passed along the ship's port side, turned, and came in close. Now the rust-streaked, tugboat-scuffed, roughly-painted, rivet-studded hull loomed over them. From an opening ten feet above the waterline, a rope ladder was tossed out to unfurl down the hull, its lowest rung awash. Terry gave Laker the nod.

He climbed out of the cockpit. The wind blew his cap off. Grasping the low railing that ran around the bow, he stepped forward and stood with feet far apart and knees bent. Terry slowed the boat further and maneuvered it closer to the ladder. She was good at this.

The boat was matching the ship's speed exactly and the rope ladder was only a yard or so away. An easy hop. He stepped over the rail to stand at the very edge of the deck. Let go the rail and crouched to jump.

The boat veered away, pitching Laker face-first into the sea.

Warm salt water filled his mouth and stung his eyes. Blindly he flung out a hand, grasped the bottom rung of the ladder. The ship's momentum almost tore it from his grip. He kicked hard and was able to grasp the next rung and pull himself up. His head broke the surface. Coughing, he struggled to breathe. The air he was drawing in was filled with spray, making him cough harder.

Two men were leaning out of the opening in the hull. Their faces were Asian. They were shouting and waving, maybe trying to tell him to hang on and they'd pull him up.

He swiveled his head the other way. The pilot boat was still there, running alongside the ship, a few yards away. He could just see Terry's head above the gunwale. She looked at him.

Only then did he realize that she had deliberately turned the wheel to throw him into the water. That her plan had never been to put him aboard the ship but to kill him. And she wasn't through trying yet.

He saw the bob of her shoulders as she spun the wheel. She meant to crush him. But it was one of the tires tied to the boat's hull that hit him. Together with the life vest it cushioned the impact. Even so the pain made him cry out. One of his hands lost its grip and his head went under.

His feet kicked, his hand probed and grasped. His

head came up. Terry was waiting for that. Her shoulders dipped as she spun the wheel. Again it was the tire that hit him. The pain in his ribs was fierce. He let go of the rope ladder and grabbed at the tire. His fingers scrabbled and found grips—on the rim of the tire, and on the rope that held it to the side.

When he was able to raise his face out of the water and take a breath, the rusty black iron hull and the dangling rope ladder were receding. Terry was satisfied. She couldn't see him and figured he was on his way to the bottom of the sea.

He knew what she'd do next. He took a tighter grip on the tire-rim and the rope. A few feet aft there was another tire he could rest his feet on. He breathed deep and held it as the boat accelerated. Terry was heading back to shore.

The next few minutes were bad. Laker's grip held, but the speeding boat kicked up so much spray that he could hardly breathe. He felt as if a spear had pierced his side and knew from experience that meant a cracked or broken rib. He was afraid he was going to black out.

That would mean he'd drown. And Terry would get away.

Unacceptable, Laker thought. He held on, and coughed, and fought the pain.

Finally the pressure of rushing water eased. The boat was slowing down. Terry must be approaching the harbor entrance. Or she was thinking about her next move. He gingerly shifted his hand and footholds till he was out of the water, clinging to the side of the boat. For a while he did nothing but breathe.

The motor cut off. The boat was slowly drifting

with the tide. Letting his legs drop into the water, Laker moved hand over hand to the stern. Raised himself till he could see over the gunwale. Terry was eight feet away, at the wheel with her back to him. Her golden-brown hair swirled in the wind. She was shrugging out of her life vest. Her Glock was shoved into the tool belt she'd taken from the pilot kiosk.

Stifling the grunts of pain from his rib, Laker clambered aboard. The noises of wind and water covered him. Terry was gazing toward shore. His eyes fixed on the nape of her neck above her collar. He took three silent steps and rabbit-punched her.

She dropped to the deck. He took the Glock, stepped back, and sat on the bench in the stern. Glanced at the harbor mouth to see if a police boat with lights and sirens was emerging. But the men in the pilot kiosk mustn't have been found yet.

Terry stirred. Opened her eyes. Took in the Glock in his fist, resting on his knee, pointed at her. He didn't say anything. She struggled onto her knees. Stood.

He said, "When did you decide to shop me to the Russians, Terry?"

She closed her eyes and let out a long breath. "I've been working for them for the last three years."

"How'd they turn you?"

"Please don't make me tell the whole story. You can fill in the details. I overreached. Didn't just walk into a trap. Ran into it. This was in Beirut. The Russians said they'd hand me over to Hezbollah. Or I could go home, as a double for them. For three years I've been doing things I hated myself for. But nothing as bad as today."

"Was it really so bad? You've always liked life on the edge. And there's no edge as thin as being a double agent."

"My controllers have never been happy with me. I wasn't maneuvering myself into the right positions to provide them the intel they wanted."

"You were in the right place at the right time when I came along. Your controller must have been delighted."

"Yes. He was. His orders were to kill you. Make sure you disappeared, so CIA would never know you'd even been in Mexico."

"What took you so long?"

Terry leaned back against the control panel. She looked weary and defeated, but Laker wasn't sure. He was watching her hands. There was a utility knife in a sheath on her tool belt. He didn't know if she was even aware of it.

"I was stalling. I kept telling my controller, what if I just keep you busy till the ship clears port? Won't that be enough?"

"Yesterday, in Chapultepec Park, you weren't talking to the embassy. It was your controller."

"Yes. He gave me the ultimatum. Carry out my orders. Immediately. Or he'd burn me with the CIA. I'd spend the rest of my life in prison."

Her left hand came up quickly. Laker raised and leveled his pistol. But she was only taking hold of the windshield frame. The wind was picking up as the sun went down and bigger waves were rolling the boat. Laker's rib throbbed.

"What's the ship carrying, Terry? Where's it going?"

"I don't know. The Russians don't trust traitors with their secrets. All I can tell you is, your instinct is correct. That ship is hot. It's the key piece in some big game Moscow's playing."

"Did you really call the ship's agent? Pretend to be Señora Montoya with her load of HVAC components for Guayaquil? Or were you just passing on misinformation from Moscow?"

"Moscow wasn't interested in misinforming you, Laker. Just killing you. Yes, I did call the agent. The information is good as far as I know. It's just my guess that only the captain and maybe his officers know what's in the container that was loaded at Magadan. And that he's not headed for Guayaquil. But I still think I'm right."

Laker nodded.

"Seems like we're through talking, Tom." She straightened up, letting go of the windshield frame, allowing her right hand to fall to her side.

"Put your hand back where it was."

Instead she grasped the handle of the utility knife.

"Stop," he said. "You know the saying. Don't bring a knife to a gunfight."

"That's if you want to win."

"Don't make me kill you, Terry. You don't want it to end like this."

"I don't want it to go on." She whipped the knife from its sheath and lunged at him.

Laker shot her in the right thigh.

She cried out as she toppled. The knife fell to the deck. Her hands caught the gunwale to break her fall. Perching on it, she grasped her bloody leg with both hands. He started toward her, but she stopped him with a fierce look.

"You bastard—Laker," she gritted out. "I would've put my bullet—right between your eyes."

Still looking at him, she leaned back and fell over the side. Laker ran to the gunwale. She'd already disappeared. There were only bubbles and a red tinge in the water. The next wave washed them away.

CHAPTER TWENTY-SIX

It would take years to sort out his feelings about Terry. Right now, he didn't even have minutes.

He turned seaward. The *Comercio Marinero* was half a mile off, and its hull was lengthening out as it turned broadside on to him, away from the harbor mouth. The two crewmen at the top of the rope ladder had witnessed the attempt to murder him. Probably assumed it had succeeded. He didn't know what they'd reported to the captain, but Korzeniowski had evidently decided not to risk going into Puerto Chiapas. He was heading straight for his next destination.

Whatever it might be.

Laker started the pilot boat's motor and spun the wheel, turning onto a parallel course with the freighter. He looked over his shoulder at the harbor mouth. Still no police boat.

Fortunately, the sun had dropped below the horizon and the light was fading fast. Tiny, bright navigation lights pricked the gloom around the distant freighter. The pilot boat had an abundant array of lights. He left them all off and opened the throttle a little. He was going to have to get closer. But not close enough that anybody on the freighter would see his bow wave or hear his motor.

Through the night he followed the *Comercio Marinero* slowly southward along the coast. The sky clouded up, obscuring the moon and stars. He could just make out the faint wake of the freighter. They would be keeping a radar watch, but he was confident that his small boat, low to the waves and moving slowly, wouldn't show up on their screen. Rummaging through compartments under the instrument panel, he found a bottle of water, which he rationed to last the night. An even luckier find was a small bottle of aspirin, which did a lot to dull the pain of his rib. He decided that it was only cracked, not broken. That way it hurt less.

Gradually the sky lightened. A thick mist lay over a calm sea. The coastline was a vague lumpy shape off to port. As the sun rose, he got an almost eerily clear view of the highest point of the freighter, the bridge topped with communication masts and dishes protruding from the mist. The ship was changing course, turning toward land. Working with Navy SEALs in the Persian Gulf, he'd learned a little about small-boat handling, but he couldn't figure out how to run the electronic chart system of the pilot boat. He could only guess that they'd left Mexico behind. This was probably Nicaragua.

The freighter headed into a narrow harbor mouth between sandy headlands. This was obviously a very small port, and Laker couldn't follow. He shut down his motor. The mist was gradually burning off, and his boat with its conspicuous paint job and glittering lights and sirens would be spotted. Anyway its fuel gauge was sinking toward empty.

He slid back the hatch lid and clambered down into the engine compartment. He had no idea what a sea-cock looked like, so he turned handles and opened valves until seawater began to pour in. Back on deck, he picked up his life jacket from the bench.

The boat was already beginning to settle. He jumped into the warm water and stroked toward the headland.

When he judged he was close enough, he put his feet down. There was ground under them. He walked through gently lapping waves to a beach littered with rusty cans and plastic bags. Then he made his way around the point.

The harbor was as small and sleepy as he'd expected. Close by on his left, he could see fishing boats lining battered wooden docks. They were shrouded in their nets. Gulls were flapping around, pecking at dead fish caught in the nets, but there were no people. This puzzled him until he remembered it was Sunday. On his right, farther off, a top-heavy cruise ship, its many tiers of balconies rising above the mist, was moored to a pier.

Straight ahead, in the main channel, was the *Comercio Marinero*, stern on to him. Its engines were off. With a clatter and splash, it dropped stern and bow anchors. He guessed that the cruise ship was taking up all of the port's pier space. A heavy chugging reached his ears, and an orange blur gradually emerged from the mist. It was a barge, with PELIGRO painted on its side in giant letters, and rows of tires to serve as fenders along its waterline. Its engines went into reverse as it maneuvered alongside the freighter, then were cut off.

Large pipes were extended toward the hull of the freighter, where crewmen were waiting to connect them. An offshore breeze brought Laker the smell of diesel oil.

It was as he'd hoped. The freighter had come all the way across the Pacific. It needed to refuel, which would take a while. This was his chance.

The yellow life jacket was too conspicuous. He shucked it and walked into the water. Its smell made him seal his lips tight. Breast-stroking so he wouldn't make splashes, hoping there was enough mist to conceal him, he swam out to the freighter and along the side away from the barge. If he was lucky, every crewman on duty would be busy with the refueling.

He raised his head, wiped the water from his eyes, and looked up. The bow loomed over him. Its edge was bare metal, the paint probably ground away by the ship's passage through the floating ice of Siberian waters. The anchor chain ran up from the water, taut and near vertical. The rusty iron links were so big that he could put his hands inside them and get a firm grip. He began to climb, and his cracked rib began to throb.

The pain worsened when he was clear of the water and his hands took his full weight. Wrapping his legs around the chain, he climbed on. The mist was dissipating. The higher he climbed, the more exposed he felt. Luckily, it seemed there was no one around to see him. Above him, the chain disappeared into the hawsepipe. The opening was far too small for him to pass through.

The chain locked between his thighs, he reached up with both hands, hoping he wouldn't overbalance. His fingers curled over the lip of the deck. He opened his legs and pulled himself up. Pain from his rib seared him. But he managed to get one elbow over the lip. Then he could swing a leg up and lock a foot in place. The rib didn't appreciate that maneuver, either. A last heave and he rolled onto the deck.

No crewmen around. In fact there was nothing to see but the sides of the containers stacked on deck, except for some sort of metal housing a few feet away. He crawled over, put his back against it, and drew up his legs.

While he got his breath back and waited for the pain in his side to ease, he looked around. The anchor chain reappeared through a hole in the deck and ran over a chock and into a slot in the metal housing, just above his head. He guessed that the housing covered a capstan that would reel in the chain when the anchor was raised. Looking down, he saw that he was sitting on a hatch.

Its dogs resisted his tired fingers, but eventually he got them loose and lifted off the hatch cover. Inside was a narrow platform with a pipe for the chain to pass through. It disappeared into the dimness below. He couldn't see the bottom. This must be the chain locker. He swung his legs into the hatch, lowered his feet to the platform, crouched and pulled the hatch cover back into place.

Total blackness. A smell of metal and grease. That was it.

A little experimenting established that the only possible position was sitting on the platform, back against the bulkhead, legs straddling the pipe. There wasn't enough head- or legroom. He had to keep his neck and knees bent. At least his rib wasn't troubling him. He waited and dozed.

A tremendous din awakened him. The chain was clanging and clattering through the pipe as the anchor was raised. A dank fog filled the locker as the wet chain fell into loops below. Laker covered his left ear. For once he was grateful that the right ear was deaf, leaving a hand free to pinch his nostrils shut. The racket went on and on.

Finally it stopped. Now he could feel the vibration of the ship's engines in the metal under him. Above him men were shouting, occasionally walking over the hatch cover. He assumed they were making the anchor fast to the side. He sensed movement and heard nearer engines laboring. He guessed there was a tugboat pushing the freighter's bow, turning her back toward the sea.

Before it got there, Laker fell asleep.

CHAPTER TWENTY-SEVEN

"Coz?" said Tilda. "I'm afraid that our little sojourn in Orlando, delightful as it's been, must come to an end."

It was early in the morning. They'd just awakened in their motel room. Ava'd made coffee in the in-room pot. Tilda accepted the Styrofoam cup, sipped, and said, "Execrable. But thanks."

She was sitting in the one comfortable chair, with her feet up on the bed. Her oyster satin robe had fallen away, revealing her smooth, tan legs. Her posture was rigidly erect, and she had an expression of intense concentration on her face, as if she were trying to thread a needle. By now Ava knew her well enough to know that she was just trying to keep her head absolutely still. She'd staggered in very late last night, and Ava'd had to get out of bed to help her with buttons and shoelaces.

Ava'd been glad that her cousin had managed to find an opportunity for dissipation in Orlando, which she'd called "the absolute low point of American banality." They weren't even staying in one of the nicer parts of the city. Determined to find a bolt-hole where Morales and Carlucci would never think of looking for them, she'd booked them into a chain motel on a long strip of other chain motels and fast-food franchises. One of those places where you turn on the TV rather than look out the window, as Tilda described it.

"Can't face the prospect of another boring day, coz?" Ava asked.

"It's not that. I can spend hours at our little pool beside the parking lot. But my lawyers—my entertainment lawyers—have summoned me to LA."

"Oh. When are you leaving?"

"Fairly soon." Tilda could afford to be vague. She had her own plane, waiting in its hangar at Miami airport. It'd be ready when she was.

"I hope it's nothing serious."

"I don't think so. Just Disney and Universal threatening to sue me."

"What? How'd that happen?"

"Very swiftly." Tilda smiled as she fingered her med-alert bracelet. It was dark green today. "You'll remember, day before last, I was looking for *something* interesting to do, and I saw that some young actors with day jobs on the theme park rides had put together a satirical revue. I found it scurrilous and salacious and good fun all around. So I went backstage and suggested to them some people I know who could help them make a podcast and get it noticed. They acted on my advice. Right away. And the thing went viral. Unfortunately, they listed me as executive producer, and—"

"Disney and Universal turned out to have no sense of humor. I'm sorry, coz. I can see why you have to go."

"Well, it's not just the lawsuit. Now Lena Dunham is after the movie rights to the podcast, and so is Seth Rogen. But enough of my frivolity. What are *you* going to do, coz?"

Ava sighed. "Time to face the question, all right. I've been calling Stan, the friend who's helping me at NSA, and Amighetti, the cop in Baltimore, and they have nothing to report. And I've been watching the news. Nothing there, either."

"Nor about Thomas Laker?"

"No. I have no idea whether he's alive or dead."

Tilda put her feet to the floor and leaned forward. The movement caused a wave of pain to cross her face, but she ignored it to pat Ava's knee. "I'm sorry, coz. I shouldn't even ask. You have enough burdens to bear. Don't you think it's time to go back to Washington?"

"I can't. I still have nothing the NSA would consider evidence that Morales and Carlucci had Ken Brydon murdered."

"Seems to me you know everything. Brydon was killed because Ruy didn't want the bad news about the toxic spill reaching Gonçalves. The great commie-capitalist partnership to remake Cuba is a lot shakier than they're letting on."

"It all looks clear to us. But at Fort Meade they'll tell me I'm just piling one guess on top of another."

"Well, fuck them. Go to Senator Chuck North."

"I started with him."

"Go back to him with what you know now. Time for him to do some work for a change. Put the screws to NSA." Tilda took Ava's hand and looked into her eyes.

"Coz, you've found out all you're going to. You're not going to get close to Morales and Carlucci again. It's dangerous even to try."

Ava squeezed her cousin's hand. "You're right. Of course you are. It's time to go back."

Tilda rose, wincing and smiling. "Time for a drink. Hair of the dog. And to celebrate that I don't have to worry about you anymore. You'll be safe in Washington."

"Nobody's safe in Washington. But I get your meaning. I've never thanked you properly for all your help. You've performed a valuable service for your country."

"How annoying. After I've tried to avoid my patriotic duty all my life. Bloody Mary or mimosa?"

Chapter Twenty-eight

Laker didn't know what had awakened him. Then he realized that it was the silence. The ship's engines were stopped. The tinkling of the anchor chain as the waves shifted it had ceased. But he had the sense that the ship was moving.

Strange.

These were all the sensations and thoughts he had time for before thirst overwhelmed him. Whenever he'd awakened, over the last hours, it had come back stronger, gradually crowding out his other discomforts, the cramping of his limbs, the burning of his cracked rib, his hunger. He didn't know how long it had been since he'd finished that water bottle on the pilot boat, but he couldn't last much longer.

He was going to have to look for water.

He felt around for the dogs, found them, twisted them open. The effort that cost told him how weak he'd become. Getting up on his knees, he cautiously lifted the hatch cover an inch or two. Light flooded in the chain locker, blinding him. He couldn't wait for his eyes to adjust, he had to see if there was anybody in the bow. Squinting and blinking, he looked in all directions, saw no feet in the vicinity. He pushed the hatch cover back and hauled himself clumsily onto the deck. Then just lay there a while, breathing the sweet, pure air.

As his pupils narrowed he could see that it was full daylight. He had no idea what time. Raising himself, he looked over the bow. The ship was in a narrow channel. Dead ahead, the tops of the great steel gates of a lock showed. Beyond was a lake surrounded by jungle-covered hills. He rose shakily and staggered to the rail. A hairy rope as thick as two fists put together ran from an opening in the hull to a boxy little electric locomotive. It was pulling the ship without noise or strain.

They were transiting the Panama Canal. That left no room for doubt. The *Comercio Marinero* wasn't home-bound for Guayaquil. It was heading into the Atlantic.

What did that mean? Laker tried to sketch out alternatives and weigh consequences, but his mind was too cloudy. He needed water. On this big ship, there were very few people. With luck he'd find it without being seen. He made his way along the stacked containers, staggering, pausing every few steps to lean a shoulder against their metal walls. Finally he reached a vacant stretch of deck. The sterncastle loomed over it. Anyone who happened to look down from the bridge would see him. Nothing he could do about that.

Running was not a possibility, but he walked as quickly as he could to the sterncastle. Leaned against a bulkhead covered with flaking white paint and rust spots as he turned the wheel of the hatch and stepped through.

He was in a dim, narrow corridor smelling of disinfectant. Were there drinking fountains on ships? Vending machines? Maybe not, but he could find a faucet somewhere. He set out along the corridor, one palm on either wall.

A crewman in light blue overalls came around a turn and stopped dead, staring at him.

Laker's right hand dropped to the cargo pocket on his thigh. But he didn't draw his pistol. Something about the man's face made him hesitate. He was a young Filipino with glossy black hair falling over his forehead, dark eyes behind steel-framed glasses, hollow cheeks and a patchy beard and moustache. His astonishment faded quickly, replaced by an expression Laker did not understand.

The crewman looked over his shoulder, then back at Laker. He put his finger to his lips. Coming closer, he whispered, "If captain find you, he throw you overboard."

Confused as he was by the man's friendly behavior, Laker didn't doubt that.

The crewman looked over his shoulder again. Putting a hand on Laker's chest, he gently pushed him back a few steps. Then he opened a narrow door and urged Laker inside. This was where the smell of disinfectant was coming from. It must be a storage closet.

"You wait," the crewman said, and closed the door.

Laker was back in the dark again. Here there was no room to sit down. He sagged against a bulkhead, and his face sank into the damp tangles of a mop. He pushed himself upright. Buckets and bottles stood around his feet and he couldn't move without knocking them over and making noise. Only the reek of disinfectant was keeping him conscious.

In less than a minute, the door opened. The crewman's arms were full. He handed Laker a banana, a Mars bar, and two bottles of water.

"Thanks," Laker croaked.

The door shut. Pocketing everything but one bottle, Laker struggled with its plastic cap for what felt like forever. Finally it was open. The tepid water was the most delicious thing he'd ever tasted. He swallowed and swallowed till the bottle was empty, then reached for the other one. He drank it more slowly and was just finishing when the door opened again.

Another man, also in light blue overalls, was standing beside the crewman. He was older, just as thin, with gray flecks in his short black hair. His large brown eyes appraised Laker closely.

"I recognize you," he said. "You are the pilot."

This must have been one of the men at the top of the rope ladder. Laker said, "I'm the man who went into the water off your port side, but I'm not a pilot."

"Who are you?"

"My name is Laker. I work for the American government."

"My name is Milaflores."

The water was already doing wonders for Laker's mental clarity. He realized he'd heard that name before—in a sidewalk café in Paris, from Lina Opalski, sole survivor of Home Port. He said, "Ramón Milaflores?"

The crewman blinked. "How do you know? Why are you here?"

"Because of the text message you sent from Magadan."

Ramón looked at the other crewman, then back at Laker. He put out his hand. Laker took it. It was small, heavily calloused, and strong.

Chapter Twenty-nine

Tilda was the first to depart, in her Avanti, while Ava wrestled with problems her cousin didn't have, like finding a seat on a flight out. Everybody in Orlando seemed to want to go to Washington today. The best she could do was a mid-afternoon flight with a stop in Atlanta. It would be night when she arrived, but people worked late on Capitol Hill, and she decided to go straight from the airport to Uncle Chuck's office.

That meant dressing in "federal rig" as Tilda called it: dark blue pantsuit, white pleated blouse, flat shoes. She was pleased to look in the mirror and see her old self again. The long, nerve-wracking masquerade was done.

She was packing her designer frocks when the maid knocked on the door. It was checkout time. She quickly gathered her belongings and went down to the front desk, where she called a cab. It got her to the airport well before her flight. She collected her boarding pass, checked her suitcase, and was looking for a place to eat lunch when her cell phone chimed: incoming email.

It was from Rodrigo Morales. The subject line was "Cruise to Nowhere." She opened it.

Hey Ava,

We're going out in my boat, how 'bout joining us? We just do a loop, an hour out and an hour back. You don't need to bring much, just the bottom of your bikini.

Directions to the marina followed. Ava was about to delete the message. But she noticed that it went on, so she scrolled down.

Your cousin's already said she'd come along. Arturo was lucky enough to catch up with her as she was about to board her plane. You know, the Embraer Phenom 300, ID number N136A, in Hangar B-10 at Miami airport.

See you,
Ruy

It was all correct. They'd flown down to Florida in that plane. She should have thought of the possibility that Carlucci would have its hangar watched. But she hadn't, and now Tilda was in their hands.

When she reached the marina, Ava parked her rental car under a No Parking sign. She picked up the papers on the passenger seat and folded them. At each stoplight along the way, she'd been scrawling her statement, everything she knew or suspected about Morales and Carlucci. She signed the statement and put it in the glove compartment, then got out and locked the car.

Crossing the parking lot, she stepped onto the floating wooden walkway that ran between berthed boats. Their rigging tinkled and clattered in the wind. She made eye contact with every person she passed, hoping that somebody would remember her when the police came around asking.

Morales's yacht was right where she'd been told it would be. Its swooping prow overhung the walkway. It was long, sleek, and white, with a band of darkened glass running around its superstructure. No one was visible on board. But by the time she reached the foot of the gangplank, Carlucci was standing at the top of it.

He was wearing shorts that revealed thin, hairy legs and a colorful print shirt. The left sidepiece of his sunglasses was, as usual, taped to his temple. The sea breeze stirred his long hair.

"Please come aboard, Ms. North."

"I want to see my cousin."

"You'll see her soon enough."

"I don't believe you have her."

Carlucci pulled something from his pocket and tossed it down to her. She caught it. It was the med-alert bracelet. The dark green one Tilda'd been wearing that morning.

A wave of weakness and fear swept through Ava. She put the bracelet away and climbed the gangplank. Carlucci fell back to give her room to step aboard. He wasn't looking at her, but at a young man coming up the walkway. When he reached the yacht he said to Carlucci, "She left her car in a tow-away zone. Put some papers in the glove compartment."

He was a dark-haired kid with inked forearms, in jeans and T-shirt. She hadn't noticed him at all. Carlucci opened his palm. "The keys, please, Ms. North."

She handed them over and he tossed them to the kid. "Put the car in long-term parking. Bring the papers to me," he said. Then he turned to Ava. "We're going below."

He pointed the way and followed her down glass steps between stainless-steel railings. It was a large room that might have been in a house, except for the view out the long windows. It had a teak floor, white sofas with lilac throw pillows, and on the walls, the familiar sepia-tinted photos of old Havana. The galley must have been nearby, because she could smell searing meat and spices.

Morales came around the corner. He was also in shorts and sport shirt. He carried a plate of chicken wings and was eating one of them. "Hey, *mio corazon*," he said. "So glad you could join us."

She flinched as he bent toward her, but it was only to kiss her, leaving a smear of grease on her cheek. "Junior cryptographer in the NSA. How much does it pay?"

"I don't know what you're talking about."

Morales looked at Carlucci. He said, "Sixty-five thousand."

"A member of the North family, working a government job for sixty-five thousand a year," said Morales with disgust. "How'd you know Brydon? Was he your boyfriend?"

"I don't know what you're talking about."

"Yeah, you were fucking him. I bet you dreamed it

up together—this plan to shake me down over that goddamn reef."

"I don't know what you're talking about."

He slapped her. The motion caused the tray to tip, spilling chicken wings over one of the white sofas, where they left brown stains. Seeing what had happened, Morales slapped her again.

"Ruy, enough," said Carlucci, in a tone of mild reproof.

"We're just getting started. You're gonna make her talk, right?"

"She wrote a statement and left it in her car. It'll tell us all we need to know. We already figured out most of it." Carlucci walked past Morales. At the end of the sofa was a small table, bare except for a smartphone.

"Come here," Carlucci said to her. "Sit down."

Ava sensed what was coming. Wished she could stay where she was and let Morales hit her some more. But she obeyed. Her movements were stiff and awkward, and she felt sick to her stomach. Carlucci looked at her and understood.

"You already know, don't you? You've sort of known all along. But you had to come anyway, because you got her into this." He picked up the phone, touched a few keys, and handed it to her.

On the screen was a photo of the Avanti. Its front end was broken into a V around the trunk of a palm tree. Hubcaps and other pieces lay on the road around it. The windshield was shattered. Carlucci bent over and flicked his finger across the screen, bringing up the next picture.

At least she couldn't see Tilda's face. She was bent over the broken steering wheel. There was a lot of blood in her blond hair. Ava tossed the phone away and put her head in her hands.

"For her it was over real quick," Carlucci said. "My guys were waiting for her outside the hangar. Hit her with a baseball bat, right in the forehead. See, with blunt force trauma, they can't tell much. They'll think it was her head hitting the steering wheel that did the damage. There won't be any problems. That old car didn't have airbags, and everybody who knew your cousin knew she didn't bother with seatbelts."

Ava began to cry. It was Carlucci's gentle manner that did it. If only he'd been as harsh as Morales, she would've been able to take it.

His strong bony hand gripped her arm and pulled her up. He walked her though the room and into a narrow corridor. "You won't have to feel bad about her for long," he said. "Just till we get to deep water."

He opened a low doorway, shifted his hand to the top of her head, bent it forward, and pushed her in. It was a small, empty storage room, triangular in shape because it was in the bow. The door closed behind her. Ava sat on the deck and covered her face with her hands. She wasn't through weeping.

The deck began to vibrate as the engine was turned on. The sound of the bow slashing through the water surrounded her as the yacht got under way.

CHAPTER THIRTY

Laker had spent the last several hours in a storage locker that was a great improvement over the first one. It did not smell of disinfectant, there was enough room to sit on the floor, and, best of all, Ramón Milaflores had a key and was able to lock the door, so Laker would not be discovered by chance. Ramón said he and the other crewman, whose name was Joseph, would return when they went off duty.

The Filipinos had explained, while conducting him to his new closet, that the other officers were cooperating with Korzeniowski. The captain had had Ramón and the other sailor who'd put out the rope ladder brought to him and threatened them if they told anyone what they'd seen. He'd made no announcement explaining why he'd bypassed Puerto Chiapas. The crew was nervous.

An hour or so after they left him, Laker felt the ship begin to rock gently again. They'd left the canal for the Caribbean Sea. Not long after that, he heard footfalls. People were passing along the corridor. A lot of people. It seemed like the whole crew. Soon it got very noisy out on deck: shouting and the whine of motors that he guessed were those of the ship's derrick. Then heavy splashes. Gradually the tumult died down. He heard more passing footfalls as the crew dispersed to their posts or their bunks.

The door opened. It was Joseph. His hands were filthy, his overalls sweat-stained. He held out a set of fresh overalls. Laker put them on. As usual, they were much too small. Joseph motioned for him to follow. They went along the corridor and out on deck.

It was still light, but the sun had set. A strong, warm wind was kicking up whitecaps. The ship's hull slashing steadily through the water was the only sound. The deck was bare all the way to the bow. Ramón was leaning on the rail. His slender frame sagged with exhaustion. Laker leaned beside him. Now he got the point of the overalls. Anyone who saw them would think they were three crewmen taking a break.

"You've been working hard," Laker said.

Ramón nodded. "The containers we loaded at Vladivostok, that we were supposed to unload at Puerto Chiapas. Captain Korzeniowski said to get rid of them. The ship's derrick wasn't meant for such a job. Some of them we had to push overboard."

Laker looked toward the bow, then up at the monkey deck. He was familiar with the ship's navigation lights from following it. He said, "You're running without lights."

"Yes. Joseph just took coffee to the bridge. Tell him what you saw, Joseph."

"Transponder off. Radio, too."

"The captain wants the ship to be invisible," Laker said.

"Yes," Ramón said.

"Captain has gun." Joseph patted his right hip to indicate a holster. "And officers."

"They're armed, too? How many of them are there?"

"Three."

"The captain made an announcement," Ramón said. "He doesn't do that very often. But he said we were nearly at our destination, where we'd be paid five times our usual wages and set free."

"How did the crew take that?"

"They want to believe in five times the usual wage. But by now they should know, Korzeniowski is not to be trusted."

"Did he explain why he wanted the containers dumped?"

"No."

Joseph pointed at the deck and said something in his native language. Ramón nodded and said to Laker, "We loaded a container at Magadan. It is on top of the stack in the forward hold. With the Vladivostok containers gone, the stevedores will be able to get to it quickly when we reach our destination."

Laker remembered something Terry had found out from the ship's agent. "Korzeniowski came aboard with that container, didn't he?"

"A little before," Ramón replied. "We had to wait for an icebreaker, to get in to Magadan. The harbor is always frozen till May at least. Korzeniowski was on the icebreaker. He came aboard and took command. Our usual captain left the ship." Ramón hesitated. His lips tightened. He went on, "Officers generally don't have much regard for us. But to Korzeniowski, we're barely human. His first order, once we tied up at the pier, was for all crew to go to quarters and stay there."

"Is that unusual?"

"Loading and unloading is the stevedores' job. The crew is generally not confined to quarters, but no one minded. It was snowing hard. And the cold was unbelievable. You thought that wind would kill you if you didn't get out of it. The only man who disobeyed was Esteban Lamon."

Joseph smiled and said something to Ramón, who smiled back. "It was Esteban's first voyage," he told Laker. "He was always curious, always getting into trouble. He came back and told us there was only one train car on the pier. We'd cut our way into Magadan to pick up one container. There were soldiers all around it. The captain was on deck, standing by the open hatch, signaling the crane operator where to load it."

"You must have wondered what was inside."

"Everybody had an idea. Gold. Drugs. Esteban thought it was the car of some Siberian oligarch. A Bugatti or McLaren. He named brands I never heard of." Ramón sighed. "I didn't dream the foolish kid would go into the hold and try to open the container."

"Is that difficult?"

"Yes. And dangerous. That is why everybody believed the announcement that he'd been killed in an accident. He fell. It's a long way from the top container in a stack to the deck of the hold."

Joseph spoke again and Ramón shook his head.

"You didn't believe the announcement," Laker said.

"I think an investigation would have showed that Korzeniowski caught him in the hold and murdered him."

"You took a chance, sending that message to his family."

"We're not allowed to have cell phones. I had to steal one from an officer's cabin. I got it back before he noticed."

"Ramón," Laker said. "I have to see what's in the container."

Joseph spoke to Ramón. Laker picked up the fear in his voice. Ramón nodded to him and said to Laker, "It's too dangerous."

"I understand. But Esteban is not the only one who's died because of that container." He told them about Home Port, and about his long pursuit of the *Comercio Marinero*. When he was finished, Ramón and Joseph had a conversation in Tagalog in vehement whispers. Then Ramón said to Laker, "We need to get hold of some tools and line. We'll hide you meantime."

They headed forward. Laker tripped over something and nearly fell. He looked down to see that it was a hatch coaming, outlining a hatch cover broad as the side of a barn. It was for unloading. They weren't going to have to open it. Joseph was already down on his knees, loosening the dogs on a smaller hatch. He lifted the cover and motioned Laker below. "You wait here," he said as he closed the hatch.

CHAPTER THIRTY-ONE

The low door opened. Ava could see Carlucci's thin, hairy legs up to the knees. His hand appeared. The fingers curled, beckoning her out. She had to crawl on hands and knees. She rose to find that he'd put on a ball cap and sunglasses. His hands were empty.

He smiled, and she realized he'd guessed her thoughts again. "What are you gonna do? Hit me and run, jump over the side? It's no good. We're miles from shore. But I'm impressed you got your spirits back. You think you're not done yet."

He gripped her arm and steered her along the corridor. "You are, though. Try to give up. It'll be easier."

A young man in a crew uniform of white shirt, shorts, and cap came around a turn. She stepped in front of him. "You've got to help me! They're going to kill me!"

He looked embarrassed and annoyed, as if she'd asked him for spare change. Stepping around her he walked on.

"I hired the crew," Carlucci said. "Made the conditions of their employment crystal clear to them. They handle the boat pretty well, considering they're deaf and blind."

He guided her up the steps, into the glaring sunlight. It was as he said, the blue horizon was empty. The sun had just set. They walked toward the bow. Carlucci gestured through the front window at a uniformed man on the bridge. He cut the engines and turned away, disappearing from view. The bow settled. There was silence except for the lapping of waves against the hull and the wind. It snatched Carlucci's cap off his head. He deftly caught it and shoved it in his pocket. His hair was blown back. So it was true. He had only half an ear, topped by hard, pallid scar tissue.

There was no safety rail along the bow. By the starboard side lay four cinder blocks roped together, with additional loops of rope beside them. Carlucci pushed her down to her knees. Told her to lie on her stomach. He pulled her hands beside her and began to tie her wrists.

"You know what this rope is made of? Kevlar. Like for body armor. Sailors use it for mooring line 'cause it's so strong." Apparently he was the kind of man who liked to talk while he worked. Her dentist was like that. "I'm tying your hands mostly for your sake. You don't want to be clawing at the water, trying to get back to the surface. Soon as you go under, breathe in. Breathe deep. It'll be over in no time. Shit—you can bust a gut trying to cut this goddamn Kevlar. I shoulda brought shears."

He was finished with her hands. Shifting positions he began to tie her ankles together. Abruptly he laughed. "So Ruy was wrong. As usual. Your statement said Brydon was just a colleague. You hardly knew him. Trying to shake us down was all his idea."

"Did you kill him yourself?"

"Yeah. You guessed right about that. I hadn't worked with the stiletto in a long time, but I did well by him, I thought. One deep, clean thrust. In fact most of your guesses were right. You should've quit while you were ahead."

"Do you always have this much to say to people you're about to kill?"

"They're the only people I can trust."

She could hear him grunting as he struggled to cut the rope. Then a clunk as one of the cinder blocks fell on its side. He was tying them to the line that bound her ankles. The last step.

"You're lucky in one way," he went on. "Fucking Ruy isn't here. He wanted to gloat over you, wave bye-bye as you went over the side. But he got a call on the radio. Gonçalves, I think. We'll be done before he is."

"You don't much like Morales."

"Total pain in the ass. He's ruthless, but he's stupid. He's gonna be worth the trouble, though, to my organization. Yemayá's just the start. Ruy will develop more Cuban properties. We'll provide financing. In return he'll deal with us exclusively. To provide the finer things in life to his guests."

"You mean drugs, gambling, prostitution."

"Yeah. It'll be like old Havana, or Vegas in its prime. The Cuban government is weak. You saw how easy it was for Ruy to push fuckin' Gonçalves around."

His work done, he straightened up. She saw his shadow move as he bent over the cinder blocks. "Remember," he said. "Breathe deep."

Abruptly the engine roared to life. The bow rose. Carlucci fell on his ass.

"Arturo!" It was Morales's voice, shouting over the engine.

"Ruy, what the fuck?"

She twisted her head to see that a glass panel in the cabin behind them was open. Morales was leaning out. His eyes were wide with excitement.

"The cross!" he shouted.

"What?" said Carlucci.

"My family's silver crucifix."

"What about it?"

"They found it."

"You shittin' me?"

"No. Gonçalves said they'd been looking since he got back from Miami. Lot of problems. But they have it now for me."

"So?"

"So we're going to Havana. Now."

"Well, okay. But I got to take care of her first. Stop the boat."

"Hey, pal, I'm not stopping for anything."

"It'll only take—"

"I don't care. Understand? We're going to Havana."

He pulled his head back in. Perhaps he took the wheel himself, because the yacht leaned into a sharp turn as it continued to speed up. Reaching for handholds that weren't there, Carlucci pitched sideways, ending up next to Ava on deck. They lay like two lovers in bed, in a gruesome parody of intimacy. She looked at Carlucci's lined face, sunglasses askew, hair blown back from his mangled ear.

"Now the thing's gonna be dragged out, I don't know how long. Sorry," he shouted over the bow's crashing through the waves.

Ava turned her face away. She didn't want him to read her thoughts again, the way he had when he'd said, *You think you're not through yet.*

Because that was still how she felt.

CHAPTER THIRTY-TWO

The hatch opened and Ramón waved down at him. The wait probably hadn't been as long as it had seemed to Laker. He'd spent it clinging to a ladder fastened to the bulkhead, which descended into the vast darkness, stinking of rust and chemicals, of the cargo hold. He had to hold tight to the rungs. The ship's motions felt more extreme here. The ladder was dancing, up and down, side to side. A stronger wave made the ship pitch violently, and he swung away from the ladder to the full stretch of his arms. This was alarming; his own weight almost broke his grip. Eventually he figured out how to bend his elbows around the ladder's uprights and lock his hands together. He couldn't see the containers, but he heard them. The racket was complex and ceaseless, groaning, squeaking, screeching, booming.

The Filipinos were descending the ladder. Ramón told him to keep climbing down. Laker did, gingerly. He didn't go far before Ramón called to him to stop.

A powerful flashlight came on, making him blink.

Ramón trained its beam on the top of a container, almost level with Laker's feet. He told him to climb onto it. Laker put out one foot. There was enough light to show that the container's edge was made fast to a metal ledge in the bulkhead. It was moving only with the motion of the ship. He put his other foot down. Let go his handgrips and dropped to a crouch. The Filipinos, quick and sure-footed, joined him. It was Ramón who had the flashlight. Laker wondered how he'd managed to descend the ladder one-handed. Ramón pointed at the next container over. "The Magadan one."

He played the light over its top. It looked no different from the others: gray metal, riveted seams, a few dents and dings. A wide steel bar held it tight to the container they were crouching on. Stepping over it, they crouched on the Magadan container. Ramón's light had shown there was no way in from the top. On hands and knees Laker crawled to the end and looked down. Could see nothing.

Ramón handed him the flashlight. The next stack of containers was ten feet away. He played the light into the gap. A tiny spot of reflection showed, in a pool of water on the deck of the hold, fifty feet below.

Joseph knelt beside him and took a loop of rope off his shoulder. "You go down. We hold you."

"I'm big and heavy."

"There are two of us," Ramón said. "We're strong."

"That's reassuring."

Joseph tied the rope around Laker under his arms. He was quick and deft with knots. Finished, he sat and braced the heels of his boots against the steel bar that held the front of the container motionless. He had the rope in his hands. He passed it back to Ramón, who sat behind him and braced his feet against Joseph's back. Once he was sure both had a sure grip on the rope, Laker crawled over the edge. The rope bit into his armpits as it took his weight. The injured rib gave its first twinge.

The Filipinos slowly lowered him. He played the flashlight over a small metal housing. Reached into it. "There's a padlock."

"There usually is," Ramón called back. "We have bolt cutters."

Laker looked up to see the long handles appear over the edge. One of the Filipinos must've had to take a hand off the rope, but Laker hadn't felt it. These guys *were* strong.

Stretching his arms up, he was able to reach the handles. Fitting the short blades into the housing, he bore down and cut the loop of the padlock. He let go of the bolt cutters. It seemed like a very long time before they hit the deck.

The flashlight beam showed him that two vertical rods kept each door closed. He lifted the handles on the right-side door, disengaging the rod ends from their keepers. He finished just as the ship rolled. The door swung open, knocking Laker out of the way. He spun all the way around on the rope. He could hear the Filipinos grunting as they held onto him.

The ship rolled the other way. Laker caught the door. With his other hand, he shone his flashlight inside. The beam showed him only a metal framework, heavily padded with rubber. Then it hit something reflective.

Laker squinted, steadied the beam. He was looking at a sphere of polished steel. Could see only half of it above the rubber-padded rack that held it. Its surface was smooth. No, it wasn't. There was a sort of nozzle on one side, a plug with protruding wires on the other. He couldn't make sense of it, and then he did.

The nozzle was a component of the assembly that armed the weapon. The plug was part of the detonator.

"Oh God," he murmured.

"What do you see?" asked Ramón.

"They're . . ." Laker played the light around. Could see four more shining spheres. Enough to kill tens of millions of people.

"They're nuclear warheads," he said.

Suddenly he was falling. He dropped ten feet and stopped. He thought the rope would cut his arms off. A bolt of pure agony shot from the injured rib up his spine into his brain, and he nearly lost consciousness.

When he came to himself, Ramón was shouting his name.

"I'm all right," he called back. "What happened?"

"Joseph. Panicked. Dropped the line—fled."

"You're holding me alone?"

"Can't for much longer."

Laker could hear the strain in his voice. Laker was dangling and slowly twisting in the loop of rope. Had to stop that. Take the load off Ramón. He'd lost the flashlight but looking down he could just make out the padlock housing of the container he was now facing. He put his foot on it. Threw out his arms to grasp the vertical rods.

"Thanks!" Ramón called. "Give me a minute. Then I'll pull you up."

"Where's Joseph going?"

"He's scared. Wants to run. But there's nowhere to run to."

"He wouldn't go to the officers?"

"He's not that stupid."

There was nothing Laker could do about it anyway from his precarious perch. Ramón called out that he was ready. A moment later, Laker began, slowly, to ascend. He didn't know where the Filipino was finding the strength.

The ship rolled again and the door of the Magadan container swung open. Ramón cried out in alarm as the rope pulled against him. Laker swung his body to the left to slide the rope off the top of the door. Pulled his legs in tight as he swung back. Now he was able to rest his toes on the foam gasket inside the container.

"I can help from here on, Ramón," he called.

Using the steel supports of the framework holding the warheads as rungs, he climbed up until he could thrust his hands above the level of the bar along the top of the container that held it in place. Ramón dropped the rope and grasped his hands. As he pulled, Laker was able to clamber back on top of the container.

He and Ramón grinned at each other, gasping. Laker noticed blood on his hands. It was Ramón's, from rope burns.

Abruptly, the lights came on. The whole vast hold was brightly illuminated. A man in dark blue overalls—an officer—was crouching on the next container. He had a pistol in his hand.

Laker's hand went to his cargo pocket for the Glock.

"No! Don't move!" The officer leveled his weapon. He seemed to know how to use it. Laker froze.

Another man in blue overalls was coming down the ladder. He turned and stepped onto the container. He had exceptionally good balance, because he was able to stand erect on a steel surface that dipped and tilted with the sea's motion. He had blond hair and beard and blue eyes. He too was carrying a pistol.

"The situation is clear," he said. "You know. And I know that you know."

He had a rather high voice, with a trace of middle-European accent. This was Korzeniowski, the captain.

"You are Laker," he said. "I can tell Moscow that now I know why their agent in Mexico City failed to report. Is she dead?"

"Yes," Laker said.

"They think highly of you in Moscow, Laker. They warned me to take you seriously. I should have. How did you get on board?"

"When you were refueling."

"And you found help." He looked at Ramón. "I don't know your name, but you work in the engine room. You've impressed me as smart, for a Filipino. But it turns out that your friend Joseph is a good deal smarter."

Laker and Ramón exchanged a look.

"I can't say it all came to him in a flash," Korzeniowski went on. "But he had a general sense of what you were going to do next, Laker. Try to seize the bridge. And if you succeeded, use the radio to call Washington. Then, in a very short time, jet fighters would have flown in, firing missiles, blowing this ship to pieces and killing everyone aboard. Including Joseph."

"No. Navy ships would have intercepted. We don't kill innocent men."

"What a shame you didn't get a chance to make that

argument to Joseph. I don't think he would've believed you. A lifetime of experience has taught him how little his life means to white men."

"White men like you," said Ramón.

Korzeniowski looked at him. "Not sure what I'll do with you. Throw you overboard is the simplest thing. But it might be interesting to find out, first, if you were the one who sent the text message that caused all my problems. As for you, Laker, you'll live. Moscow is interested in you."

A third officer was descending the ladder. Korzeniowski waited until he turned and drew his pistol. "Now," he said. "Stand up. And put your hands on your heads. Do it very slowly, Laker. You mustn't take your survival for granted."

CHAPTER THIRTY-THREE

At last the low door opened. Ava backed away from it, panting for breath, rubbing her sore knuckles. Carlucci's long-fingered, hairy-backed hand appeared, beckoning her. She crawled out on hands and knees, then rose.

"You must be tired," Carlucci said. "You've been banging on the door and shouting since we cut the engine." The lined, lean face bore a sardonic smile.

"Are we in Havana?" Ava asked. Her throat was raw.

"You know we are. Gonçalves is aboard. I'm supposed to bring you topside. But it wasn't all your noise that did it. He never heard. It was fucking Ruy. He couldn't resist telling him all about you. C'mon up."

He took her elbow and steered her along the corridor and up the steps. It was night. The yacht was tied up at a pier, but aside from the lights of a ferry boat crossing their stern, there wasn't much to see of Havana.

She'd heard Morales's petulant, bullying voice before she could see him. He sounded overexcited and irritable. He was pacing among the deck chairs in the stern while Gonçalves watched impassively. Morales was wearing a white linen suit and open striped shirt, Gonçalves olive-drab fatigues.

"So I come into the harbor, I'm expecting to see Morro Castle, and what do I see?"

"Morro Castle," said Gonçalves.

"Only the silhouette. 'Cause it's not floodlit. Disappointment Number Two, I couldn't see the Malecón."

"Oh, it's there. But too far from the harbor mouth."

"Well, we can do something about that. Carlucci, remember this for me. We're gonna have big color photos in the elevators at Yemayá, with Morro Castle floodlit, viewed from the Malecón. We'll photoshop it so they're right next to each other. People will love 'em. We'll sell 'em in the gift shop for twenty bucks. With frame, a hundred."

A crewman in his immaculate uniform stepped up to Ava and offered her a tray of mojitos. One of those who'd been deaf to her pounding and screaming of a few minutes before. Now it was her turn to ignore him.

Gonçalves walked over and studied her face. He seemed a lot different on his home ground, erect and confident. Funny how his suit had been shabby and ill-fitting, while his army fatigues looked custom-tailored and freshly pressed.

"Yes," he said. "It *was* you who approached me in Miami."

"That's what I told you," said Morales. "We were

pretty sure right away that it was her, because she'd been hanging around for weeks, poking around in my business. Didn't take my people in D.C. long to find out she was NSA. *Former* NSA. The agency doesn't know what she's been up to."

Gonçalves's deep-set black eyes were fixed on hers. "Is this true?"

"Yes. I quit to investigate a murder. Morales killed a colleague of mine to prevent you from finding out about the toxic spill at San Fernando."

Gonçalves turned to look at Morales. "I'd never have known at all, except for her."

Carlucci sighed. "See, Ruy? I told you it was gonna get complicated if we brought her up here."

"No complications. Ivan Diegovich and me are tight. He's found my family cross." Morales lifted his mojito to Gonçalves, who couldn't respond, not having one. "Hey, speaking of the cross, what are we standing around here for? Let's go."

"I have a request," said Gonçalves. "Turn the North woman over to me. We would like to interrogate her."

"Ruy—" Carlucci began.

Morales waved him off. "Fine. We'll never have to worry about her again, Arturo. The *Fidelistas* are experts at making prisoners disappear."

The remark didn't dismay Ava. She had the sense Gonçalves was up to something. Didn't try to figure out what. All that mattered was she was walking down the gangway, off that yacht from which she'd nearly gone overboard, and into a night city. A chance to escape was bound to come.

On the pier, two Jeeps were waiting, one empty, the other with soldiers in it. Even in the darkness, she could see how ancient and dilapidated they were. It was easy to imagine them being made in Detroit, shipped across the Atlantic in a Liberty ship, carrying Red Army men all the way to Berlin, being sent to Cuba as part of a military aid package, lasting through Fidel's long reign, and serving still. But when Gonçalves got behind the wheel and pressed the starter, the engine came to life immediately and ran smoothly.

She climbed into the back with Carlucci beside her. He wasn't armed, as far as she could see, but he was watchful. Any sudden move and those strong hands would grasp her. In the Jeep behind them were four soldiers, and all but the driver had Kalashnikovs in their hands. Ava postponed her break for freedom.

Morales swung into the front passenger seat, planting his right foot on the Jeep's mudguard, in imitation of the hero of a favorite World War II movie, she assumed. "Let's go by way of the Malecón," he said. "Or—wait. Are the waves breaking over the seawall?"

"I wouldn't think so," Gonçalves replied. "Not windy enough."

"Then I'll wait till tomorrow. I want to see the waves breaking. And the fishermen. And couples strolling arm in arm." His moods were as mercurial as ever. The irritability had passed, and he was happy and excited. "After I see the cross. I wanna have dinner. Been too excited to eat. And cocktails. First, Hemingway daiquiris at Sloppy Joe's. Then the best *palador* you know. We'll eat *lechón*. And *congri*. And *ropa vieja con sofrito*."

"All at one meal?" asked Gonçalves. Again Ava noticed his equanimity. Morales no longer oppressed him. Only amused him a bit.

"Better have somebody call Coppelia. Tell 'em to stay open."

Gonçalves had been waiting patiently with the engine idling, looking sideways at Morales. He raised a hand, and one of the soldiers from the Jeep behind came running. He stopped beside Gonçalves and presented arms. Gonçalves rapped out an order. Spanish was one of Ava's weaker languages, and she didn't catch what he said, but she didn't think it had anything to do with Coppelia.

He thrust the Jeep's long crooked gearshift lever forward, and they set off. At the *punta de control* where the pier joined the land, the soldiers raised the barrier and came to attention. "We will waive the customs and immigration formalities," Gonçalves said.

He turned into a narrow street. The pavement was rough, the lights few. Morales was leaning dangerously far out of the Jeep, looking around. "It's *so* gloomy," he said. "No advertising. It's so dark you can see the stars," he said with disapproval.

Abruptly he ordered, "Stop! Turn off the motors!"

He got out of the Jeep and stood turning in a circle, sniffing the air. "I can smell the gardenia . . . and, yes, the lavender. Just like Tía Luisa said. The scented nights of Havana." He cocked his head. "But it's so quiet. There should be music coming from every window. *Guajiras* and *boleros* and *pachanga*."

"Too early. Havana has not come to life yet," Gonçalves said, in the same amused, tolerant tone.

Though it was the middle of the night, this seemed to mollify Morales. He climbed back in, and they got going again. After a few minutes they turned onto a broader street with more traffic, enormous old American cars and tiny box-like Soviet cars. Motorcycles and bicycles. Even a *cocotaxi* or two, the egg-shaped three-seat motor-scooters Ava'd heard about. The sidewalks were full of strollers. Wherever there was a working streetlight, people were sitting under it, playing dominoes or checkers, or selling their wares. Morales turned in his seat, pointing at a wizened man with a tray of carved wooden dolls hanging from his neck.

"Hey, there's a guy going into business for himself," he said. "Creeping capitalism, Gonçalves. You want to stop and arrest him? We'll wait."

"Not necessary. But I will wait if you want to bargain with him. See how ill-fed he looks. You can probably beat him down to a few pesos."

Morales gave Gonçalves a long look as they drove on. He wasn't a sensitive man, but even he was now noticing the old Cuban's lack of deference.

Seeing a woman in high heels and tight pants standing alone under a streetlight, Morales pointed and said, "*Jinetera!* You people brag about opening all the professions to women. But I bet there are still plenty who are in the oldest profession."

"Yes," said Gonçalves. "You and Señor Carlucci will find it easy to staff the brothels you will soon be opening."

Carlucci said nothing. But he shifted in his seat. He was a wary man, and Ava could tell that his focus had shifted from her to Gonçalves.

They passed another *punta de control*. Again they were recognized and not stopped. The Jeep turned into a narrower, quieter street. "Welcome to *Vieja* Havana," Gonçalves said. He was wrestling with the wheel as the car bounced and jounced over broken pavement, avoided furniture lying upended in the street or piles of brick and rubble. There were fewer working street-lights, but she could see bits of the fine old houses they were passing: pillars holding up round arches, colon-nades, pedimented windows, balconies with wrought-iron railings. But many windows were covered with sheet metal, colonnades were crumbling, railings bent. Either because the decaying grandeur made him thought-ful, or simply because he was only minutes from seeing his family crucifix, Ruy Morales's manner was sub-dued. He slumped in his seat, saying nothing, darting glances about the unevenly lit streetscape.

Gonçalves slowed and turned between noble stone posterns. He switched off the engine and lights. The other Jeep pulled up beside them. "*La casa Morales*," Ruy whispered. He climbed out and looked up at the ghostly white stone villa. Pointing up at a wrought iron balcony. "That's where my Tía Maria was serenaded. I ever tell you that story, Arturo?"

"Yes," said Carlucci, distractedly. He was watching the soldiers pile out of the Jeep. He said to Gonçalves. "They can stay put, can't they?"

"They are here for your protection."

Morales was still gazing dreamily upward. "A cer-tain Señor Villardo sent musicians to serenade my aunt. They no sooner finished than another band ap-peared, sent by Señor Montero. The two most eligible bachelors in Havana, as Tía Maria was the most beautiful girl. She would have made the marriage of the season—if the Revolution hadn't interfered."

"Not to one of those two," said Gonçalves. "Villardo was murdered in '58, by another gangster who was jealous of his special relationship with Batista. Montero was homosexual and so determined to hide it that he had the poor peasant boys murdered as soon as he was finished with them."

Morales threw him a hurt look. He was too lost in the past to think of a comeback. He turned away and mounted stone steps that looked as if they'd been gnawed by a giant. The banister was gone. Its fluted supports stood there like a row of tree stumps.

"Maybe you want to tone it down," said Carlucci confidentially to Gonçalves. Ava had noted before his ability to sound mild and menacing at the same time. "This is a special moment for Ruy. After all the trouble you went to, to find that cross, you don't want to spoil it."

Gonçalves walked on as if he hadn't heard. Carlucci followed Ava. The four soldiers were close behind them.

Morales said, "I'm gonna fix this place up. No matter how much it costs. And then I'll move back here. There should be a Morales living here. I'll get married again. Fill it with kids. What do you think, Arturo?"

"Sounds good, Ruy."

The door was standing open, with only shadows behind it. Morales entered and said, "This was where Abuelo Francisco had his office, right by the front door. He didn't want the womenfolk to bother him when he was sitting in here with his business associates, smoking cigars. When she was four my mom snuck in. Abuelo Francisco was very stern. But Tío Gusto laughed and let her sit in his lap and cut his cigar."

"That would be Gustavo Latro," said Gonçalves. "Who ran your father's loansharking business. An excellent manager. Your father would order him to break the leg of a man who fell behind in his payments. But Latro would only break his left thumb, so he could go on working and paying."

"Those are all lies! My family had nothing to do with loansharking." Morales turned and came back at Gonçalves, arms swinging. The latter stood his ground. Morales tapped him on the chest. "Hey, *camerón*. You've about used up the points you've earned for finding the cross. And I haven't even seen it yet. Let's have less talk and more action."

"Finding the cross was quite difficult," the Cuban observed. "There were half a dozen families living here, until the place became structurally unsound. It was standing empty when I returned from Miami. Since then, it's been full of diggers, archeological consultants, guards."

"Six families living in my family's house."

"You find that disgusting."

"Who wouldn't?"

"Me, for one. I find your family taking up space for six disgusting. This way."

He was standing in the doorway. Rather than entering, he led the way along the side of the house. Morales held back a moment, glaring after him, lips pouting, fists clenched.

"I don't get you, pal," Carlucci said quietly to

Gonçalves. "You figure the project is so far along, Ruy can't pull out? Don't count on it."

Morales was still hanging back. "Where the hell are you going?" he shouted. "The cross was buried in the courtyard."

"No, I'm afraid it wasn't," Gonçalves called back, over his shoulder. "Family stories are unreliable. That's what held us up so long. We found it in the back-yard, near the smokehouse."

Carlucci was hesitating too now. He glanced at the soldiers behind them, then turned to his employer. "I think we ought to come back tomorrow, Ruy."

"Twenty feet from the cross and you're trying to pull me back?" Morales walked past him.

In the overgrown backyard, earth-moving equip-ment was standing in the shadows. A work light on a stand threw glaring light into a large hole next to a di-lapidated shack. A pair of soldiers with slung Kalash-nikovs were standing by. One had something under his arm.

"The lead box!" Morales hurried forward. "It was buried in a lead box, my grandfather told me. Who says you can't trust family stories?"

"Awful big hole for such a small box," said Car-lucci, following his employer.

"We weren't sure where it was," said Gonçalves, also moving up.

Ava was about to follow when her elbow was grabbed from behind. She turned to look at the young soldier who'd done it. He didn't speak or return the look.

Gonçalves was adjusting the work light. "Open the

box and show him," he said to the soldier holding it. In what looked like a rehearsed move, the soldier smoothly unlatched the lock and swung back the lid.

The box was empty.

All the soldiers, including Gonçalves, burst out laughing.

Carlucci recovered first. "Ruy, let's get out of here!"

"What the fuck?" Morales said. "Where's my cross?"

"It would be my guess that your grandfather could not bear to get his hands dirty." Goncalves was still chuckling. "Never having done a day's work in his life. He ordered a servant to bury the cross. The servant sold it. It was melted down to make fillings for the teeth of workers. That is my hope, anyway."

"That's it, *camerón*," Morales was spitting with rage. "You forgot, you need me more than I need you. I'm pulling all my money out of this fucking country. Tell the workers they got their last paycheck. They might as well put down their tools and go home."

"They have already stopped work," Gonçalves said. "The project is finished."

"What are you talking about?"

"I don't need you anymore," Gonçalves said. He turned to Carlucci. "You were right about the size of the hole. It's big because it's your grave."

Carlucci lunged at the soldier behind him. The long thin blade of his stiletto caught the light. But the soldier was even quicker. Back-pedaling, he fired a burst into Carlucci at point-blank range. The bullets knocked him over backward. Before he hit the ground, all the soldiers were firing. The one who was standing next to Ava ran forward, also firing. The muzzle flashes were almost continuous in the near darkness. On Morales's white suit bloodstains like crimson hibiscus flowers bloomed. He fell to his knees. Gonçalves walked toward him, firing his pistol. Morales's face turned to pulp.

Ava spun and ran up the driveway to the Jeeps. Nobody'd been left on guard. Everybody'd wanted in on the firing squad. The shooting was still going on, the reports almost continuous. Ava jumped over the low door of the Jeep Gonçalves had been driving. Her hands swept the dashboard in search of dangling keys. It took her far too long to remember that Gonçalves had simply pressed the starter button. She did so and the engine roared to life. She stamped on the clutch pedal. Where was reverse? It was too dark to see the pattern on the gear knob, if there was one. She guessed down and right. The gears ground. She tried up and left. The long crooked gear lever slotted into place. She backed up into the street.

As she drove away, the shooting continued.

Others were hearing it. Heads were leaning out of windows. She wove to avoid little knots of people standing in the street, cyclists who'd stopped and put their feet to the ground. Ava's heart was pounding and her mind's workings were gummy with shock. Once she could no longer hear the firing but only the Jeep's busy engine, she began to feel a little calmer.

She spun the car's wheel to make a turn. She was heading for lights and people, trying to get away from the murder scene. That was enough for the moment. Up ahead were the lights of the *punta de control*. She didn't think they were going to raise the barrier and salute for her.

She swung the car right, turning into a narrow *calle*. Switched off the Jeep and walked away from it. She walked for a long time, through mostly empty streets. She retreated from checkpoints and turned away from sirens. The sky began to grow light. She had no idea where she was, but over the tops of buildings she could see a dome that was a small replica of the U.S. Capitol.

That could have been taken as a bitter joke on her. She was still wearing the clothes she had put on to fly to Washington and go to the Capitol in search of Senator Chuck North. Here, she was conspicuous: a tall, pale redhead in a navy blue pantsuit and a filthy blouse that had once been white.

That would be the description given to the police and the army, who were looking for her. She expected they were looking for her hard. The soldier who had held her back from the killing ground had been acting on Gonçalves's orders. He wanted her kept alive for some purpose she couldn't guess at.

She was walking down the cracked pavement of another of those streets of once beautiful, now crumbling houses Havana seemed to have so many of. She passed concrete walls covered with mold or moss, broken columns, collapsing arches, peeling paint, and cracked and holed stucco. And enormous and brilliant bougainvillea and hibiscus that hadn't been cut back in a long time.

A clothesline was strung across a wrought-iron railed balcony, on the second floor, just above her. The pants and blouses hanging out to dry among bras and panties looked like they would fit, at least from a distance. The window was dark. Ava glanced around. The street was empty, but that wouldn't be the case for much longer. The city was awakening. This was her best chance.

A thick and flourishing vine looked strong enough to take her weight. In fact it looked more substantial than the building. She took hold with both hands, placed the soles of the feet against the wall, and climbed hand over hand. When she was level with the bottom of the balcony, she grasped one of the wrought-iron uprights and started to swing toward the balcony. The iron support tore out of the concrete and she nearly fell. She got both hands on the vine again, climbed higher, and swung a leg over the balcony. Then the other. She was happy to see that the blinds of the window were drawn. She unpinned a pair of blue jeans and a pale-blue blouse and a floral print scarf. Bundling them under her jacket, she climbed down and breathed a sigh of relief as she walked quickly away.

The next street was busier. People were on their way to work on bicycles or motor scooters. A truck with a flat bed and wooden railings was loading passengers who'd stand all the way to work. A barber with immaculate white smock and gleaming moustache was trimming a customer's hair on the pavement. Fruit merchants were filling the bins outside their shops. A bike repair shop was opening its doors. So was the café next door. A woman was watering the flower boxes while a man was plucking a chicken for lunch. The place smelled agreeably of coffee. Ava ducked in.

Ignoring tables and chairs, she went into the women's room. It was very clean, but the toilet was a reeking hole in the ground between footpads. Ava changed quickly. The jeans were too big for her in the waist and short in the leg. She stripped the belt from her pantsuit and cinched it tight. The blouse was a pretty thing, hand-embroidered with a scoop neck, but it was much too low and kept revealing her bra, no matter how much she tugged it this way and that. She draped the scarf over her conspicuous hair and tied it under her chin. Stepped back into her leather pumps, and went out.

The proprietress smiled and offered her café con leche.

It smelled wonderful, but Ava mumbled apologies and went out. She had no money, no identification, nothing. Her purse was on Morales's yacht.

She walked on, feeling less exposed now. She didn't even dart into a shop or alley when a police car or army Jeep went by. The streets and sidewalks were becoming more crowded.

She turned a corner and entered a park. Rows of tall, straight royal palms and benches lined a path. On the worn, dusty grass to her left, some teenagers were playing *beisbol*, using a stick for a bat and milk cartons cut in half for gloves. On the right, smaller children were playing a wild game of *fútbol*. The ball was so flat it was visibly misshapen. The kids had to kick it with all their force to make it wobble downfield. Their book bags marked out the goals.

Ava joined the solitary readers and cooing couples on the benches. She thought about what she ought to do. The United States now had an embassy, but not an ambassador in Havana, she'd read, though she had no idea where it was. There was nothing for her to do but go there, somehow get in to meet the non-ambassador, and tell him that Rodrigo Morales had been murdered by his supposed partner in the Cuban government. She would also repeat that baffling remark of Gonçalves, that the project was finished. She hoped they would take her seriously, even though she had no identification to prove that she was a former employee of the NSA.

Decision made, she rose and walked to the street. A glossy yellow 1957 Chevrolet pulled up at the curb and a smiling man leaned out. He must have noticed her air of urgency.

"Taxi?" he said.

Ava was tempted to accept the offer. Get in, and let the embassy pay him. But there seemed to be a *punta de control* at every major intersection. And they would be on the alert for her. It was going to be just as obvious to Gonçalves as to her that the embassy was her only possible destination. She'd have a better chance of reaching it on foot.

Guessing the embassy might be somewhere near the Capitol building, she turned toward its dome. As she passed a dilapidated church with a tall, leaning bell tower, an old lady in a black dress came out, stowing her rosary in her purse. She had a lined and puckered face with bright, kindly eyes. Ava asked her the way to the U.S. Embassy. The woman smiled and said she would show her. Ava offered her an arm to lean on.

They chatted. The old lady disapproved of Ava's not being married and a mother yet, but was complimentary of her Spanish. She stopped abruptly and said, "That's funny. There didn't use to be a checkpoint here."

It was a temporary one. Two police cars were parked bumper to bumper, blocking the street. In the distance,

Ava could see the American flag waving over a building. She blurted, "Is there another way?"

Her tone, even more than the question, gave her away. The old lady's eyes widened and became fearful. With a wordless cry, she backed away, pointing a thin finger at Ava.

Ava was about to make a run for it. Too late. The police at the checkpoint already had their weapons leveled on her. She slowly raised her hands.

CHAPTER THIRTY-FOUR

Ava was sitting on the floor in an empty room. Unlike everyplace else in Cuba that she'd seen, it was new and clean. So recently built that it smelled as if the concrete hadn't fully dried yet. Strips of fluorescent in the ceiling provided the light; they were underground.

Her captors had put her in the backseat of a car, the newest she'd seen on the island. Soldiers flanked her and another drove. They handled her gently, even respectfully, and did not even bind her hands, as if she was a valuable property they were eager to present to their officers. They did not speak to her and ignored her questions. The car took her out of the city, past fields of sugarcane and tobacco, over bad roads. The broken pavements eventually gave way to dirt. Noticing her coughing at the dust, a soldier closed the windows and turned on the air-conditioning. The car had delivered her to a cinder-block structure with a steel door. They'd descended stairs, put her in this room, and left her.

The door opened and a soldier, one of her escort, entered. He was carrying two steel and plastic chairs, cheap and new. He put them down facing each other and retreated to stand in the doorway. A moment later Gonçalves entered. He was wearing fresh olive fatigues, with high laced boots and a flapped holster on a web belt. He motioned her to sit facing him.

She doubted he'd had any sleep last night, but he looked none the worse. He gave the impression that something, his mission or perhaps just his great age, had taken him beyond the need for rest or food. The deep-set black eyes below tufty gray brows regarded her. The dense but close-trimmed gray beard concealed his expression.

"You have a good chance of survival," he said. "At least in the short term."

"If you think I possess valuable information, you're wrong."

He looked puzzled, but only for a moment. "Oh, yes. I told Morales I wanted to interrogate you. In fact, I do not. But you are going to serve my purpose."

"Not if I can help it."

"You cannot. I am so glad we were able to find you again. It was unforgivable that you were allowed to slip away. My men . . . lost control of themselves."

"So did you. You were trying to blast Morales's corpse apart with bullets."

"Yes. I admit that. I hated Morales. I didn't hate Carlucci, oddly enough, though he was a bad man and deserved to die. Their idea for the Cuban people's future was . . . their past. Serving foreigners who've come to enjoy a tropical paradise. Being preyed upon by gangsters and corrupt politicians. It was agony to play along with them."

"I can believe that."

He was silent, his head on one side, studying her. With his long nose and black eyes, he was like a bird of prey. "The toxic spill," he said. "We haven't been able to determine if it was freon for the air-conditioning system or fertilizer for the golf course."

"So that's what you've been working on. Instead of trying to find Morales's cross."

"It's a matter of great interest to me, this thing that almost brought our efforts to ruin. You are a brave woman, taking on Rodrigo Morales all alone."

"I wasn't alone."

"Yes, your aunt—no, cousin. Morales told me Carlucci had her murdered. I've read about your family. The Norths. Like the Bushes and the Kennedys. First you exploit the people to build up a great fortune. Then you go to Washington to serve the people."

He saw her reaction and held up a hand. "I'm not mocking you. America once had ideals. And people who believed in them. But now you are in the hands of Morales and his kind. He was doing something that would profit his cronies in Washington, and they made sure that he would not be hampered. Not even questioned."

Ava wanted to contradict him. Couldn't.

He continued. "Morales's offer—to build a resort— had been on the table for a long time. I knew about it, but I must confess I failed to realize how useful he could be. Finally realization dawned. I did not call him at once. First I went to Moscow."

Gonçalves rose. "Come with me."

He turned and walked out into the corridor and up the steps. The other two guards who had brought her fell in behind them. They stepped out. It was late afternoon, the shadows long and the day's heat ebbing. She could smell the sea but not see it. Gonçalves led the way through a copse of giant ceiba trees. On the other side, they began to ascend a slight hill. Here and there lay felled and sawn-up trees. Scars gouged in the red earth by bulldozers. They passed an empty swimming pool, a bank of tennis courts without nets. Ava stopped. There was something wrong with the courts.

Gonçalves noticed her reaction. He waited patiently as Ava went closer. The high fence surround the courts was real, but the courts weren't. Canvas tarps had been painted with what looked like concrete and lines, then smoothed out on the grass and weighted.

Ava felt a chill. She began to understand. But she said nothing, only followed Gonçalves as he walked to the top of the rise. Now she saw roads scraped but not yet paved, dry fountains, the beginnings of garden beds. And YEMAYÁ RESORT HOTEL, *A Rodrigo Morales Property*.

The building had a large concrete footprint. The first and second floors were going up. Trucks and bulldozers and cement mixers stood around piles of construction material. But the site was quiet today, no people in sight.

"Come closer," said Gonçalves.

She did and understood. There was no hotel here.

Only the rebar framework was real. The walls were plywood. She turned to Gonçalves. He smiled at her expression.

"Oh, a great deal of work has gone on. Almost all of it underground."

He beckoned her and they walked closer. The soldiers were silent, but she noticed the smiles on their faces. It was pride in accomplishment, she thought. They stepped into the shadow of the fake hotel. The plywood panels creaked and shuddered in the wind off the sea.

Underfoot was a gray concrete apron. The concrete was thick: you could see a yard of it above the earth level. There were ventilator housings, manhole covers surrounded by railings. These things she recognized. Another feature she didn't. Waist-high circular coamings topped by lids, with heavy steel and concrete hinges. They were numbered, one to five.

Gonçalves gave a nod to one of the soldiers, who raised his walkie-talkie and spoke into it. The response was immediate. The cover labeled 1 slowly rose on its hinge. A steel lid underneath smoothly retracted with a whine of electric motors. Ava walked closer to the edge.

She looked down at the conical nose cone of a missile. A ladder led down to a retractable metal platform. Men in white protective suits and helmets were kneeling on it. They were working on a panel in the missile and did not look up.

"ICBMs," Morales said. "We also have medium-range cruise missiles on mobile launchers, capable of hitting Miami, Atlanta, Houston. These are for targeting Washington and New York. For them range is not an issue. They could hit Seattle if we chose."

Ava gazed into the depths of the silo. Her head spun. She turned and staggered away, out into the sunlight. The beach and the sea stretched out before her. Her voice sounded hollow in her own ears as she said, "They're Russian."

Gonçalves and the soldiers had followed her. "Yes. Don't be alarmed," he said. "Your cities will not be destroyed. These missiles will not be fired. A move is being made in a chess game, that's all. America is about to be put in check by Russia."

"The Baltic invasion," Ava said.

"Yes. The Baltic states used to be part of the Soviet Union, and Russia wants them back. So Russia will take them. Their army is poised. At the order, the tanks will roll."

"NATO will stop them."

"NATO will hesitate and fumble, because what is the transatlantic alliance without the United States? And the United States will be throwing all its weight and will against the defense of the Baltic states." Gonçalves swept a hand across the launch site. "America will break its word, because the Russian threat will be too fearsome. These missiles could reach your cities within minutes. Your anti-missile defenses would be useless."

Ava stared out to sea. There was a tiny ship on the horizon, like a bug crawling along a shelf.

"Don't look so stricken, Ms. North. It will be all right. In Europe, there will be some resistance. A few thousand will die. But America, sitting on the sidelines, will come out unharmed. That is not to say there won't be consequences. The world will see America bend the knee to Russia. Desert its European allies. Your reign as the only superpower will come to an end."

"Is that your reward?" Ava asked. "For letting the Russians put their missiles here? It doesn't seem like enough."

Gonçalves said, "It will please me to see America brought low. Why shouldn't it? Your country backed an invasion of Cuba. Tried to assassinate El Líder. Your embargo has choked us, kept us in poverty, for more than half a century, and is still doing so. But this operation is not about settling grudges. The deal I made in Moscow will bring us far more."

Ava saw it at last. "The Russians will start paying your subsidy again. Of course. Their rubles kept your misfiring socialist economy going for decades—"

"We would have thrived if not for the embargo."

"Dream on. You would have gone under long ago, if the Soviet Union hadn't kept you going to serve as an outpost of world revolution in the western hemisphere. When the Soviet Union fell, you got Chávez of Venezuela to prop you up for a while. Then he died, and you've been withering on the socialist vine ever since. But I have to hand it to you, Gonçalves. There are very different men in the Kremlin now, but you found something they would pay you for."

The soldiers exchanged a look. They unfastened the flaps of their holsters, rested their hands on the butt ends of their guns. Ava didn't think they could understand what she was saying, but they didn't like her tone of voice.

Gonçalves snapped a curt order. The soldiers shifted to parade rest, hands clasped behind their backs. He smiled at her again.

"No harm must come to you, Ms. North. You have an important role to play tomorrow."

"I will not cooperate with you."

"All I want you to do is your job. Report to your government. We will be at work all night, making everything ready, tearing down this sham construction over our heads. So that when the NSA's satellite comes overhead tomorrow, it will see what is here. But we want to make sure there is no misunderstanding. When the moment is right, I will put you on the telephone to your chief in Washington. You will tell them you have seen the missiles. We will arrange for you to witness the arrival of the warheads, watch them fitted in the nose cones. We want your leaders to be in no doubt that a loaded gun is now aimed at their heads, at point-blank range.

"It has fallen to few intelligence agents to announce to their country that its glory days are over. Your name will go down in history, Ms. North."

"No," Ava said.

"You have no choice."

"It won't come to that. You just admitted, as of now your gun has no bullets. The warheads aren't here yet. You said Morales's view of Cuba's future is its past. Well, you've made the same mistake. This is October 1962, the Cuban missile crisis. You're trying the same thing. And again, you won't get away with it. America will realize what you're up to. We'll put a naval blockade around Cuba. Search every ship that approaches. Send back the one carrying the warheads."

Gonçalves smiled. "How desperate you are. You imagine all this will happen in the next few hours, when it hasn't happened in the months we were pouring concrete, laying out roads, dredging the harbor to receive the ships full of building materials. And, of course, the missile components. Your satellites passed over and took no interest. If the NSA had sent a drone, it would have uncovered what we were doing. But it wasn't just plywood and cardboard we were hiding under. It was Morales's reputation. The dealmaker. The money-spinner. Washington wanted him to succeed."

Ava backed away, breathing heavily, looked at the soldiers. The only thought in her head was that she would not make that call to Washington. Better to die first.

Gonçalves's black eyes looked into hers and understood. He made a weary gesture to his men. One drew his pistol as the others closed in, each grasping one of her arms. She kicked and struggled in vain.

"Stop that, Ms. North," said Gonçalves. "I don't want you to harm yourself, so I will tell you, it's too late. The U.S. Navy cannot stop us this time. The ship carrying the warheads is here."

Goncalves pointed at the ship she'd been watching. It was no longer crawling along the horizon. It was steaming steadily toward them.

CHAPTER THIRTY-FIVE

The drive to the harbor didn't take long. The wide, smooth road, paid for by Morales, was the best she'd seen in Cuba. She was sitting behind Gonçalves, in another Word War II–vintage Jeep. The young soldier beside her was watchful—more watchful than he needed to be, considering she was tied hand and foot. Ahead of them was a heavy-duty flatbed truck, for transporting the container of warheads back to the launch facility.

The road took a sharp turn and headed downhill. They were descending to the bay of St. Ferdinand. The sun had just set and its waters were deep blue. On the other side, she could see the shacks, ramshackle wooden docks, and net-shrouded boats of the fishing village. Directly below was a long concrete pier with tall gantry cranes above it, Morales's state-of-the-art cargo-handling facility. The freighter was already alongside. It was old, battered, and rust-streaked. At the side of the bow was its name, *Comercio Marinero*.

She thought what a smart idea it had been—proba-

bly Gonçalves's own—to smuggle the fateful cargo to
Cuba aboard the most ordinary-looking of commercial
freighters. No one had tried to stop it, she supposed; no
one had even noticed.

When they drove out on the pier, the ship was tying
up. Long, thick mooring lines dropped almost straight
down from the bow and stern to stanchions on the pier.
Spring lines sloped from both ends of the ship to the
middle of the pier. An accommodation gangway was
angled against the hull.

By the time Ava was lifted out of the Jeep and set on
her feet, the pier was busy. Soldiers with slung Kalash-
nikovs were guiding the truck as it backed up under the
gantry cranes. Stevedores in helmets and hi-vis vests
were climbing the gangway. A trio of men wearing
white overalls, whom she guessed were Russian missile technicians, idled and smoked, looking down at
the water.

Gonçalves approached her. "Come along. I want
you to see everything, so you can make a full report to
Washington."

The rope binding her ankles gave her about a foot of
slack. She hobbled after Gonçalves to the bottom of
the steep, narrow gangway. Looked up it and said to
him, "You'll have to untie me."

The old Cuban frowned. But a glance at the steps
showed him she was right, and he summoned a soldier
to cut her bonds. Then he mounted the gangway, followed by Ava, then the soldier.

Nearing the top, Ava's steps slowed. She felt an irre-
sistible fatigue that she knew was really defeat. Her
call to Washington would be recorded, then released or
leaked. As Gonçalves said, she was going to be fa-

mous. The cashiered NSA employee who told America that the trap was sprung. It was too late. Laker, if he was still alive, would hear that tape. What would he think of her?

There was only a single railing. She could throw herself over it and fall into the water. Not that she had any hope of sabotage or escape. She'd just open her mouth and swim for the bottom. Drowning was an easy death, Carlucci had told her.

The soldier behind her grew impatient and poked her in the back. That made her angry. Which was an improvement. She raised her head, squared her shoulders, and climbed on to the top.

Gonçalves was shaking hands with a taller, younger man. He had a blond beard and a captain's white peaked cap. The stevedores were either standing with their hands on their hips or down on one knee, examining the hinges of a large hatch cover. Abruptly, a man came running toward her. He was a skinny East Asian in light blue overalls. His face looked terrified. He passed her, dodged the stevedores, ran to the ship's railing, and jumped. Two men in dark blue overalls were chasing him. They had pistols in their hands. Reaching the rail, they leaned over and started shooting.

The captain ran to the rail. After a moment, the shooting stopped. The captain strode back to Gonçalves. They spoke in Russian, a tongue in which they both seemed to be fluent. So was Ava.

"Got him," the captain said.

"Who was he?" Gonçalves asked.

"One of the crew. They aren't needed anymore, and my officers are rounding them up, putting them in the galley. So they'll be out of the way till we decide what to do with them. Do you think some of your men could help?"

Gonçalves ordered the soldier standing next to him to join the officers, who were crossing the deck toward the sterncastle. He turned to the railing and gestured. The soldiers at the foot of the gangway began to climb it.

"Has the crew been giving you problems?" Gonçalves asked.

The captain wearily closed his piecing blue eyes. "You can usually count on Filipinos to do as they're told. They're too stupid to do anything else. But there were troublemakers in this crew. We even had a stowaway. We caught him, but rumors spread. The crew's been very agitated."

"Well, you're here now. Let me know if you need any more men."

"Thanks." The captain shifted his blue-eyed gaze to Ava. "Who is this?"

"A former employee of the NSA, who luckily dropped into my lap. I want her to witness everything we do in the next few hours. She will be useful in making the situation clear to Washington."

The captain shrugged. "You want her to watch the unloading? Fine. But there will be a delay. We had to push some containers overboard, and apparently the hatch cover was damaged. Where do you want to put her?"

"This stowaway—is he in a secure place?"

"Yes, the ghost deck."

"Put her in with him."

The captain turned to beckon an officer in dark blue overalls. Then he hesitated. "Perhaps it would be better to separate them?"

Gonçalves smiled. "I don't see that we have anything to worry about."

The officer received his orders. Drawing his pistol, he grasped her arm with his other hand and pulled her toward the hatch of the sterncastle. Stepping back, he told her to open it and go up the steps. At the top of the third flight, they stopped and she waited while he opened a hatch and pushed her inside.

She regained her balance to find that she was in a large bare room with steel beams supporting the ceiling. Tied to one of them was a tall, broad-shouldered man. His dark hair disordered, his clothes torn and dirty. He raised his head to look at her. His bristled face was cut and bruised. It took a full second for her to recognize him.

"Laker," she said, and fainted.

CHAPTER THIRTY-SIX

"I was so *dumb*," Ava said. "I told you at the beginning, look for the bear under the bed. But I never thought to take my own advice. Never dreamed Ken Brydon's murder was connected to the Russians until it was too late."

"I don't feel all that bright myself," Laker admitted. "I was trying to keep you out of trouble with the NSA by not contacting you. Turns out that was pointless."

The surprised officer had picked Ava's limp form up from the deck and put her back against a support beam facing Laker. Grabbing a loop of line hanging from a hook, he tied her up. Then he left without a word. By then, she was conscious. They'd spent a bewildering, frustrating few minutes recounting their actions over the last couple of weeks.

"I guess I shouldn't say I'm happy to see you, considering," Laker said. "But . . ."

She smiled. That oval face, with the level brown eyes and the long, straight nose, made his heart turn over. As always. She was wearing a cheap embroidered blouse with a scoop neck that revealed her bra straps and baggy jeans that ended inches above her ankles. "I like the new look," he said.

"You're one to talk. At least they're clean. I stole them off a clothesline."

"Are you feeling better?"

"Yes. Sorry for fainting. They called this the ghost deck. I guess I thought you were a ghost."

"They call it that because it's only here to raise the bridge, so the officers can see over stacks of containers on deck. There's nothing here that we can use to . . ."

He broke off, because the wheel on the hatch behind Ava was turning. It opened and Ramón stepped through. His face was as battered as Laker's. He closed the hatch and spun the wheel that locked it. Laker was relieved. When Ava had told him about the crewman jumping into the water and being shot, he'd feared it was Ramón.

"Ava, this is Ramón Milaflores, whom I told you about," he said. "Ramón, this is Ava North. A friend."

Ramón nodded to her. Stepping behind her, he began to untie the knots that bound her wrists.

"They put me in the bosun's locker," he explained. "After they got tired of beating me. It was Joseph who freed me."

"Joseph?"

"His way of apologizing for his stupidity in believing the captain. When they started rounding everyone up, shoving them in the cafeteria, he realized that it was all a lie. They were never going to set us free and pay us five times our wages."

"Where is he now?"

"They caught him. I think everyone else is under guard in the galley now—except the poor bastard who jumped over the side. I don't know who he was. Sorry, ma'am," he said to Ava. "These knots are tough. I wish I had a knife."

"Wouldn't be any easier. This is Kevlar mooring line." To Laker's questioning look, she replied, "I've been tied up a lot lately."

Ramón finally finished with Ava. She stood rubbing her wrists as he came around to untie Laker. "You have our thanks," Laker said to him. "And the thanks of the U.S. government. What will you do now?"

"You are going to try to stop them," Ramón said.

"Yes."

"If you succeed, will Captain Korzeniowski go to prison?"

"At the very least."

"Then I am with you."

Laker's hands were free. He clapped Ramón on the shoulder and said, "All right. Can you get Ava onto the bridge?"

"I think so. Most of the officers seem to be on deck."

"Be careful. We need to get Ava to the radio." He turned to her. "Go on frequency 1153. Say 'Gettysburg.' That will get you Sam Mason."

"What do I tell him?"

"Send in the Marines. Preferably by helicopter."

"But he can't order that. It's a violation of Cuban airspace, to start with, and—"

"You'll be amazed what Mason can do." He took her hand and let it go. That was all they had time for. As he stepped through the hatch, she was saying to Ramón, "You go on, I'll be right behind you."

Laker glanced back, to see her picking up the ropes

they'd been tied with. It puzzled him, but he didn't stop to ask why.

It was fully dark now, and no one noticed Laker as he slipped through the hatch onto the deck. Near the bow, powerful work lights on tripods showed that the ship's derrick was lifting the big hatch cover. An old man in fatigues was watching the work intently. That would be Gonçalves. Laker didn't see Korzeniowski. Ava had told him there were about a dozen soldiers; four of them were here. He could see only the helmeted heads of the stevedores. They were in the hold, standing on the container of warheads, unfastening the locking pins with long-handled hooks. One of them made a gesture, and with a whining and rumbling a heavy, complicated steel framework descended.

Laker looked up. The gantry crane was a huge structure, consisting of vertical metal frames supporting a horizontal component. On this bridge were runways along which ran the hoist that lifted the container out of the ship's hold, shifted it sideways over the pier, and lowered it to the truck. In a small, brightly lighted cab attached to the hoist, he could see the operator, the one man who controlled all this potent machinery. The bridge projected over the water on the other side of the pier, so it could unload a ship moored there. At present, there was no ship.

That gave Laker an idea.

Everybody on deck was focused on the hold and the job to be done. He made his way quickly across the dark deck to the top of the gangway and began to descend the steps. An armed guard was standing at the bottom. His job was to keep anyone from mounting the

steps, so he was facing away from Laker. All Laker
had to do was get down without being noticed by any
of the men standing around the truck. Good thing his
clothes, face and hands were so dirty; he didn't stand
out against the dark hull.

The soldier was a small man with an angry red boil
on his neck above his shirt collar. Descending the last
few steps Laker was sure he was going to sense something and turn. He didn't.

Laker dropped him with a rabbit punch. Lifted him
enough to slide his Kalashnikov out from under him.
Slung it over his own left shoulder. This area of the
pier was dark. He'd be almost invisible. He ran to the
nearest upright of the crane, looked up to find it
smooth. He went to the next one. Here were the rungs.
He started climbing.

Ava too was climbing, up the stairs to the bridge.
Shouts and noises of machinery were coming from the
bow, but it seemed quiet in the sterncastle. She reached
the top to find Ramón crouching by the door, peering
in the glass panel. He motioned for her to get down.

"Korzeniowski is on the bridge," he whispered. "And
he's armed."

"What can we do?"

"Wait."

Halfway up the gantry crane, Laker heard the whining of machinery again and saw that the container was
being lifted out of the hold. Time was running out. His
sense of urgency made his foot slip. He had to scram-
ble for new hand- and footholds and nearly lost the
Kalashnikov.

He reached the bridge and climbed on top of it. The

pier was seventy feet below. He decided not to look down again as he set out along the narrow steel beam. It was tempting to get down on hands and knees and crawl, but there wasn't time. He walked.

The container seemed enormous as it rose steadily toward him. Laker crouched, looked down on the cab. There was a platform for the operator to stand on while he opened the door. Laker took a second to plan his next moves. No room for error.

He dropped onto the platform. His left hand pushed down the lever and opened the door while his right unslung the Kalashnikov from his shoulder. He leveled it on the operator. His face was astonished and frightened. He wasn't going to resist.

"Salí!" Laker said. *"En seguida!"*

The man obeyed at once. Fear made him clumsy and he nearly fell off the narrow platform. Laker took his place in the seat and shut the door. The man's feet disappeared as he climbed to the top of the bridge. There was a bare light bulb in a cage in the ceiling. He broke it with the rifle barrel, to make himself less of a sitting target. The container swung gently from its chains below him. It blocked the view of him from the ship's deck, but the men down there would quickly catch on that something was wrong.

He reached for the controls on his right. Nudged a lever at random. The container began to descend. He released it and pushed another lever. This was the one he wanted. The hoist and cab began to slide over the pier. In a moment they were over the flatbed truck. The container didn't shield him from the view of the men around it. He looked straight down at the upturned faces of the workmen and soldiers, shadowy in the glaring work lights. He held the lever down and the hoist continued to slide.

The soldiers reacted quickly. They unshouldered their weapons and pointed them up at him. Laker braced himself. There was nothing he could do. He was trapped, a fish in a barrel.

The glass exploded as the bullets hit, showering him with fragments. Some of them cut deeply. He felt a tremendous blow on his right arm, knew a bullet had hit him.

Pain and weakness threatened to engulf him. He shook his head. Realized the container had stopped because the fingers of his wounded arm were too weak to hold the lever down. He reached across with his good arm. The container began to move.

Ava heard gunfire. So did Korzeniowski. Kneeling beside Ramón outside the door, she watched as he ran out onto the open bridge wing on the pier side. Stepping onto a ladder, he disappeared from view.

"Now," Ramón said. He opened the door and they entered the bridge. There was no one else here. She scanned the many instrument panels helplessly. Ramón grasped her arm and led her to the radio. She was surprised at how small it was. Just a screen, keypad, knobs, and a telephone receiver. She sat and lifted the receiver while Ramón worked the keypad. He nodded to her.

"Gettysburg," she said.

Laker could see the muzzle flashes on the pier, hear the ricochets of bullets from the metal body of the cab. But the shooters didn't have a good angle on him anymore, because cab and container were now out over the black water on the other side of the pier. The hoist banged against the end of the bridge and stopped. Laker let go of the lever. Began pushing and pulling other levers, pressing buttons on the consoles on either side of his seat. None of them had any effect. The container continued to sway gently right below him.

He found the right lever. The hoist released. The container didn't descend slowly but dropped like a stone. It hit the surface with a thunderous splash. By the time the water settled, there was nothing to be seen of the container but the chains holding it to the hoist.

He opened the door and stood on the platform. Bullets were pinging and clanging against metal, but the soldiers were shooting at random. They'd lost track of where he was. He reached up. The wounded right arm responded, but his hand was too weak to grip. Using his left arm he was able to lift himself until he could get his knee, then his foot, onto the ledge of the shattered glass window in the door. Halfway. Straightening up, he repeated the maneuver and pulled himself onto the bridge. Now he was shielded from gunfire from below. He put the Kalashnikov across his lap. The container was still recoverable, but anybody who wanted to try would have to climb the upright supports and run along the bridge toward him. Laker figured he could hold off a battalion from this position.

As long as he didn't lose consciousness from loss of blood.

On the ship's deck, Korzeniowski ran up to Gonçalves, who was standing at the side, gripping the railing, anguish on his face.

"Laker?" the captain said.

Gonçalves pointed. "He dropped the container into the water. But we can raise it. We need more men. I have to call the missile base."

Korzeniowski gave him a look. "You think the warheads will still function? After the impact and immersion? The container isn't watertight."

Gonçalves grasped the taller, younger man by the shirt collar. "I will use the ship's radio."

Korzeniowski didn't argue. He waited only for Gonçalves to release him to turn and run to the nearest hatch in the sterncastle. He climbed the steps at a run, Gonçalves right behind him. At the top, he threw open the door.

Ramón turned. Korzeniowksi ignored him. Ava swiveled her seat around. She was still holding the receiver to her ear. Korzeniowski grasped the handle of the pistol holstered on his hip. Ramón crouched and sprang, hitting him hard and low. The pistol clattered to the floor. Korzeniowski toppled and Ramón was atop him in an instant, pummeling his face.

Gonçalves walked toward Ava. His pistol was already in his hand.

"Too late," she told him. "Helicopters are coming from the Guantanamo Bay base. They only have to fly across the island. They'll be here in minutes."

Gonçalves shot her twice in the chest. The impacts knocked her from the chair. She spun and fell, landing facedown on the deck. Gonçalves grasped the dangling receiver and jabbed keys on the pad. When he got through to the missile base, he ordered more troops to come to the harbor immediately. The man on the other end was confused, and Gonçalves had to go through it twice.

Korzeniowski had managed to regain his feet. But Ramón was punching him, driving him back, out onto the open bridge wing. Gonçalves replaced the receiver, picked up his gun, and started to go to Korzeniowski's aid. Then he heard a sound that froze him in his tracks.

The wump-wump-wump of jet helicopter blades.

Ramón was dazed and bloody. The captain was landing his punches, making the most of his longer reach. No use hanging back. Ramón surged toward him, throwing both fists at Korzeniowski's midsection, ignoring the blows to his own head. The rush knocked Korzeniowski back against the waist-high rail. His arms flew up as he tried to get his balance. Ramón seized the opportunity, throwing an uppercut at the point of his chin. The impact lifted Korzeniowski off his feet. He toppled backward over the rail and fell forty feet to the water.

Ramón was spent. Panting and grunting with pain, he leaned his forearms on the rail, clutched his head. His knees almost buckled.

A shot made him flinch. Wiping the blood from his eyes, he looked around. Stepped back inside the bridge. The body of Ivan Gonçalves lay on the floor. A pool of blood was spreading on the linoleum floor around his gray head. The pistol with which he had shot himself was still in his right hand.

Ramón looked up. Saw Ava's body near the radio console. He went to her, turned her over. Her eyes were closed, but she was still breathing. He looked at the front of her blouse, saw bullet holes but no blood. He pulled up the blouse.

Her entire torso was wrapped in mooring line. He could even see a flattened bullet in its tight coils. Her eyes slowly opened. She said, "I noticed it was made of Kevlar. Thought I'd put it to use."

"You're all right?"

"I feel like I've been kicked by a mule. A large mule wearing iron shoes. Let me just lie here for a minute, okay?"

Ramón gently lowered her to the floor and sat beside her, leaning his back against the console. In silence they listened to the helicopters coming closer.

The lead chopper swept past, almost at a level with Laker atop the gantry crane. He had no trouble reading USMC on its door. Four more followed in loose formation. The leading one circled over the harbor and came back, searchlights sweeping the pier and the ground in search of a place to land. None of the Cubans chose to fire on it.

Laker put the Kalashnikov on safe and laid it across his lap. Then he lay down on his back on the top girder of the bridge and closed his eyes. He would be just fine right here until someone came to help him down.

CHAPTER THIRTY-SEVEN

The top of Laker's restored 1964 Mustang was still stuck in the down position. But that was okay, because spring had come to Washington.

He and Ava were cruising along Rock Creek Parkway on a mild, cloudy day. He glanced over at her, wanting to see her auburn hair flowing in the wind. In the old days, she used to wear a hat and hold it down tight. But he'd noticed she was different in small ways since she'd spent so much time with her cousin Tilda. It'd loosened her up a bit.

The hair was a swirling red-brown mop, all right. But she was turned to him and her lips were moving. He couldn't hear a thing. He slowed down.

"What?"

"That's one advantage of being deaf in your right ear, Laker!" she shouted. "You can't hear when you're driving!"

"Do you want to stop?"

"Yes! Let's find a place and cuddle for a while!"

When he could, he pulled over to the side of the road. They got out and walked to a bench under a willow tree. It was Saturday, and traffic was calm. Ava sat on his left side. That was the good ear, but the wounded arm. Though it was healing, he couldn't lift it high enough to put it around her. She put her arm around him and kissed his cheek.

He picked up the conversation where wind roar had interrupted it. "You said the NSA had offered you your job back, with ample groveling."

"Yes. They want to make sure my confidentiality agreement is still in effect."

"Hopeless. It's all going to come out. Too many journalists are digging too hard. A guy like Ruy Morales can't just disappear."

"I've heard that everybody in the Havana government is preparing to swear up and down they had no idea what Gonçalves was up to."

"I doubt that'll hold up."

"But you have to admire the way Moscow is trying to brazen it out."

Laker chuckled. "Maneuvers in the Baltic area have been a complete success, and now the troops have returned to base."

"I see that NATO has announced maneuvers of its own."

"With American troops proudly participating."

Ava was scrutinizing his face. "Your cuts are healing. I'm glad there won't be any scars."

"So is Mason. He hates identifying marks on his agents."

"You haven't said if he's hired you back yet."

"He never fired me. Or even suspended me. I was drawing my salary the whole time the FBI and CIA were chasing me."

"Mason's such an ornery cuss. You've got to love him." Ava fitted her little finger in the cleft of Laker's chin. He loved it when she did that. "What's the latest on Captain Korzeniowski?"

"Recovered from his fall into the harbor. Telling the interrogators interesting yarns about his days in the Russian Navy. But they're not making any deals. Eventually he'll stand trial for the murder of Esteban Lamon and other crimes. Ramón Milaflores says he's looking forward to testifying against him."

"And you're looking forward to seeing Ramón."

"I owe him my life, several times over. Can't wait to buy him a Speyside Cardhu."

"Ah," said Ava and jumped to her feet. She returned from the Mustang with a bottle of his favorite single malt and two glasses. This surprised him, and not just because she usually called it Old Tooth Dissolver.

"This is a national park," he said as she poured him a glass. "We're probably breaking federal law."

"My cousin Tilda would approve. We're about to toast her." Ava poured her own glass. "You know, I am eager for this whole mess to be dragged into the light. However embarrassing it'll be for the various D.C. spy shops. I want to tell Tilda's children what she did for her country."

Laker nodded. He knew Ava was haunted by thoughts of her cousin. As he was haunted by thoughts of Terry. He hadn't mentioned them. Knew what Ava would say. Terry had betrayed her country and tried to kill Laker.

All true. But he'd never forget that last look before she threw herself into the sea.

Ava lifted her glass. "Matilda North, hail and farewell," she said.

"Hail and farewell," Laker said and drank.

Adding silently, *Theresa Lydecker, rest in peace.*

ACKNOWLEDGMENTS

When a new book is published, there are many people to thank. No author does it alone. As always, I want to thank Kensington Publishing for our long standing relationship, and Michaela Hamilton, an editor to treasure. Thanks to Dominick Abel, my agent and my friend. Proofreading, research, editing, and suggestions from David Linzee, Marilyn Davis, and of course, my wife, Barbara, have been enormously appreciated.

Special Bonus!

First Time in Print!

Keep reading to enjoy a short story featuring
Thomas Laker and Ava North.

PARANOID ENOUGH
FOR TWO

Sunday night in Washington, D.C., and the clubs and restaurants of the Adams-Morgan district were brightly lit, the sidewalks thronged. Every parking space was taken. Many diners and drinkers had to park on distant side streets and hike back to their cars at midnight when these streets were dark and deserted.

A fact well known to the city's predators.

As one couple, strolling arm in arm, left the lights and people behind, a skinny kid in jeans was trailing them. His T-shirt bared heavily inked arms. His face had a wispy beard and dark, deep-set eyes. They were fixed on the couple. The woman had a willowy figure set off by a long, full skirt that she had to hold down against the wind with her free hand. Her purse hung from a strap over her shoulder. The man was tall and broad-shouldered. He was old, though. Which to someone the kid's age meant forty.

The kid decided to take them.

His right hand slipped into his jeans pocket, and with swift quiet steps he closed the distance.

The woman turned, a look of concern on her lovely face. "Young man, no closer, please. My boyfriend spotted you two blocks ago. He's just waiting for you to come in reach to break your arm."

The mugger hesitated, but only for a second. His hand came out of his pocket and flicked his gravity blade open. Holding it poised for the underhand thrust, he stepped closer.

"*That's* not going to do you any good," said the woman. "Now he may kill you. He knows fifteen ways to do it with one blow."

The kid looked at the man. He was standing quite still, arms at his sides, face expressionless. The kid took another step.

"Oh God—here!" the woman said, and tossed him her purse.

The kid caught it. Surprise held him motionless for a moment. Then he spun and sprinted into the shadows, arms pumping. Within seconds he'd vanished.

"I wasn't going to kill him, Ava," said the man. "Just disable him."

"Yeah. For life. It's only money. In this case, only twenty-four dollars."

"Assuming that's what he was after."

Ava laughed. "You actually think this was an enemy op? The Russians or the North Koreans sent that kid? He's still in his teens. Laker, you are so paranoid."

"Paranoia is a secret agent's best friend, my boss likes to say."

"Which explains why everybody's paranoid in the agency whose name none dare speak." That was the

Washington insiders' nickname for The Gray Outfit, for whom Laker worked. It wasn't entirely a joke.

Laker was staring into the darkness with narrowed eyes. "I would've liked to ask the kid a few questions."

"Laker, it's the city. Once in a while, even secret agents get mugged."

Ava's apartment was on New Hampshire Avenue near Dupont Circle. On her salary as a junior cryptographer at the National Security Agency, she'd never have been able to afford a place in one of the capital's choicest neighborhoods. But she was a North, offspring of the celebrated political dynasty, and the apartment had been in the family for decades. It had served various Congressmen as a Washington pied-à-terre and at least one cabinet member's mistress as a love nest.

"Care for a nightcap?" she asked as they entered. "I bought a bottle of Old Tongue-Shriveler in honor of your visit."

"You shouldn't have, but thanks."

She returned from the kitchen with a bottle of Speyside Cardhu, his favorite single malt, and a glass. He always took it neat.

"Thanks," Laker said. "What are you going to have?"

"Nothing. I want to finish up that report. It's due tomorrow."

She went to her laptop, which was sitting on the coffee table in front of the sofa. Ava had a home office with a desk but didn't use it much. "Oh! The flash drive's not plugged in."

"You mean the thumb drive?"

"Funny how people can't agree on what to call these things. Especially when 'flash drive' is so obviously the correct term."

"But they don't flash."

"Sure they do. When you plug them in."

"That's a wink at best. On the other hand, they're just the size of your thumb."

"*Your* thumb. You have mutant thumbs."

"Not so. Just measure one against your thumb."

"I would if I could find it," Ava said. She'd been rummaging through drawers as they'd talked. She stopped, put her head back and closed her eyes. "Oh, shit. It was in my purse."

Laker had poured a glass of single malt. He set down the glass and the bottle and looked at his watch. "We should call NSA at once."

"There you go again, Laker. It was just a mugging. Anyway, I would never put classified information on a flash drive and take it out of the NSA."

"Or a thumb drive?"

"Or a thumb drive."

"What about the draft of your report?"

"It's on an Iranian code we broke last year. Mathematical and linguistic analysis might help us break the next one. But it's not top secret. Or even bottom secret. It was just a lot of work."

"Do you have a backup?"

"Sure. It's on the system at the office."

"So no harm done—except you can't work tonight." He held up the bottle. "Care for a bracing dram of single malt?"

"Ugh. I'll make myself a Black Russian."

They were halfway through their drinks when the intercom buzzed. She pressed the button. "Yes?"

"I'm looking for Miss Ava North," said a soft wheezy voice through the grille. An old woman's voice.

"Speaking."

"Miss North, I have your purse. I found it on the street."

"Oh, that's wonderful! Thank you. Please come up. It's 6-J, left off the elevator."

She walked over to Laker, who was sitting on the sofa, and clinked glasses with him. "Here's to good luck and good Samaritans."

"I'll be interested to see what's left in your purse."

A few minutes later there was a knock on the door. Ava opened it to a woman in her seventies, who was leaning on a cane. She had white hair under a thin faded scarf, and she wore bifocals.

"Please come in," Ava said.

"I don't want to be any trouble," the woman said, almost inaudibly, and held out Ava's purse.

"No trouble at all. Thank you so much. Here, let me give you something—"

"There's no need."

"Just for your time and inconvenience." Ava had taken her wallet out of her purse. She frowned. "The cash is gone. Should've expected that."

Laker rose and came over to the door. "Better check what else is gone."

The woman peered up at him in alarm. "I didn't take anything!"

"No, of course you didn't," Ava said. "We didn't mean—"

"I'm sorry," Laker interrupted. "Please come in and sit down."

But the woman was already shrinking back. Ava took a step toward her, which only made her turn and hobble toward the elevator. Giving up, Ava glared at Laker.

"You scared her."

"I didn't mean to. I really wanted to talk to her. At least find out her name."

"Oh, you think she's an enemy agent, too? That little old lady?" Ava was pawing through the contents of the bag. "Everything's here except the cash."

"The thumb drive?"

Ava plucked it out and flourished it. "The flash drive."

"Are you sure it's the same one?"

"Of course. It's a yellow Lexar."

"Maybe slip it in your laptop just to make sure."

"Laker! No foreign power was after my little essay. You can't be suspicious of everyone we meet and everything that happens to us. You're driving me crazy!"

She spun on her heel and went into the bedroom, taking the purse with her. She didn't slam the door, though. Laker figured that meant he could join her once he'd finished his single malt. But if he didn't want to be sent back to his place for the night, he'd better not mention the thumb drive again.

Even if he called it the flash drive.

The Gray Outfit was on Capitol Hill, but the NSA was located in Fort Meade, Maryland. Which meant that Ava had to leave for work before Laker did. Ordinarily he rose with her and set off for a jog. But on this Monday morning, he fell back asleep as soon as she shut off the alarm clock. He'd had a restless night.

He'd been trying to figure out what hostile nation would be interested in an analysis of a broken Iranian code. Hadn't gotten anywhere. Maybe he *was* paranoid. But even when he awakened the second time and got out of bed, his suspicions wouldn't let go of him.

As he made coffee, he tried again to shake them off. If this had been an enemy op, it had been an elaborate one to stage just to get hold of a thumb drive. And why would a foreign agency assume it would have valuable intel on it? As Ava said, she'd have to be pretty stupid to put secrets on a drive and take it out of the NSA.

As Ava also said, secret agents could get mugged, too. Considering the street crime statistics in Washington these days, it wasn't even that unlikely.

What *was* unlikely was the purse being returned.

The thought brought Laker up short. He sat down with his coffee and let his paranoia, if that's what it was, rip. Allowed himself to be suspicious of a little old lady. With a headscarf and a cane and bifocals and a querulous voice and timid manner. It was all a bit much, come to think of it.

Say the little old lady *was* an agent. That would mean that returning Ava's purse was as important as stealing it. Which would mean that the purpose of the op wasn't to steal her thumb drive.

But to substitute another one for it.

One that carried a virus.

It hit Laker with sickening force. When Ava plugged

the drive into her desktop computer, the virus would infect the NSA system.

He ran into the bedroom, grabbed his cell phone from the table, and speed-dialed her phone. Heard it ring. Looked across the room to see that it was plugged into its charger.

Next he called the entrance security checkpoint at Fort Meade. Glanced at his watch as the phone rang. This was going to be close.

"Front gate."

"Has Ava North passed through yet?"

"Maybe you have the wrong number, sir."

"No, I don't. You're the NSA. I'm Thomas Laker. My ID code is J for John 1749. Now has Ava North passed through? This is urgent."

"Give me a minute."

It took more than a minute. Laker paced. Naturally the guard was verifying his ID before answering his question about Ava.

Finally the line opened. "Ms. North went through ten minutes ago, Mr. Laker."

He ended the call and speed-dialed her desk phone. Got the recording. He said, "Ava, call me right away."

Leaving his cell free for her callback, he went into the kitchen and picked up the receiver of the wall phone. Dialed NSA Security.

"Extension 317."

"This is an emergency. Send somebody to the desk of Ava North in cryptography and—"

"Hold it. Let's start with how you got this number."

"I'm Thomas Laker, J for John 1749. You've got to—"

"Sorry, did you stay J for John? You'll have to slow down, pal."

* * *

Ava had gotten into the office early. She was passing empty desks on her way to her own at the end of the row, near the window. Just as well she didn't have to chat with anybody. In the car she'd been running over her report in her mind and knew just what revisions she wanted to make. She sat down, switched on her desktop computer. While it booted up, she removed the flash drive from her purse and laid it on the desk.

The message light on her phone was blinking. That was bound to be Major Thornton, the project director, wondering where her report was. She'd wait until she could truthfully tell him it was done and on its way.

The screen was asking for her password. She typed it in. The NSA screensaver appeared, an eagle with spread wings, a golden key in its talons. She picked up the flash drive.

She thought she heard footsteps and voices behind her, but before she could turn to look, the phone rang. She leaned forward and reached for it left-handed. Her right hand was extending toward the CPU under the desk, to plug the drive into the USB port.

It was two inches away when a tremendous force hit Ava and she and her chair toppled over. She found herself lying on her back, with two burly U.S. Marines on top of her.

A man in a suit loomed over her. His eyes were staring at her right hand, as if she was holding a stick of dynamite with a burning fuse. He said, "Ms. North, please drop the thumb drive."

"You mean flash drive," she said and let it fall.

* * *

"NSA took no chances," Ava told Laker that evening at his loft. She was drinking straight Speyside Cardhu. It had been that kind of day. "They inserted the drive into a nonnetworked computer. The effect was amazing. It was like a tiger hurling itself against the bars of its cage. Our cyber warfare experts say it's the most effective virus they've ever seen. It would have spread from my computer to the whole NSA system in nanoseconds. Before we could have reacted, it would have swept every shelf in the cupboard bare. All our secrets would've been shooting across the Internet."

"To where?" Laker asked.

"As yet undetermined. They're tracing the route from servers in the Cayman Islands to Warsaw to Tokyo to . . ."

"It may be a while till we know who was behind this."

"In the meantime, new regulations have already been announced. All USB ports on desktop computers are being sealed. Employees are forbidden to bring in flash drives from outside."

"And thumb drives?"

"Those, too."